DAMAGE

by Brandy Echols

This is a work of fiction. The authors have invented the characters. Any resemblance to actual persons, living or dead, is purely coincidental.

If you have purchased this book with a 'dull' or missing cover—you have possibly purchased an unauthorized or stolen book. Please immediately contact the publisher advising where, when and how you purchased this book.

Compilation and Introduction copyright © 2011 by
Triple Crown Publications
PO Box 247378
Columbus, OH 43224
www.TripleCrownPublications.com

Library of Congress Control Number: 2011920036
ISBN: 978-0-9832095-6-0

Author: Brandy Echols
Graphics Design: Hot Book Covers
Editor-in-Chief: Vickie Stringer
Editor: 21st Street Urban Editing: Niccole: M. Simmons

Copyright © 2011 by Brandy Echols. All rights reserved. No part of this book may be reproduced in any form without permission from the publisher, except by reviewer who may quote brief passages to be printed in a newspaper or magazine.

First Trade Paperback Edition Printing 2011

10 9 8 7 6 5 4 3 2 1

Printed in the United States of America

ACKNOWLEDGMENTS

Firstly, I wanna to give thanks to God for giving me this wonderful talent and opportunity. I'm very blessed and thankful for everything He has done for me, and & I'm gonna continue to use this wonderful talent to the best of my ability.

To my parent's, Angela & Joe Echols, I love y'all so much! I know I probably was getting on y'all last nerve bugging y'all about this book, but no matter what, y'all helped me & supported me the whole way! God blessed me with two of the most wonderful parent's a child could ask for. There's no better feeling then knowing that you have a mother & father who will love and support anything you want to do. Y'all are truly my biggest fans & the best parents ever man!!!! There's no way I could've came this far without you guys. I love y'all to death.

To my little cousin Bri'anna, I really appreciate you little cuz! You were one of the first, if not the first person to read this book when I first wrote it. You gave it a chance & I love you for dat!!! To my sister Brianna, you were right behind NaeNae when it came to reading my book. I love you & by the time you read this, my niece should be here, Yay! Lol. To my cousin's Lyntonia, Dominique, Shelisa, & Jacinta, thanks so much for reading my book & giving me honest feedback on it. That meant a lot to me! To my wonderful cousin Raymond (TJ) I love & miss you so much! Even from miles away you support me like crazy. Do yo thing over there big cuz & be safe. And to the rest of my wonderful cousins, big ups for the love and support y'all always show me! I love all y'all trust & believe dat! To all my lovely aunts, uncles & wonderful grandparent's, I just wanna thank all y'all for the support! My whole family was behind me on this book & I'm so grateful to have y'all. Definitely wanna shout out my girls Shay, Zanashay, NueNue, Lola, & Raiine! Thanks for reading my work y'all! Each and every opinion mattered to me. To one of the most influential people in my life, Jamall, thank you for always supporting me and sticking with me no matter what. I know you got my back when nobody else don't. Thanks to all the supportive people that I work with. It makes me happy to know that I have you guys support. Special thanks to Sabrina Eubanks, Deja King, & Shavon Moore and the rest of the authors who reached out a helping hand to me whenever I needed it! I really appreciate that.

To all the TCP staff that helped bring this book to life, big thanks to you guys. I am so blessed to have the opportunity to be under the Three Crowns! To all the wonderful editors, including Niccole M. Simmons & Marian Nealy, thanks so much for being a part of this book. To Caitlin McLellan, thanks for all your help! A special thanks to Ms. Vickie Stringer for believing in this book from the start. The fact that you told me yourself that you felt my work had great potential meant so much! I just have to say thank you so much to everybody who had anything to do with me & this book! This is like the hardest part because I'm afraid I'll leave someone out. So as I said, I have to thank EVERYBODY who stood behind me on this. I promise this is only the beginning to something major. Me & my pen have special plans for the future, & everybody will find out soon enough! I hope you guys enjoy my debut novel. Nothing but blessings & love this way!

DEDICATION

I wanna dedicate this book to people who are scared to go for their dreams. I was the same way, but God didn't bless me with this talent for it to be hidden. Whatever you wanna do, DO IT! The sky is the limit & I'm here to prove that. I was a little girl who loved to write; now I'm a young lady with a published novel.

To my lil bro Joe (Tra). No matter if it's football, basketball, or whatever
you decide to do, go hard lil nigga! You something special and big sis can see that already!
I love you Bro!

1

Tader kissed Wesley on his cheek while holding her hand out to collect her prize. When he placed a hundred dollar bill in her hand she looked at him like he had lost his mind. Her treasure was worth more than a hundred dollars so Wesley needed to act like he knew. She kept her hand out until she saw him go back in his wallet for more cash. A smile spread across her face when he placed four more hundred dollar bills in her hand. Three hundred was what she was used to, but she wasn't gonna argue with five. She got up from her bed fully nude and walked into the bathroom. She turned the shower on and waved for Wesley to come in. She liked for her men to shower before they left her house. Wesley walked in and smiled as he stepped into the shower. He wanted Tader to join him but he knew that he would have to come out his pockets once again for that opportunity. Tader shut the door to let

Triple Crown Publications *presents* . . . **DAMAGE**

him shower in peace while she crawled back into her bed. She glanced at his Black Berry when she heard it ring on the floor next to his clothes. Being the nosey person that she was, Tader got back out of the bed and grabbed the phone. When she looked at the screen it displayed a new text message from a contact labeled 'Tasha'. Tader knew that was his wife because she heard him talk about her on many occasions. Before she could read the first text, Tasha sent four more. Tader hated nagging wives so she decided to be ignorant.

With the phone still in her hand, she tiptoed into her living room. Without even reading the texts, she searched for the camera icon. Once she found it, she positioned the camera so that you could see her face as well as her naked body. She smiled while snapping the picture and saving it. Once she was done, she scrolled through the contacts and found Tasha's name. She clicked the 'Send Message' button then sent her the picture that she had just taken. *Nag about that bitch,* she thought to herself. She turned the phone off so that it wouldn't ring and crept back into her room and placed it in the pockets of his jeans. When Wesley finally came out of the bathroom, Tader was laid back on her bed with a look of innocence spread across her face. All Wesley saw was an angel when in actuality Tader was more so like the devil.

"I had a good time," she said smiling.

"So did I, Ta'Ronna," Wesley replied, searching for his clothes.

Tader hated when people called her by her government name but she let Wesley get away with it this time. She watched him get dressed then walked him to the door. "We have to do this again sometime." She smiled knowing that it would be the last time she ever saw him. Once his wife got the picture, she knew he would never mess around

Triple Crown Publications *presents* . . .   DAMAGE

with her again. She could care less because she already hit the jackpot in his pockets.

"I agree," Wesley stated. He headed for his car as Tader shut her door and locked it. She cleaned out her tub before taking a long hot bath. Once she got out, she flat ironed her hair and slipped into her all black strapless Freak'um dress. She damn near drooled over herself in the mirror as she admired the way that the dress hugged her toned figure. While heading to her closet for her stripper heels, she heard her house phone as it started to ring. She got nervous thinking it was Wesley until she remembered that he only had her cell number. When she reached for the phone, she realized that it was her main man Terrell.

"Hey, babe," she spoke softly into the phone.

"We still on for tonight?" He asked.

Tader balanced the phone between her ear and shoulder, trying to hold it in place. "I'm sick Terrell," she lied. "Just call me first thing in the morning, and maybe I'll be better by then."

"Here you go with that bullshit."

"What bullshit Rell? I said I was sick. Now whether you believe me or not, I'm 'bout to take my ass to sleep." Tader hated when people didn't believe her lies. She got so angry that she started to believe that her lie was actually true.

"Yeah, well sweet dreams." Terrell hung up the phone before Tader could respond. She knew he was mad but she had already made plans to kick it with her girls tonight. Terrell was what you would call Tader's main squeeze. She went back and forth between men but Terrell was her keeper. She knew she would have to clear her schedule in order to make more time for him. After putting the final touches on her makeup, Tader hopped in her all black Tahoe and pulled out her cell phone to call her best friend Spencer. After three rings, Spen finally answered the phone.

"Hello?"

"I'm on my way, so be ready 'cause I'ma just blow the horn."

"Girl, you can come in for a minute," Spen stated, frustrated.

Tader was annoyed. She was ready to party and she refused to bicker. "Girl we already late, and we still have to get Chatt."

"A'ight, damn!" Spen hung up the phone before Tader could say anything else.

"That bitch get on my nerves," Tader said aloud to herself as she closed her phone. After stopping at the gas station around the corner from Spen's condo, she pulled up and blew the horn.

Spen looked outside her window and saw Tader waiting for her. "Baby that's Tader outside, I'm 'bout to go." She leaned in and gave her boyfriend Devon a peck on the lips before heading out the door.

"Don't get outta hand at that damn club tonight," Devon yelled out to Spen as she left.

"Relax boo; you know who I'm coming home to." She blew him a kiss and headed out the door. Devon and Spen had been dating since high school. They were off and on for a few years, but lately the couple had been going strong. Devon, determined not to live a life of selling drugs, graduated from law school after four years in undergrad school and three long years in law school. He was now working at a law firm and living in a beautiful condo with Spen. He helped her dreams come true by purchasing her the perfect property to open her hair salon, 'Hair Desire'. Spen's salon had been open for two years now, but she was still unsatisfied with the outcome of the business. She hoped that in due time her salon would make great progress and turn out to be the image that she had been

Triple Crown Publications presents... DAMAGE

seeing since she was little.

Devon looked out the window and watched Spen's hips shift from left to right as she walked toward Tader's truck. He knew his girl was the shit. Spen was a naturally beautiful black woman with a body to die for. With a hazelnut skin complexion, an hourglass figure and those lovely almond shaped brown eyes, she was sure to grab any man's attention. She got in Tader's truck looking gorgeous as usual, wearing a silk gold halter top, a pair of black skinny jeans and matching gold pumps. "Heifer, you could have come in and spoke to my man," she told Tader jokingly.

"Girl ain't nobody got time to be talking to his stuck up ass," Tader replied, thinking about how much she couldn't stand Devon. *Damn, I just wanna clock that nigga!* She thought to herself.

"You know, till this day, I still don't fully understand the beef between y'all. If it's about him calling you a hoe, Tader, you need to drop that shit."

Tader rolled her eyes. "I been dropped that shit girl. I know the life I live and Devon can kiss my ass if he don't like it."

Spen shook her head knowing where the conversation would lead to if she didn't change the subject. Tader was her girl true enough, but she was starting to get fed up with her constantly dogging her man. "Fuck it, new subject. Did you tell Chatt we were on are way?"

"Yeah, I let her know," Tader responded, still thinking about Devon. She didn't wanna drop the conversation. "Spen, why you ain't found a new man yet?"

"Tader, we already been through this plenty of times, damn!"

After a long discussion about Spen and Devon's relationship, they pulled up in front of Chatt's apartment. "Chatt need's to get the fuck up out these projects," Tader

Triple Crown Publications *presents* . . . **DAMAGE**

said, looking at the raggedy apartments. Chatt came out the apartment wearing a pair of jeans and a white tee. Her hair was pulled to the back and she obviously added a sock to make her donut look bigger than it actually was. When she approached the truck, Spen and Tader both stared at her, confused. Finally Tader couldn't hold her tongue anymore and asked, "Chatt," she paused trying to get her words together, "why are you wearing that shit?"

Chatt looked annoyed. "I'm comfortable," she assured her.

"Well, yeah, but I mean that's not..."

Seeing that Tader couldn't get her words together Spen spoke for her. "Chatt, where yo pumps girl? You know we don't do gym shoes at the club."

"My feet can't handle another night in pumps."

Tader shook her head eying Chatt up and down. She didn't wanna be seen at the club with a chick wearing a white tee and jeans. It just wasn't right and even though the club didn't require a dress code, Tader still was against the sloppy wardrobe. "Well damn, could you at least try to be classy?"

Chatt was getting irritated. "Look, I'm not changing my clothes," she stated firmly. "We going out or not?"

"Girl, just get in," Spen told her getting impatient. She was ready to party regardless of Chatt's wardrobe. Hell, she looked good so why bother trying to help somebody else.

The girls arrived at club Chaos ready to party. Tader walked inside demanding any attention that she didn't already have. The place was packed. Tader didn't waste any time migrating to the dance floor. She was ready to get down and catch a buzz in the process. Moving her hips to the beat, she could feel a pair of eyes watching her. She smiled and continued to move to the beat of one of her

Triple Crown Publications presents... **DAMAGE**

favorite songs. When she finally looked up, she couldn't help but speak on the guy she noticed watching her. "Damn, that nigga breaking his neck to look at me," she said to Spen over the loud music.

Spen peeped the guy she was talking about. "Nah girl, he's definitely looking in my direction," she assumed trying to dance extra exotic just in case he was. "Oh, shit. Don't look now, but he's coming over here."

The mysterious man approached them, clutching his drink in his hand. He was even more handsome up close. "What's up, ma?" He spoke, looking directly at Chatt. Tader smacked her lips, a little pissed that his interest wasn't in her.

Chatt glanced at him and rolled her eyes. She quickly put a story behind his good looks and automatically labeled him as a player. "Hey," she replied under her breath.

"You looking kind of good in them J's," he complimented, noticing her footwear. Chatt didn't respond but that didn't stop him from speaking to her again. "So, can I get you a drink or something?" He asked, trying his chances once more.

"No you can't get me a drink," Chatt snapped. "And I'm not shipping out free pussy either, so you can just stop now."

Both Spen and Tader were astonished with Chatt's response. They couldn't believe she had just crushed this man's ego so harshly. They knew she didn't bite her tongue, but damn! They never expected her to snap the way she did.

"Damn," he replied. "I was just trying to be nice, ma."

"Yeah, I bet," Chatt said, looking bothered by his presence. She didn't care that she was being nasty. Her whole purpose was to try and get him to leave her alone.

Spen was ready to go upside Chatt's head. She hated

Triple Crown Publications presents . . . DAMAGE

when she acted stuck up for no good reason. "She'll meet you by the bar," she assured him. He nodded and walked off while Tader busted out laughing. After she came out shock she found the entire situation to be hilarious.

"I don't know why you told him that," Chatt said addressing Spen's comment. "I'm not going over there."

Spen grabbed Chatt's arm, and drug her into an empty corner in the club. "Now look here," Spen told her, "I don't know why you're acting all stuck up tonight, but you need to fix the problem."

Chatt crossed her arms and faced the ground. She was ready to go. She wasn't really in the mood for the club scene at the time. She only agreed to tag along because she didn't want to be the member of the clique that killed the night. Chatt was the youngest of the crew. She was in the fourth grade when she met Spen and Tader who were in the sixth grade. They all hung tight, graduating from the same middle school and high school. Chatt moved out of her junkie parents' apartment when she turned eighteen. She moved into an apartment complex known as "West Brook". She was dead broke and working a minimum wage job to try and make ends meet. She tried to make it look as if she weren't struggling. She knew she was, but she didn't want anybody feeling sorry for her because she damn sure didn't feel sorry for herself.

"Chatt just let the man buy you a drink. He's not asking for pussy girl, stop trippin'," Spen advised. Chatt looked over at the bar and saw dude waiting for her. She didn't want to talk to him, but Spen was getting on her nerves about it. She figured one drink wouldn't hurt, but it would definitely shut Spen up.

"Okay," she confirmed, "but just one drink and nothing else."

Spen gave her thumbs up and shoved her in the direction

Triple Crown Publications *presents* . . .   **DAMAGE**

of the bar. Chatt wasn't nervous because she didn't care how she came off towards anybody. No matter who you were, she would do her at all times. She approached the bar and took a seat in front of dude. "Look," she began, "my bad for going off on you a minute ago. I just know how these nigga's are and I'm not on it."

"I feel you one hundred percent ma," he responded, nodding his head.

"My name is Chatt, a'ight? You don't have to call me 'ma' every time you say something to me." She laughed a little, making him more comfortable.

"Chatt?" He restated. "I know that ain't written on your birth certificate."

"Actually, it's short for Chasity. Me and my girls shortened our real names back in middle school."

"Well, it's good to meet you, Chasity. I'm DreStar."

Chatt smacked her lips. "Quit playing. What's your name fa'real?"

"I'm serious as fuck, DreStar."

"Oh." Chatt felt a little embarrassed for laughing. She looked away, feeling awkward.

"But that shit ain't on my birth certificate," he joked, putting her at ease. She turned back around grinning.

"Just order my drink already," she demanded, waving the bartender over.

Tader was dropping it low when she felt someone grab her from behind. She immediately turned around to see Terrell standing there. If her ass was big enough, she would've shitted three bricks. "I guess you're feeling better," he said nonchalantly.

"Oh shit," Tader whispered. She tried to remain calm. If she panicked, she was sure to give herself away. "Rell babe, what are you doing here?"

"Same thing you doing, but I could have sworn you told me you were sick."

"I was sick," she lied, conveying a fake cough.

"Don't lie in my face, Tader."

"Babe, I promise..." Tader stopped in mid-sentence when she noticed one of her sideline men approaching. She knew she was in trouble if she didn't act fast. *What the fuck is going on?* She asked herself. *What, all of a sudden these niggas wanna party?*

"What's good Ta'Ronna, baby?" David yelled over the loud music. David was Tader's second main man. He bought her the truck she was riding around in. She told Terrell the truck was a gift from her parents for her twenty-first birthday. He didn't believe her, but he also didn't pressure her for the truth. Terrell knew Tader messed around. He would be stupid not to know, but he accepted it as long as it never happened in front of him.

"Hey David," Tader greeted him. "How you been, big bra?"

"What you mean big bra? Get over here and give me a kiss girl. I see how you been avoiding me lately," David spoke, pulling Tader in for a kiss. She turned her head causing him to miss her lips.

"Who the fuck is this nigga up in here kissing you and calling you by your government name and shit?" Terrell shouted, snatching Tader away from David.

"Nobody babe," Tader explained. "This is just a friend."

David laughed, though the situation didn't strike him as funny. "So I'm just a friend, Ta'Ronna? Was I just a friend when I put you behind the wheel of that truck?"

"David, just go," Tader told him through clenched teeth. *His ass tryna' get me fried!*

"Yeah ma'fucka, beat it!" Terrell barked, getting in David's face. He felt so disrespected by having another nigga claim

Triple Crown Publications *presents* . . .   DAMAGE

Tader right in front of his eyes.

"Nigga, I ain't a fucking child. I'm a grown ass man," David roared back. The club bouncers began to approach the scene. David nor Terrell were concerned with the security.

Tader was shook up. She didn't want to get put out the club, nor did she want Terrell and David to start fighting. Although it would have been lovely to have two handsome men fighting over her, she tried to avoid the major conflict. She looked at David and said, "Just go, okay? I don't want any trouble."

David glanced at Tader then back at Terrell before making his way out of the club's nearest exit. It was far from over but fighting Terrell in the club wasn't the way David wanted to do things. He made the decision to dismiss himself before things got ugly. Tader looked at Terrell and she knew he was pissed. She had no clue how she would get herself out of this one. She opened her mouth but he quickly silenced her putting his finger to her lips.

"Have your ass back at home within the next hour," he ordered. He then walked off without saying anything else.

Tader looked at Spen and spat, "This shit is hectic girl! Rell is gon' fry my ass."

"You damn right," Spen said trying to hold back laughter. She loved Tader but she knew sooner or later she was bound to get caught up. She messed around with too many men to get away with it forever. Tader didn't find the situation funny. She was ready to leave the club not wanting to disobey Terrell's orders. She had already fucked up once, so she didn't want to make the situation any worse. She spotted Chatt still sitting at the bar talking to DreStar. She hated to interrupt, but it was time to go.

"It's time to bounce girl," Tader said, walking up behind Chatt's chair.

Chatt turned around feeling really bothered. *First they*

Triple Crown Publications presents . . . DAMAGE

mad because I play the dude, but now that we're chattin' it up; they wanna say it's time to go! "What are you talking about?"

"I just got caught up in some shit. Terrell told me that I need to be home soon and you know I don't question my man's authority."

Chatt grabbed her drink and took a sip before she spoke. "Well, I'm not ready to go."

"Well, ride home with him then," Tader replied, nodding her head towards DreStar. *This bitch done got a lil liquor in her and wanna talk slick!* Tader thought as she watched Chatt chill.

Chatt looked at Dre and asked, "Can you give me a ride home?"

"Yeah, it's not a problem," he assured her.

Tader looked sideways at Chatt. She had either loosened up or she was trippin'. Either way, she had a whole new attitude towards DreStar and Tader was not mad at that.

"Call me when he drops you off." Tader wanted to know everything that was going to go down between the two; and judging by Chatt's new attitude, something was bound to go down.

"A'ight," Chatt answered, taking another sip of her drink.

"Tader, who the hell you got beef with?"

Tader turned around to see Chelae, a friend from her job. "It's plenty of females I don't like, but I wouldn't say I got beef wit' nobody. Why?"

"Girl, I think you might wanna see this," Chelae said, waving for Tader to follow her.

Tader and Spen exited the club, following behind Chelae. Although Spen didn't want to get caught up in any drama, she was ready to get back home to her man. She looked over at Tader and noticed that for some reason she had

Triple Crown Publications presents... DAMAGE

blood shot eyes. Her hands were shaking and she opened her mouth to speak, but no words would come out. Spen looked up ahead to see what had her so shaken up. She placed her hand over her heart when she saw that Tader's truck was engulfed in flames. "You can't be fucking serious," Tader sobbed, shaking her head. She knew exactly who was responsible for her misfortune.

"Girl, you better tell one of these police officer's what happened. You know David did this shit," Spen stated, shaking her head.

"He has lost his fucking mind!" Tader yelled. "Why the fuck would he do this?"

Spen looked at her like she was stupid. "Probably because you just tried to shit on him in front of another nigga. You know how crazy David is, so don't act like you didn't know he was gon' do something stupid." She started laughing while Tader got more upset. She had a look on her face that meant she didn't find anything funny.

"We gotta find a ride and get the hell up out of here."

"Tader, you need to call the insurance company or something. Your ride is fucked up," Spen reminded her, pointing to the truck.

"I ain't calling them ma'fucka's so they can blame this shit on me."

"You ain't do this shit Tader, David did!"

"I can't tell them that without any proof," Tader informed her. "The truck's not in my name anyway."

"What?" Spen was shocked yet pissed at the same time. How could Tader be so stupid? She knew for a fact that she should have gotten the truck registered in her name. "Tader, why the fuck didn't you get the truck in your name?"

"David told me that if anything ever happened, he didn't want it to fall back on us, so he got some other bitch to put it in her name."

Triple Crown Publications *presents* . . .   DAMAGE

"Unbelievable," Spen explained. She began pacing the parking lot, while Tader stood calmly. "So the fucking truck is stolen?" Spen continued.

"No, Spencer!" Tader blurted, getting frustrated. "It's just in somebody else's name, a'ight?"

"Whatever." Spen didn't care anymore. Her car was at home safe and sound and in her name; that's all that mattered.

"Let's go back inside before these pigs start questioning me," Tader said, heading back towards the entrance.

She and Spen walked backed inside the club and re-approached the bar.

Chatt eyed them confused and a tad bit annoyed. "I thought y'all was leaving."

"I thought we were too," Spen answered while looking at Tader.

Tader rolled her eyes and walked off. Spen was on her last nerve. One more word out of her and they were gonna be squared up.

"Look," Spen continued, "we need a ride. David set Tader's truck on fire and you know we don't do the bus."

"He set her truck on fire? Why the fuck would he do that?"

"Because he's a fucking nut!" Spen snapped. She realized that she was taking her frustration out on the wrong person and tried to speak calmly. "Look, we just need a way home okay? And soon because Tader's trying to avoid the Po-Po."

"Y'all need to call the insurance company or something," DreStar stated.

Spen snapped again, "The fucking truck ain't even in her name."

"Oh, hell," Chatt mumbled. She shook her head in disbelief.

"Damn, sounds like a sticky situation. Let me give y'all a

 Triple Crown Publications presents... DAMAGE

ride then," DreStar offered.

Spen's eyes lit up. She was waiting for DreStar to offer a ride for the longest and finally he did. "You sure?" Spen asked, not wanting to seem too obvious to the fact that she was waiting on him to offer.

"Yeah," he assured her. "Y'all gon' have to give me the addresses though."

"Okay, thanks. At least let me give you some gas money," Spen insisted, digging into her wallet. Hell, gas was so high she felt stupid for even offering.

"Nah," DreStar told her. "Keep your money."

Spen looked at Chatt and noticed that she had developed an attitude. She didn't even bother to ask her what was wrong because she didn't care at the moment. She was just ready to go home. She searched the club for Tader and when she found her, they left for DreStar's whip.

"Thank you for the ride," Chatt said politely. She rushed out of DreStar's truck, in a hurry to get inside her apartment.

"Hold on," he called out. "Can I at least get your number before you run away from me?"

"I'm not running," she informed him. "I'm just a little tired."

He gave her a flirtatious grin. "You mind if I tuck you in?"

"Yes I mind," she quoted him. "My place is a mess."

"I don't care what your place looking like ma. I'm not judgmental."

Chatt blushed. "I told you not to call me ma," she paused, facing the ground, "but I guess you can come in for a minute." Chatt didn't invite men into her apartment often. Although she always kept it neat and clean, the apartment itself needed much work done. Paint was peeling off of the walls and when it rained hard enough the ceiling would leak. Not to mention it had a few mice or two that she had been trying to get rid of since she moved into the place. Oddly, she invited DreStar in anyway. "I know you're probably used to shit fancier than this, aren't you?" Chatt asked as DreStar walked into her living room.

"I told you I'm not judgmental. You could live in a box for all I care."

"Well, let me just be thankful that I don't," Chatt joked. "Make yourself at home," she continued. "I'll be right back." She went into her bedroom to change her clothes. She put on a white wife beater and a pair of black booty shorts. She took the sock out her hair and let it fall to her shoulders. Then she popped two Mentos in her mouth and applied a thin layer of Carmex to her lips.

DreStar couldn't help but grow excited when he saw Chatt walk out of her room wearing booty shorts. "You look nice," he teased.

She looked down at her shorts and grinned. "I like to sleep in these; they're comfortable," she defended herself.

"You ain't gotta explain yourself to me," DreStar laughed, throwing his hands up in his defense. Chatt took a seat next to him on the couch. She grabbed the remote and started flipping through the local channels.

"So DreStar, where you stay?" She scooted closer to him.

"I gotta place out in Kettering; and call me Dre if you don't mind."

"Okay Dre," she restated. "Why so far away?"

"Dayton got a little too much going on for me. Kettering's quiet, no drama comes my way."

Chatt nodded her head. "I feel you. You live alone?"

"No females, if that's what you want to know."

"I was just asking," Chatt told him rolling her eyes

Triple Crown Publications presents . . .   DAMAGE

playfully. "Besides, if you had a girl, I'm sure you wouldn't be up in here with me."

He smiled. "Maybe, maybe not."

"So you do got a girl?" Chatt asked. She crossed her arms and waited for his response. He looked down at her then grabbed her chin to bring her lips to his. Chatt pulled away. "I already told you I wasn't doing this," she whispered.

He spoke in a soft tone. "We don't have to do anything."

Chatt looked away. She didn't know what she wanted at the time. A part of her wanted to just let go, but another part of her was still holding on to something. *Let go Chasity, just let go,* she told herself. She looked up at Dre and went in for another kiss, this time inviting his tongue in her mouth.

"Let's go in my room," she told him. He got up and followed her into the bedroom, closing the door behind him.

"You sure you want to do this?" Dre asked.

"Yeah," Chatt answered. Dre turned out the lights and Chatt knew her episode at the club was now pointless. She felt stupid for telling him she wasn't giving out free pussy because that was exactly what she was about to do.

Triple Crown Publications *presents*... **DAMAGE**

2

"Devon, we need to talk before you leave." Spen got out of her bed and grabbed her robe. She followed Devon downstairs into the living room as he was getting ready to leave.

"What is it baby?" Devon questioned. "You know I'm rushing."

"Look, I've said it more than once but damnit I'm saying it again. I'm ready to start a family Devon. You keep saying your too busy or whatever but I'm getting sick of waiting baby. I know you want a little Devon running around here one day."

Devon tried to easily change the subject. "Let's talk about this when I get back. Have you seen my phone?"

"You know what Devon, fuck it! Whenever you want to talk about something I listen to you." Spen was frustrated. She was sick of Devon always blowing the subject over.

 Triple Crown Publications presents . . . DAMAGE

"There you go pouting and shit," he pointed out. "I said we would talk about it when I get back."

Spen sighed. "Whatever Devon," she hissed, walking towards the stairs.

"Look at me when I'm talking to you girl!"

"Don't be fucking yelling at me!" Spen shouted down the steps. She walked back inside her room and lay down on the bed. Devon walked in behind her. He crawled on top of her smiling.

"You better get off me," Spen warned, knowing good and well she didn't want him to move.

"Chill out girl," Devon told her. He began kissing her neck and loosening her robe. He knew a good orgasm was exactly what she needed. He kissed her all the way down to her already soaked clit. He put his tongue to work until it was swollen red. After making her come more than twice, he went into the bathroom to freshen up.

"I gotta bounce baby. I'm 'bout an hour late." He walked over to the bed and pecked Spen's lips. He knew he had satisfied her needs sexually, but he could still tell that she was unhappy. He lifted her chin and placed another kiss on her lips. "I promise I'ma put one in you soon okay? When the time is right, you'll have your stretch mark belly."

Spen gave him a half smile. She then gave him another kiss and told him to leave seeing that he was already late. When Devon finally left, Spen took a shower then picked up her house phone to three with way Chatt and Tader.

"Hey loves," Tader said answering the phone.

"You sound a little too jolly for someone who got her whip set on fire last night," Spen reminded her.

"I ain't trippin'. Me and David are done so I don't need his whip anymore."

Spen didn't believe Tader's comment one bit. She knew her like the back of her hand so she knew she wasn't done

Triple Crown Publications *presents* . . . **DAMAGE**

with David. "Yeah, I hear you Tader."

"Don't say it like that. I'm serious when I say I'm done with his ass."

Spen just laughed. "Chatt, why you so quiet?"

"No reason," Chatt answered. "Let me call y'all back."

"Why?" Tader chimed in. DreStar took the phone out of Chatt's hand. He told both Tader and Spen that they would have to talk to her another time; and then he hung up.

Spen looked at her phone. "I know he didn't just hang up on us."

"Hell yeah he did."

"Niggas these days, I'll tell ya. What time you coming in today?"

"Probably two," Tader told her. "My first client's not scheduled until two forty-five."

Spen eyed the clock on her bedroom wall. It read ten minutes after ten. "I think I'ma gon' and head up there. I got two clients that come in at noon, so I better get moving."

"Okay. See you in a few hours."

"Okay." Spen hung up the phone and headed downstairs.

Spen was putting a roller set in her client's hair when she spotted Tader getting out of Terrell's truck. She shook her head because she knew Tader had fed Terrell a bunch of lies in order for the two to have reconciled so quickly. Tader flipped her hair over her shoulders and smiled as the sum beamed down on her chocolate skin. She walked inside of the salon with all smiles.

"Hey ladies," she greeted, headed for her station. Spen eyed Tader confused as to why she was so happy. With everything that took place the night before, happiness was the last thing Spen expected from her. She put her client under the dryer and then walked over to Tader's station.

Triple Crown Publications presents . . . **DAMAGE**

"You wanna tell me why you're so happy."

Tader smiled and said, "Life is too short not to be happy Spen. You better get hip girl."

"He believed everything you told him, didn't he?" Spen asked.

"Actually he's still trippin'. But I know Terrell; he'll get over it."

Spen crossed her arms and began shaking her head. "So what's the deal with your truck?"

Tader revealed a sneaky grin. "I'm meeting with Anthony this weekend. Some good pussy should have that nigga digging deep in his pockets to purchase me something nice."

"You're crazy." Spen walked back over to her station to start her next client. Moments later Chatt was walking through the door. Spen eyed the clock and noticed that Chatt was hours early. She tried to read her facial expression, but had a hard time because Chatt was always so nonchalant about everything. When she heard the door's open again, she turned around to see DreStar coming in. The women inside the salon immediately began whispering to one another. Chatt smiled because she knew she was about to be the new topic of gossip.

"Aren't you a little early?" Spen asked.

Chatt's expression was still blank as she spoke, "Yeah, a little."

Spen glared at DreStar suspiciously. "Hey DreStar," she greeted him, trying to break the ice.

"He'd prefer if you call him Dre," Chatt stated.

Spen turned up her lip, rolling her eyes. She felt embarrassed, but tried to play it cool. "Sorry Chasity, but I don't believe I was talking to you."

"Actually, she's right," DreStar informed her. "I prefer Dre if you don't mind."

Triple Crown Publications presents . . . DAMAGE

Spen shook her head and returned her attention back to her client. She knew DreStar didn't mean any harm, but she felt as if Chatt came off a little rude. Tader laughed when she noticed that Spen was a little upset. "You salty," she mouthed at her. Spen silently laughed and continued flat ironing her client's hair.

"It was nice seeing you ladies again," DreStar said heading towards the doors.

"You too Dre," Tader replied, saying his name with sarcasm in her tone. The minute he walked out, the whole salon started talking. Chatt just shook her head and grabbed the broom. She began sweeping the floor while listening to rumors float around. Chatt didn't have a Cosmetology license, but Spen helped her out by paying her on the side to help keep the salon in order.

"So," Tader began, "what you and Dre do last night?"

"We ain't do anything," Chatt answered. She searched for the dust pan and continued, "after he dropped me off, he left."

Spen smacked her lips. "Girl, we know that's just the code for he came in and y'all fucked the night away."

Chatt couldn't hide her grin. She put the broom and dust pan away, and then took a seat. She knew everybody was waiting for her story, but she remained silent.

"Tell us what happened!" Tader ordered. "We know he spent the night because he hung up on us from yo phone earlier."

"Y'all know what happened. No need to tell a story that's already been read." Chatt didn't want to discuss what had happened between her and Dre because she still felt a little stupid. She made a scene at the club in front of everybody, letting him know that she wasn't giving it up, but when they were alone, she did the complete opposite.

"Magnum or Trojan?" Tader questioned. Everyone in the

Triple Crown Publications presents... DAMAGE

salon was silent, waiting on Chatt's response. Their eyes were glued to her as she searched for the words to speak.

"I'm gonna take raw for five hundred," Chatt joked, nervous to hear the girls' opinions.

Spen's mouthed dropped. "You fucked that nigga raw?"

"I believe that's what the child just said," spoke Chelae, who was another stylist in the salon.

"What y'all trippin' for?" Tader asked looking around the salon. "Shit, raw is my favorite brand of condoms!" She raised her hand in the air for Chatt to meet her high five, but Chatt left her hanging.

"You nasty little girl," Chelae said pointing her curling iron in Chatt's direction.

"You nasty!" Chatt fired back, taking her comment personal. At that moment, she wished she would have kept her mouth closed.

"She ain't nasty! I know half of the chicks in here done fucked on the first night." Tader was determined to defend Chatt's case.

"Yeah, but at least we have the decency to use condoms. Shit, I keep me a Trojan in my purse in case of emergency." Chelae high fived her client.

Tader smacked her lips. "Chelae, please! Any nigga you fucking with gon' need a Lifestyle. Magnum's and Trojan's are for real men."

"You would know," Chelae mumbled under her breath. Tader heard her comment, but didn't feel like bickering at the time. She was too focused on Chatt's situation. In a way, she was proud of her. Chatt was never the one to go out on a limb, so Tader was excited.

"So Chatt, you like this Dre nigga?"

"He's a'ight. I've only known him for a day though, so it's nothing serious."

Spen decided to re-enter herself back into the

Triple Crown Publications presents . . . DAMAGE

conversation. "You plan on getting serious?"

Chatt shrugged her shoulders. "I don't even know him like that. Why y'all going so hard?"

"Because you fucked him Chasity. We all know how you are and that's not like you," Chelae stated. "You must be feeling dude."

"From what I know, he seems cool. I don't plan on being in a relationship with him though."

"Why?" Tader questioned. "You ain't had a steady man in forever girl."

"I know you ain't talking," Chatt laughed. "Ms. I got niggas burning my truck up and shit!"

"Okay, but at least I'm involved with men. You been solo for how long?" Tader looked at her watch to add dramatics to her joke. Everyone laughed; everyone but Chatt.

"I been single for a while by choice. Don't act like nigga's don't be eyeing me when we go out." Chatt rolled her brown eyes and turned around in her chair so that she was facing the mirror. She stared at her reflection trying to convince herself that she was beautiful. Her self-esteem had been low ever since she was little. Chatt's crack-head mother Shawan never failed to insult whenever she was around Chatt. No matter what Chatt wore or how hard she tried to present herself as a young lady, Shawan always knew the perfect combination of words to tear her self-esteem in half. What Chatt didn't realize was that Shawan only tore her down to build her own self up. Every random nigga that invaded their apartment always had eyes for Chatt. Although Shawan informed them that Chatt was off limits, she still couldn't ignore the attention they would give her. Shawan got fed-up and started telling Chatt that she was ugly almost every day. She told her that she was the most unattractive little girl that she had ever seen and no man would ever want her. Chatt would never forget those

Triple Crown Publications presents . . . DAMAGE

words in all her days of living. Throughout high school, the guys never paid her much attention as they would the other girls. Chatt believed it was because of her looks, but in actuality, it was because of her insecurities. Everyone knew how insecure she was, and it became a turnoff for most people.

"Chasity!" Spen yelled, snapping her fingers in Chatt's face. "What are you looking at?"

"Nothing." Chatt turned away from the mirror.

"Well, if you don't mind me putting my two cents in, I think it's great that you might like this man. Just because you haven't had a past with anyone, doesn't mean it's too late to create a future."

"I don't know if he'll even be in my future. How many times I'ma tell y'all that I just met him?"

"We know you just met him girl. We were with you last night," Spen reminded her. "I have an idea."

"Oh, hell! Take cover," Tader said, joking around again.

"Shut up!" Spen told her. She looked at Chatt and continued. "Since we didn't fully finish our night out yesterday, how about a drink tonight at my place?"

"As long as Devon's not there, you know I'm down," Tader stated seriously.

"Don't start with the Devon shit Ta'Ronna. You and Terrell better have y'all black asses at my spot tonight, no bull-shit."

"I can't." She sighed. "Terrell is still trippin'. I know he ain't gon' come."

"Well, at least ask him. Chasity, should I be looking forward to seeing you and Dre tonight?"

Chatt shook her head. "Nah, don't plan on it."

"Girl stop acting like that! You ain't working at that damn food joint tonight, so you don't have shit else to do." Spen was tired of Chatt always saying no to things. She

Triple Crown Publications presents . . . DAMAGE

knew she was going to have to start forcing her, in order to get her to cooperate.

"Come on, Chasity." Tader began to pout. "Don't make me go alone."

Chatt lowered her head. She knew that if she said no like she really wanted to; she would be the one ruining the night. She hated when she was put in the position as the third person. "I might come, but don't expect Dre to be with me."

"Why not? That's the whole point." Spen preferred a date night, rather than just a girls night. She loved spending time with her girls but sometimes she wanted to share those good times with Devon. With his job at the law firm, Spen had to work around his busy schedule to get as much quality time in as she could.

"I don't know Spen. I can't just ask him to come; I mean what if he's busy?"

"If he's busy, then fine. But try to invite him, okay?"

"Okay." Chatt finally agreed because she knew Spen wouldn't stop if she didn't. She honestly didn't know if she would ask Dre or not, but she didn't plan on it. Chatt saw him as nothing more than a one night stand until the women in the salon filled her head with ideas about them spending more time together. She wasn't really looking for a relationship because she felt like she would have to devote all of her time into her partner. Chatt was the type that needed her space and hated to feel smothered.

"So I guess ain't none of us invited, huh?" Chelae asked, referring to her and the other women in the salon.

"Of course you're invited," Spen stated. Chelae just laughed because she knew that meant no. She rarely hung out with Spen, Tader, and Chatt outside of the salon anyway, so it didn't bother her. She was more associated with Tiffany, Benita, and Shaquana, the three other stylists

Triple Crown Publications presents . . . DAMAGE

that worked in the salon.

"So what time should we be coming?" Tader asked.

"About nine-thirty, ten," Spen replied. "And let's try to dress classy," she added looking at Chatt.

Chatt chuckled. "You know me and you have two different meanings of classy, but I'll do my best."

Spen turned the shower off and grabbed a towel to dry her wet body. When she opened the bathroom door, she entered her bedroom and sat on the bed. She grabbed the bottle of baby oil off of her dresser and began rubbing her body down. She smiled when she noticed headlights beaming through her bedroom window because she knew Devon was home. She peered through the blinds, watching him until he reached the front porch. She jotted down the steps still naked, to greet him at the door. Once inside, Devon brushed past Spen as if she was invisible. "Well, hello to you too," Spen said, following behind him.

"What's up baby," he replied, continuing into the living room.

"What's wrong with you?" Spen asked. She knew something was wrong, because it wasn't like Devon to just walk in and ignore her presence, especially with her being naked.

"Long day," he answered, plopping down on their Italian leather sofa. Spen stood up behind him and began massaging his shoulders...

"Well, I know exactly just what you need," she told him.

Devon politely guided Spen's hand away from his shoulders. "I'm not in the mood right now, Spen."

"Devon, ain't nobody trying to fuck you," Spen spoke, raising her tone. She was offended because sex was not what she wanted from him.

Triple Crown Publications *presents* . . . **DAMAGE**

"My fault baby, but can you blame me for thinking that's what you wanted? I mean you but ass naked, touching on me and shit."

"Whatever." Spen went back upstairs to put her clothes on. Devon sighed, knowing the routine way too well. In order for Spen's attitude to disappear, he would have to follow her upstairs and basically kiss her ass; but tonight, Devon was not in the mood. He was tired and all he wanted to do was chill, without having to please anybody but himself. Spen was a little irritated when she realized that Devon didn't follow behind her, but she didn't trip. She knew that if she could convince him to have a drink, then he would loosen up. She put on her black lace *Armani* dress, and then grabbed her house shoes, not wanting to walk around in heels until her guest arrived. She walked back downstairs into the kitchen, purposely walking through the living room so that she could get Devon's attention.

He glanced up at her and said, "Have fun, baby. You look gorgeous."

"I'm not going out," she stated. "We're having company."

"Come on Spen, not tonight a'ight? I'm tired," Devon nagged.

Spen grabbed two glasses from out of the kitchen cabinet, then grabbed her favorite liquor and poured them both a shot. With both glasses in her hand, she walked into the living room and handed one of the glasses to Devon. He sat it down on their crystal coffee table, not in the mood for a drink. Spen rolled her eyes, becoming annoyed with his slight attitude. "Why are you acting all stuck up? All I want to do is have a drink with my man."

"Then we can have a drink baby, but why we gotta have people coming over? It's a weekday; we all got work tomorrow."

Triple Crown Publications presents . . .   DAMAGE

"Because Devon, we need some fun for one night." She sat on his lap and wrapped her arms around his neck. "Please baby," she whispered in his ear. "I promise we can do whatever you want afterwards." She kissed his lips.

Devon looked at her, and gave her a half smile. "Go turn the shower on for me," he said. When he saw her eyes light up with excitement, he knew that was the only reason he had agreed to have a drink with her; just to see that light in her eyes, the light of happiness. As long as Spen was happy, Devon was happy.

Tader got out the shower and put on an all-black spaghetti strap dress, a pair of diamond studs and a diamond necklace. She pinned her hair up in a bun and grabbed her silver pumps. That was one thing about Tader; no matter what the occasion, her wardrobe was on point. She grabbed her cell phone and called Terrell, hoping his attitude towards her had disappeared. Tader knew Terrell was mad, but she didn't understand why he couldn't just brush the situation off. He knew she messed around with other men, and she knew he fooled around with other females, so she couldn't get why he was still tripping.

Tader was the wildest between herself, Chasity, and Spencer. She never liked to settle with just one thing because her life quote was, 'The more, the merrier'. When it came to men, she lived by her quote to the fullest. She figured, why have one man when you could have four or five? As long as they were coming out the pocket for her, she had no problem opening up her legs to return the favor. When she met Terrell, she fell for him in a different way than from other men. They messed around in high school, but never got serious until they were older. He demanded the most attention from her, causing her to spend more time with him, rather than with the other men she fooled

Triple Crown Publications *presents* . . . DAMAGE

around with.

Tader grew fond of Terrell, and even decided that he was her favorite out of all the men she messed with. Their relationship was very unique, sort of like they were together, but not yet official. But no matter how much Tader was feeling Terrell, she never fully dismissed any of her sideline men. Terrell had her attention, but he didn't have her *full* attention.

Tader pressed the send button on her cell phone, and waited for Terrell to answer.

"Yeah," he answered on the third ring, sounding annoyed.

"Hey babe. Where are you?"

"Handling bid'ness. Is this important?"

"You didn't get my message earlier about having a drink tonight at Spen's?" Tader asked, her tone sounding as if she wanted to cry.

"Yeah, I got it," Terrell stated. "But I never said I was going."

"But I want you to come Rell. Why are you acting so damn stubborn?"

"Look girl, I ain't 'bout to sit here and argue wit' you 'bout this shit a'ight? I'm not coming, so where do we go from here?"

Tader lowered her tone. "No where, I guess."

Terrell could hear the disappointment in Tader's voice as she spoke. He knew she was upset, and he felt bad for snapping at her the way he did. "Call me when you come back in, and I'ma come see you." Tader remained silent. "Did you hear what I said?" Terrell asked.

"Yeah Rell, loud and clear." She hung up on him before he could say anything else. She was frustrated because he was acting so stubborn, and she felt like the whole situation was petty. She huffed, thinking about how she had planned

Triple Crown Publications *presents* . . . **DAMAGE**

on Rell being her date and transportation as well. With him not going, Tader didn't have a ride to get over Spen's house. She thought about calling Spen to come and get her, but immediately decided against it because she didn't want anybody knowing that Terrell had bailed on her.

Ding-dong!

Tader's heart jumped when she heard the doorbell ring. She knew it was Terrell, and smiled inside for letting herself think that he would actually still be tripping. She grabbed her jacket, and headed towards her front door.

Ding-dong!

"I'm coming babe," Tader hollered out loud. When she opened her front door, she was completely surprised to see David standing there. "What the fuck are you doing on my damn porch, David?"

"You look nice," he complimented. "Going somewhere?"

"Yes I'm going somewhere, so you need to leave right now."

"Damn Tader, that's how you gon' play me? After all the shit we been through," he reminisced.

"Fuck you, nutty ass nigga!" Tader slammed the door in his face, and then locked it. She looked up at the ceiling and sighed thinking about her actions. Even though David had crossed the line to Tader's bad side, she could never forget what they had been through. David played a huge part in the lavish shopping sprees that Tader went on, not to mention the fact that he provided her with transportation, even though it wasn't in her name. It kept her from riding the bus, so Tader was grateful either way. She wasn't in love with David, but in love with the money he spent on her. David, on the other hand, swore he was in love. What he failed to realize was that it wasn't Tader he was in love with; it was the coochie that had him sprung.

Tader opened the door ready to apologize to David for being so rude. "Look David, I'm sorry, but you're crazy ass is gon' have to...." Tader was silenced by David's hand covering her mouth as he shoved her into the house and threw her against the wall. He shut the door and pulled out his 9MM pistol.

"You didn't think I was gon' let you get away with that, now did you?" David asked, pointing the gun in Tader's face.

"You are a crazy fucking bastard!" Tader tried to stand up, but David sent the butt of his gun across her face, almost knocking the wind out of her.

"You wanna tell me where you were headed this evening?" David asked.

"Over Spen's," Tader replied, holding her chest area.

"Over Spen's?" he questioned. "Y'all grown ass women having sleep over's and shit."

"I was just going to have a drink," Tader confessed.

David laughed. "Alcoholic ass bitch! All you do is drink. You need to slow down before you find yourself in rehab."

"Thanks for the advice."

"You're welcome Tader." He lifted her chin, and placed a kiss on her forehead. "I love you," he told her.

Tader shook her head in disbelief. How in the hell did she let nutty ass David barge into her home, and pull a gun on her? "David, Terrell is on his way over here and if he walks in and see's you here, he's gon' go ham!" She boasted.

"Fuck Terrell!" David shouted, hitting her with the gun once again. "Don't ever threaten me with another nigga, you hear me?" He grabbed her neck, forcing her to face him.

"Yes," she whimpered. "I hear you."

"Good. Now let me ask you something Tader." He let her

neck loose. "How come you didn't choose me?"

Tader looked at him confused. "What?"

"I thought we had something. Why you try to play me out in the club the other night?"

"I'm sorry," she stated.

"Really?" He asked.

"Yes." Tader looked in David's eyes and began to contemplate a plan to help her escape her impending demise. She took her right hand and brushed it across his cheek. "David, we can be together if that's what you want baby. Fuck these other nigga's; let's be happy together."

David smiled. "Fa'real? You wanna be with me, even after all the shit I've done?"

She nodded her head. "Everybody deserves a second chance David."

David kissed her lips then said, "You full of shit bitch!" He swung the gun across her face again, this time leaving blood gushing out from her nose. Let's take this party downstairs," he ordered, kicking her in the ass. She began crawling through her living room, headed towards the basement with David behind her laughing. "Get a fucking move on bitch! I don't have all day," David said, kicking her once more. She reached the basement door then stood up to open it. David had a tight grip on the back of her neck while they both walked down the steps. Tader had all types of gym equipment in her basement such as a tread mill, a bike, jump ropes and even a weight bench. She didn't play when it came to keeping her figure right.

"So this how you stay in shape huh?" David asked, letting the grip of her neck loose. Tader stood silent, terrified of what David's next move would be. "Not talking now huh? Well let's have some fun baby girl. Take them clothes off."

Without saying a word, Tader slowly took her clothes off. She figured that she would just give him some pussy

Triple Crown Publications *presents* . . . DAMAGE

33

and then the night would be over. She stripped down until she was standing in nothing but her underwear.

"Bra and panties too bitch! You know I like to see you naked!" David yelled. Once Tader was fully naked, he turned her treadmill on. "Get on here," he demanded.

"Can we please just fuck and be done with it," Tader begged, holding her hands together as if she was praying.

"Get on the fucking treadmill, bitch!"

Tader got on the treadmill with a bloody nose, fully naked, and began walking on it. Minute after minute, David increased the speed. After five minutes, Tader was running full speed on the treadmill. It was as if she was running for dear life. Sweat began to drip from her forehead and she began breathing heavily. David watched her and found the whole scene hilarious. He laughed hysterically while he watched Tader run.

Spen got excited as she looked through her blinds and saw Chatt and DreStar approaching her front porch. She couldn't wait to get Chatt alone so that she could ask her all the details about how she convinced Dre to come. "Baby Chasity's here," Spen yelled, hoping Devon could hear her from up the stairs.

"I'll be down in a minute," he shouted back.

Chatt rang the doorbell and waited patiently for someone to answer. Spen opened the door, all smiles. She was so happy to see her best friend finally branching out. Spen knew that Chatt had only known Dre for a short amount of time, but she hoped that they would work out in the long run.

"Hey guys," Spen spoke excitedly.

"Hey," both Chatt and Dre replied in unison.

"This a nice crib y'all got," Dre complimented. "I know y'all had to come out the pockets for something like this."

Triple Crown Publications presents . . . **DAMAGE**

Spen smiled. "Thank you, and yes this was a pocket breaker," she joked.

Spen invited them inside the condo and hollered again for Devon to come downstairs. He came walking down the steps, his swag demanding attention. He was rocking a gray Emporio Armani polo with the matching five pocket blue jeans. Spen smiled, eyeing her gorgeous, tall brown skinned boyfriend as he made his appearance.

"How you doing Chasity?" Devon asked, giving her a friendly hug.

"I'm living," she replied, embracing his hug.

"Baby, this is her friend Dre," Spen introduced.

Devon looked at Dre. "What up fam'?" He said, giving him dap.

"Nice meeting you partna'," Dre responded.

Everyone headed into Spen's favorite section of the house, which happened to be the living room. She designed the room on her own, and was more proud of herself every time she stepped foot inside what she called her masterpiece. She picked out everything from the Monaco dark brown Premium Italian Leather Sofa and Loveseat, to the Beige and Cream colored walls and carpet. She wanted a regular T.V with the matching stand, but Devon opted to get a 51-inch Plasma Flat Screen. Spen didn't wanna argue with him, seeing that he was covering most of the expenses of the room.

"So," Spen began, her tone filled with much excitement, "me and Chasity are gonna go in the kitchen and whip up some drinks and you two can stay in here and get better acquainted."

Devon grinned showcasing his deep dimples. He knew how excited Spen was and it made him feel good to see his girl so happy. Devon loved Spen unconditionally and he would give her the world if she asked. She captured his heart at a young age and he did the same with hers. "Yeah, gone 'head and have y'all little women talk," Devon said. He grabbed the remote control and turned the T.V on to watch the Lakers take on the Nuggets. Spen smiled, as she migrated into the kitchen with Chatt.

"You and Devon don't play when it comes to y'all Armani," Chatt stated, admiring Spen's dress.

"Girl you ain't know? Me and my babe dress to impress, no matter the occasion."

Chatt giggled. "True, cause y'all dressed like we going out."

"Yeah, that's how we do." Spen smiled. "So tell me how you convinced your new boo to come over here."

"My new boo?" Chatt blushed.

"Yeah, girl! Your new boo."

"Well," she paused; peeking into the living room to make sure Devon and Dre weren't listening in on their conversation. When she saw their eyes glued to the Lakers game, she continued. "Dre is a sweetheart. I told him I was coming over here to have a drink, and then I asked him if he wanted to join me, and he said yes with no question's asked."

"He is so sweet," Spen cooed. "I like him Chasity. You've only known him for what a day or two, and I already like where this is going."

"Yeah, I guess." Chatt faced the ground. She wanted to change the subject because she didn't want Spen going on about how she and Dre could have a future together. She knew that Spen was just excited for her, but it bothered her when people tried to rush things in her life, including men. She preferred to move at her own pace, and no one else's. "So where's Tader? I expected her to beat me here."

"I don't know," Spen stated, shrugging her shoulders. "I called her, but got no answer."

Triple Crown Publications presents ... **DAMAGE**

A devilish grin spread across Chatt's face. "You know what that means right?"

Spen chuckled. "Hell yeah. If I know my girl Tader, Terrell came over and their black asses are having a makeup sex session."

"That girl loves her some dick." Chatt shook her head. "She would go nuts if all the men on earth disappeared over night."

"Yeah right," Spen spat. "Her ass would be walking out the Sex Shop with every dildo they got in stock."

Chatt burst out with laughter. "Girl, you ain't never lied."

"Hell nah." Spen grabbed two extra wine glasses from out of the cabinet. "You know I'm the truth teller." She held the glasses in the air. "Now let's go get drunk!"

"Amen to that," Chatt said, grabbing a glass from Spen's hand.

Tader's body ached as she lay on the hard concrete floor of her basement. She held her eyes closed tightly as she waited for David to finish raping her for what seemed like the thousandth time. She opened her eyes when she felt him let off his semen inside her. He looked down at her causing the sweat from his forehead to drop onto her face. Tader was so disgusted. She looked into David's eyes, hoping that he could feel the hatred she had for him. He smiled informing her that he didn't give a fuck how she was feeling at that point. Tader turned her head and began to think about the phone conversation she and Terrell had earlier that day. He told her to call him once she got back from Spen's place so that he could come over. Tader could only hope that Terrell would show up without receiving her phone call. "Go take a shower and clean yo' nasty ass up," David ordered, rising up from on top of Tader. She jumped up as if he had just told that she was free. "Let me tell you something," David continued, "when you get out of the shower, I'll be gone. But don't get it set in your mind that you free from me. I will always be watching every fucking move you make." He gripped her jaws, demanding her undivided attention. "Now dig this, if you tell anybody, and I mean any fucking body that I was here, you won't see another fucking day in your life! And that goes for your ugly ass friends, the feds or whoever you decide to run your mouth to. I'll kill you, Ta'Ronna, I promise."

He kissed her forehead before letting her jaws loose from his grip. Tader watched him put his clothes on and walk out the door. She immediately jumped up to lock it, then she fell on the floor ready to release the tears that had formed in her eyes. She wailed and wailed until she cried herself to sleep. When she woke up the following morning, she heard a loud banging at her door and prayed like hell that it wasn't David.

She looked out her window to find Terrell standing on her porch. She opened the door, her blood steaming with anger. "Was your fucking business so important that you forgot to come over last night?" she hollered, her tears gathering back up.

He ignored her question and focused on her bruised face. "What the fuck happened to you?"

Tader wanted to tell him the truth badly, but David threats never left her mind. "Me and some bitch got in a scrap yesterday," she lied. "Why the fuck didn't you come Terrell? You knew I was waiting on you!"

"I told you to call me when you got back." He grabbed her arms. "What the fuck is wrong with you?"

"Don't touch me Rell," she said, pulling away from him.

"Tell me why you acting like this," Terrell demanded.

Triple Crown Publications *presents . . .* **DAMAGE**

"Rell, what are we?" She blinked, letting the tears relocate to her cheeks. "I mean seriously, what are you and I?"

"Shit, you tell me Ta'Ronna. I think you're the one confused as to what role I play in your life. I mean let's be honest baby, no games. I mean, I thought we agreed that those are for kids, right?" Terrell was always so calm when he spoke.

Tader stormed back inside the house and crawled into her bed. Terrell followed right behind her, still confused as to why she was acting funny. "Terrell, I don't want us being friends with benefits, babe." She wiped her tears. "I need a steady relationship."

Terrell sat on the bed and pulled Tader into his arms. He was so confused by her actions and wanted to know why she was acting so shook up. "What's going on Tader? I need you to speak up on whatever's got you shook."

Tader wrapped her arms around him. "I just need you Rell. I need us to work babe." She buried her head in his chest and continued to cry. Her body trembled as she had flashbacks of David raping her, and how she thought Terrell was going to walk in and save her. Terrell seen the pain in Tader's eyes and he knew something wasn't right with her, but decided to not pressure her about the situation anymore. When the time came, he would most definitely get to the bottom of it.

Triple Crown Publications *presents . . .* DAMAGE

3

Chasity smiled as she laid next DreStar, watching him sleep; the sun creeping through her blinds, glistening on his dark brown skin. She giggled, noticing his long legs hanging off of the edge of her bed. She knew he had a hangover and decided to take care of him. He was way past drunk when they left Spen's place, and Chatt knew that he was in no condition to drive, so she took it upon herself to drive him safely back to her place for the night. She eyed his muscular frame as his chest inhaled and exhaled.

"Wake up Dre," she said, tugging on his shoulder. He yawned, opening his light brown eyes. Chasity never paid attention to how attractive DreStar was until now. Her smile turned into a frown when she thought about her past experiences with men. *I wonder why he chose me*, she thought to herself. *There were plenty of other women in the* club that night, including Tader and Spencer, but the nigga chose me.

"What's wrong?" Dre asked, noticing Chatt's change in emotion.

"Nothing." She didn't want to tell him that she questioned why he chose to talk to her instead of one of her friends. Chasity was so used to guys approaching the women around her, that it surprised her when a guy actually was interested in her. "Look, I have to work later so you might want to head on out."

He was taken aback by her comment. "To be honest, I don't even remember coming here last night."

"You were drunk and in no condition to drive, so I...."

"You decided to bring be back to your place?" He interrupted.

"Well, it's not like I know where you stay." She had an attitude. "That's the only reason I brought you back here."

Dre was confused with her sudden change of heart. "Whoa, did I say something to upset you?" He looked sincere.

Chatt rolled her eyes. "No, but I think you should go, okay?"

"I'll go, but not until you tell me what it is that I did to upset you."

"I don't even know you," Chatt exclaimed, "but here you are lying in my bed like we been together for some time now." She shook her head. "And I even fucked your ass not knowing shit about you!"

DreStar was stunned. "Calm down, Chasity."

"No!" She got out of her bed and began pacing the floor. "Why did I do this? I should have never let you in that night."

"What are you trying to say?" Dre asked.

"Just get out!" Chatt yelled, pointing towards her

bedroom door. "Get the fuck out of here nigga!" Dre got out of the bed, and started walking towards her. "Get away from me," she screamed.

He grabbed her hand. "Can you just listen to me for a minute?"

"Listen to you so you can make me feel more stupid than I already do?" She snatched her hand away. "I don't think so."

"I'm not trying to make you feel stupid," he explained. "I'm just trying to be real wit' you." Chatt sat on her bed and buried her face inside her hands. "Chasity, if you don't battle your insecurities now, they'll always fight with you in the future," DreStar preached.

"I'm not insecure," she stated.

"Well that's how you're coming off. I told you we didn't have to do anything if you didn't want to." He grabbed his shirt from off of the floor, and pulled it over his head. "I would have enjoyed myself either way, but now it starting to seem like we only had sex because you thought I wouldn't be interested in you if we didn't."

Chatt looked up. "Would you?"

"Yeah, and I'm sorry you couldn't see that." He searched for his shoes. "What you do wit' my keys?"

"I sat em' on the living room table." She watched him walk out of her room. "Wait!"

He turned around. "Yeah?"

"I don't want you to leave," Chatt confessed.

"You're confusing me."

She sighed. "Can you just stay a little while longer?"

"Nah, I think it's best that I get going." He walked into the living room to retrieve his keys from the table. Chatt followed behind him.

"Don't leave," she begged, snatching the keys from his hand.

Triple Crown Publications *presents* . . . **DAMAGE**

"Come on ma, give me the keys."

Chatt dropped the keys on the floor. "So I'm back to 'ma' now?"

"I meant Chasity." He picked the keys up from off of the floor. "I'll see you later."

"I'm sorry for going off on you. Just don't leave yet."

He asked, "Why should I stay when you think sex is all I want from you?" He was serious. "Besides, we barley know each other right?"

"Then let's get to know each other," Chatt suggested. DreStar put his keys in his jacket pocket, and then sat on the couch. He patted the seat next to him informing Chatt to sit down. She sat next to him with her eyes watering. She was so embarrassed with how she was acting, but she couldn't control herself. Her emotions were on overload as she thought about how many men used her in the past. She had never met a man who didn't want more than sex from her. Her past relationships were nothing more than a hit and quit situation. That was the reason she went off on DreStar at the club, because she thought she knew what he wanted. Once they got back to her place and talked a little more, she realized that he was a cool person and figured that she would have to open her legs in order to get to know him better. As far as she knew, you had to spread em' to keep em'.

"So tell me about yourself," Dre requested.

"Well, I got plenty to tell," she replied.

Chrisette Philips stepped foot inside *Hair Desire* looking flawless. All eyes were on her, and she couldn't deny the fact that she was loving the attention. Although she was used to it, Chrisette never got tired of people admiring her top model looks. Every morning when she woke up, the first thing she would do was look in the mirror to see if her beauty sleep paid off. She moisturized her Vanilla skin every night and washed her long black curly hair, every two days. She was at the gym five days a week making sure her physique was on point. In her eyes, she was a hundred and thirty-five pounds of pure perfection. She removed her Gucci shades from her face, enabling everyone to see her hazel eyes. The low-cut jeans that she wore made it easy for everyone to see the tattoo that read 'Crispy' on her lower back.

She actually got the nickname when she used to hang out with Chasity, Spencer, and Ta'Ronna, back in school. The four of them hung tight, but Crispy always knew that she was the outcast. She knew she didn't have the bond that the other three girls had, but it never fazed her. She was still popular; regardless of whom she hung out with. Crispy partied hard throughout high school until the tragedy of her mother's death hit her heart. The two were extremely close and the thought of not ever seeing her mother again left Crispy's heart scarred forever. After her graduation, she moved to California to live with her grandmother, causing her to lose touch with everyone. She knew she would miss her past, but she moved to California to build her new future. "Well hello ladies," Crispy said, as she swung her hair over her shoulders.

"Chrisette? I mean Crispy," Spen asked, eyeing her up and down.

Crispy smiled. "Yeah, girl. "How you guys been?"

"We've been good." She looked over her shoulders at the other women in the salon. "Well I can only speak for myself."

Crispy glanced at Chatt. "Hey Chasity, how you been?"

"Living life, one day at a time." Chatt was nonchalant.

"That's great." Crispy looked at Tader and grimaced, noticing her bruised face. "And Ta'Ronna, how are you?"

"I'm good," Tader replied, rolling her eyes. She knew what Crispy was looking at but she didn't care. Tader had told everyone the same lie about getting into a fight to explain her sore face and if Crispy asked, she would get fed the same story. Between the three girls, Tader couldn't stand Crispy the most. Crispy was pure plastic in Tader's eyes, and she didn't trust her one bit. Spen noticed the tension between the two women and tried to ease the vibe.

"So Crispy," she said, breaking intense staring contest between her and Tader, "I thought you moved to Cali. What are you doing here?"

"I'm in town on business," Crispy informed her.

Tader smacked her lips. "Well if you're in town on business, what are you doing here?"

"I'm actually free today." She flaunted a fake smile. "I ran into Terrell earlier and he told me about the salon, so I had to stop by."

Tader's facial expression displayed anger. "Terrell? Where the fuck did you happen to see him?" She asked, almost burning her client with the curling iron.

"I ran into him around the way."

"Where the hell is around the way?" Tader was serious. She didn't like the fact that Crispy had exchanged words with her man.

Crispy sighed. "At a food joint, Ta'Ronna."

"Yeah, I hear you." Tader decided to drop the conversation, but she promised herself that she would confront Terrell the first chance she got.

"So Spen, how long you been running this place?" Crispy asked.

"About two years now. I'm just getting started though." Spen knew her salon wasn't up to high standards, and she knew Crispy was judgmental, so she felt the need to let her know that she was just getting started. Spen's image for

Hair Desire was not how she pictured it, due to low funds. She wanted so much more for her salon, and she knew that a better image would increase her clientele. "I got plenty more to do around here."

Crispy nodded. "Sounds interesting."

"It is interesting," Tader stated. She didn't mind speaking her mind, especially when it came to those she didn't like.

"Well, the hotel I'm staying in is having a party tonight. You guys should be my guest."

"I have house cleaning," Chatt blurted.

"And I promised to help," Spen added.

Crispy didn't even face Tader, already knowing what her response would be. "Well I guess I'll be on my way."

"Nice seeing you," Chatt stated as Crispy left.

Crispy smiled as she walked out of the salon, knowing that she had haters out the ass. She was used to females not liking her, so she didn't sweat it. She actually liked when people gave her a negative attitude because she knew that they were envious. She got in the driver's seat of her black Benz, and pulled her cell phone from out of her Gucci purse. She went to her recent calls, and then pressed send on the first highlighted number.

"Hello?"

"Hey you!" Crispy spoke excitedly into the phone. "What are you into?"

He was nonchalant. "Money."

"What about later?" Crispy asked.

"I don't know."

"Well, I want you to join me tonight. My hotel is having some sort of party later and I don't want to attend it alone."

"Then don't go."

"Please," Crispy begged. "I want to go, just not alone. You don't even have to stay that long."

"Fine," he agreed. "Hit me in a few hours, I'm busy."
Crispy spoke happily. "Great, talk to you then."

The minute Crispy left the salon; the gossip began to fill the air. Chatt smiled, knowing the routine to well. No one said anything while Crispy was present but they were about to grill her ass now that she was gone. In a room full of females, you really couldn't expect anything else but good gossip. "That girl ain't changed one bit."

"You damn right," Tader stated. "Who does she think she is, just walking up in here like that?"

"It was just a friendly visit," Spen noted.

"A friendly visit my ass! Ain't shit friendly 'bout that bitch and Terrell is gon' hear a mouth full when I talk to his ass."

"You shouldn't cuss him out till you know what happened," Chatt advised.

Tader smacked her lips. "Girl you know I act first and ask questions later." She kept it real.

"Who was that girl?" Chelae asked.

Spen did the honors. "That was Chrisette Philips, better known as Crispy. She actually got that nickname from us when we were younger."

"So why y'all don't like her?"

Tader spat, "Because the bitch is fake. I can see right through her plastic ass, with all that long pretty hair. I ought to sneak in her hotel room and cut that shit off tonight."

Spen chuckled. "No, Ta'Ronna. Let the woman have a peaceful visit while she's in town."

"Fuck that!" Tader wanted Crispy's trip to be hell.

"Go sit at my station," Spen told her client as she was walking away from the shampoo bowl.

The sounds of bells chiming, informed that someone

was walking through the door. "Hello ladies," David greeted with a Kool-Aid smile.

Tader damn near shitted brick's hearing his voice. She kept her head low as she packed her client's hair with mousse. Without even looking up, Tader could feel David approaching her station and she wanted to scream. She had no clue what he had up his sleeve and sure as hell didn't want to find out. By the time he reached her, Tader had caked the entire bottle of hair mousse in her client's hair. She didn't even realize that she had done it, until her client spoke up. "Girl, why you packing so much foam in my hair? It's gonna be super hard."

"Sor...sorry," Tader managed to say, still holding her head low. She could feel David's body heat gaining up on her.

He wrapped his arms around her waist, and whispered in her ear, "Don't act so nervous or they'll suspect something."

Tader swallowed a gulp of salvia down her dry throat, and then produced a fake smile. She looked at Spen who appeared to be confused, as well as Chasity. Although they didn't know about the torture that David had put Tader through, he still was disliked from his actions at the club. Spen eyed Tader suspiciously. Why was she still communicating with the man who destroyed her only transportation?

"Girl, why is he here?" Chatt asked.

"I don't know, but I'm gonna find out," Spen stated, eyeing David's every move. "Tader, let me talk to you for a minute."

"Wait," David said, grabbing Tader's hand as she tried to walk towards Spen's station. "I want to make an announcement."

Tader was nervous. "David, please don't do this," she whispered, still conveying her fake smile.

David smiled, kneeling down on one knee. "Tader," he paused digging into his pocket, "be my wife baby." Without hearing her response, he slid the ring on her finger, keeping a hold on her wrist, until he got his answer. Tader was speechless as she eyed the tarnished gold ring, with four diamonds missing. She wanted to snatch it off her hand and throw it in his face.

"Gon' girl!" Chelae was excited, not knowing the situation behind closed doors.

Tader remained silent until she felt pain shoot through her arm, caused by David squeezing her wrist. "Alright," she stated through clenched teeth.

"I can't hear you." He heard her loud and clear, but wanted the women in the salon to hear as well.

"I said alright," she repeated.

Spen couldn't believe her ears. "Tader, we need to talk now!"

"She'll have to call you later," David said, standing up. "I'm taking her somewhere special to celebrate."

"She can't leave." Spen was becoming irritated. "She still has clients for the day."

Tader tried her best not to look nervous. "Spen, I'll call you later."

"What am I supposed to tell your clients?"

David said, "Just cover for her. She just got engaged and y'all don't seem too happy."

"Yeah Spen, let her have her fun," Chelae chimed in.

Spen sighed. "Fine."

With that said, David and Tader were out the door, leaving Spen beyond upset. There was no way possible that she could be happy for Tader's engagement, because she didn't like David one bit. Spen was definitely a little skeptical about the whole situation, and she planned on keeping her eyes open to find out what she didn't know.

She knew there had to be something that was being done in the dark, and it may only come to light in the nick of time. When she left the salon for the night, she went home ready to tell Devon about the unpleasant news. Realizing that he hadn't made it home yet, she ran her some hot water and took a long needed bath. She folded her hands and rested them on her flat stomach, imagining that she had a baby bump. Her thoughts about Tader's engagement to David escaped her mind when she closed her eyes, and pictured her unborn child.

Spen couldn't control her overwhelming desire to become a mother. Each time she and Devon had sex, he would always pull out, knowing that she wasn't taking birth control. She always hoped that one day he would forget to pull out, but never once had he forgotten till this day. All she wanted to do was be the mother that she never had. Spen never knew her biological parent's, only her foster care providers. Now that she was older, she realized that being raised by strangers could never amount to the feeling of being raised by an actual family. Although she was taught to believe that the people around her actually loved her, Spen knew that she was just another child in the system, being used to collect government money. She couldn't wait to have a child of her own, so that she could demonstrate the love she never had.

Spen inhaled the delicious scent of breakfast food, and then opened her eyes to a plate of bacon, pancakes, and scrambled eggs with cheese. Devon was standing over her smiling, with a cup of orange juice in his hand. She grabbed the cup and took a sip, before sitting it on her dresser. "What's all this?" she asked, nibbling on a piece of bacon.

"It's breakfast baby," Devon replied. "Eat up."

Spen spoke with a mouth full of eggs, "What's the

Triple Crown Publications presents . . . DAMAGE

rush?"

"Today is all about you." He kissed her forehead. "I got shit planned."

"Devon?" She eyed him suspiciously. "What's the deal with you baby?"

"Damn, I can't spend time with you?"

Spen blushed. "Of course baby." She grabbed the back of his neck and brought him in for a kiss. "You never have to ask to spend time with me."

"Then shut up with the questions and eat!" He shoved a pancake in her face, leaving whipped cream smeared all over her nose. She laughed and playfully nudged him away from her. Once she was done eating, she and Devon took a shower together, followed by steamy shower sex. Just like any other time, Devon pulled out on time, but Spen didn't pay it any mind. She was too excited about spending the entire day with her man. Once they finished in the shower, they got dressed and headed for the door. As Spen sat in the passenger's seat of Devon's ride, she smiled watching him nod his head to the music. Devon grinned knowing that she was watching him, but he never took his eyes off the road. *My man is so cute,* Spen thought to herself. She loved it when he smiled because it showed off his dimples.

"We're at the first stop," Devon announced, pulling into the parking lot.

"Code Credit Union?" Spen was confused. "Why are we at this bank?"

Devon smiled. "Just stay here."

"Whatever you say," Spen stated, still confused. She waited patiently, while Devon handled his business inside the bank. When he returned, he got back in the truck and handed Spen four envelopes. "What are these?" she questioned.

"I promised you I would help finish it didn't I?" He kissed

her lips. "Have I ever broke a promise?"

Spen shook her head. "You're confusing me, Devon."

"The salon, baby." He ran his fingers through her hair. "I promised you that I would help finish it."

"My salon?" She had to be sure she heard him correctly.

"Just open the envelopes," he told her, smiling.

When Spen opened the first envelope, she saw nothing other than Benjamin Franklin's lined up perfectly. "Baby what is this?"

He laughed. "It's money."

"I know it's money, but why?" She was beyond surprised.

"I told you why." He grabbed one of the envelopes. "There's five stacks of cash, in each one of these."

"That makes twenty grand!" Spen stated, not realizing how loud she was.

"I'm glad you know your math," Devon joked. "But seriously baby, I want you to finish your salon with this money, a'ight?"

Spen didn't know what to think. "Devon why, I mean how...where?"

"Shhh." He grabbed her hand. "Don't worry about any of that. Your only focus should be the changes that you plan on making to make *Hair Desire* a bigger success than it already is."

Spen found herself getting teary eyed. "Tha... thank you," she said, stuttering through her words. "You don't know what this means to me."

"Yes I do."

"No you don't Devon." She tried her hardest to hold back her tears but she failed. "I can't believe you did this."

"Well believe it baby." He wiped the tears from her cheeks. "You deserve it."

Triple Crown Publications *presents* ... DAMAGE

Spen blushed. "Get your sexy ass over here." Without knowing what else to do, she gave him a passionate kiss that lasted for almost ten minutes.

"The day ain't over," Devon informed her, restarting the ignition. "Time for the second stop."

Spen took a deep breath and tried to understand everything that was happening around her. True enough she was happy; but something tugged at her mind, leaving her feeling robbed of unanswered questions. She knew Devon had money considering his occupation, but she never knew his money was sitting so high, that he could take out twenty thousand dollars at once. She wanted to question him about it, but she didn't know how to go about it without coming off as ungrateful. *Stop tripping Spencer,* she told herself. *This man loves you; don't make him feel unappreciated.*

Tader sat on her bed thinking of all possible ways to get rid of David. After another long torturous night, she couldn't possibly see herself letting him do this to her any longer. Her mind set was determined on finding a way to free herself from a prison with no bars. She felt as if Terrell had left her hanging once again, because he didn't show up when she needed him. She sat up straight in her bed; her movements slow because of the pain. Tader knew she would have to tell somebody soon, because eventually the bruises would speak for themselves. She knew she couldn't continuously tell the lie about getting into fights over and over.

When Tader tried to stand, she felt the soreness in between her legs, caused by David's constant rape sessions the previous night. She leaned against the wall for support as she made her way into the living room. She reached for her cordless phone, letting her body fall onto the couch as she grabbed it off the hook. She was exhausted and all she wanted to do was sleep; but the thought of David popping up randomly, gave her more than enough strength to stay awake. She gripped the phone tightly, thinking about who she wanted to call. She didn't know who to possibly tell, without David finding out about it.

When Tader looked down at her hand, she noticed that her finger was turning green from the ring that he had put on her finger. With all her might, she snatched the ring off, and threw it across the room. Tears of frustration filled her eyes, but she fought the urge to let the tear's fall. She wanted to be strong in this situation, and prove to David that he was nothing. The only problem was; she didn't know how to do that. David was definitely in control and his threats played in Tader's mind, over and over.

Ring...ring...ring

Tader jumped, the sound of her ringing phone scaring the shit out of her. She swallowed hard, looking at the caller I.D. When she saw, *'Chasity Banks'* flashing across the screen, she answered immediately. "Chatt...Chasity?"

"Sounds like somebody's excited to hear from me," Chatt stated from the other end of the phone.

"You have no idea." Tader laid back on her couch and closed her eyes.

"You a'ight?" Chatt asked.

"No," Tader confessed, "I don't think I am."

"I don't think you are either Tader. Me and Spen were talking yesterday and something's not right with you girl."

"I know."

"So what's up?" Chatt asked, sounding concerned.

Tader sighed. "Are you busy?"

"I'm at Dre's place." There was an uncomfortable silence. "You there?"

"Yeah," Tader spoke dryly. "What are you doing over

there?"

"He invited me over," Chatt informed.

"Oh." Tader was surprised with how fast Chatt was moving. "What, you in love or something?"

Chatt chuckled. "Nah girl, you trippin'."

"Yeah, I guess. When are you leaving?"

"I don't know, why?"

"I want you to come over; that is if Dre doesn't mind sharing you with your friends."

"Oh, he won't mind," Chatt stated, looking at Dre as he sat across from her. His facial expression was unreadable. "You won't mind, right?" Chatt mouthed, holding her hand over the speaker of the phone.

Dre shook his head. "Nah, it's cool."

Chatt smiled. "Thanks." She removed her hand from over the phone's speaker. "I'll be over soon girl."

"Don't take forever Chasity. We need to talk."

"I'll be there," Chatt said. "Give me time."

Tader cracked a slight smile. "Okay." She hung up the phone and rose up from the couch. She then glanced at her front door, making sure it was locked before she took a shower. Although Tader was still nervous about David popping up, with Chasity coming over, it sort of put her at ease. *Shit, if his nutty ass comes over, at least I won't be alone,* she thought to herself.

Devon and Spen pulled up to the Down Town River Front around noon. There were couples getting boat rides in the river and other couples getting horse rides along the bike path. Devon got out of the driver's seat and walked around to the passenger's side to open Spen's door. "Baby, what are we doing here?" Spen asked.

"I need to talk to you about something important. I wanted a calm environment so we're taking a boat ride."

Spen was nervous. "Is it bad?"

"Don't worry 'bout it right now." He grabbed her hand and led her to the River Front where a tall white man approached them.

"How can I assist you today?" The man asked.

"What's the price on the rides?" Devon questioned.

"Thirty bucks, thirty minutes; sixty bucks, sixty minutes."

"Let me get sixty minutes."

"Right this way sir," the man said, guiding them towards the boats. Once inside, they were given life jackets and seated across from each other. When the ride started, Devon grabbed both of Spen's hands and placed her fingers in between his. They kissed passionately, for about half of the boat ride. Spen tried to let go of everything, and be happy for the moment; but she couldn't help but be nervous about hearing what Devon had to tell her. Whatever it was, she prayed they could move past it.

"Spen, where do you see us in the future?"

She grinned. "Where ever we are, I hope were happy and I hope I'm pregnant."

Devon laughed; knowing that Spen wasn't gonna let him forget that she wanted kids. "I was kind of hoping the same thing." He kissed her forehead. "There's something you need to know."

"What is it?" Spen asked, growing even more nervous. A part of her didn't even wanna hear it.

"You know I love you, right?"

"You're scaring me Devon." Spen's heart was pounding heavily in her chest at this point. She was sure to have a heart attack if Devon didn't hurry and deliver the news.

"Relax," he told her.

"I can't baby, you're scaring the shit out of me."

"Just answer my question." He was serious.

"Yes," she paused, "I know you love me."

"You don't sound too confident."

Spen pulled away from him. She couldn't take the heat any longer. "Are you cheating on me?" She asked, her eyes starting to water. "Don't tell me you got another bitch pregnant!"

"Whoa, whoa, slow down baby." He caressed her cheek. "I know I'm not perfect, but I would never cheat on you, let alone get another girl pregnant knowing how bad my fiancée wants kids."

"Fiancée?" She didn't think she heard him correctly.

"That's right," Devon confirmed. "All I was trying to tell you was that I want you to be my wife."

Before Spen could blink twice, she was looking at a four kt. platinum ring with channel set diamond side stones and a matching V-shaped band. The tears in her eyes were now on her cheeks, but instead of tears of hurt, they were tears of joy. "It's beautiful," she whimpered.

Devon grabbed her hand. "Spencer Janay Brooks, will you..."

"Yes, yes, yes!" Spen interrupted before he could finish. She couldn't help but become more emotional as he placed the ring on her finger. "I love you, Devon."

He stood up and wrapped his arms around her. "I love you too." They held each other tightly until Spen got a little over excited and tried to jump on Devon, causing them both to fall in the River. "Well ain't this a bitch," Devon said laughing. "I propose and yet I still get pushed in the water."

"I'm sorry baby. You know how I am when I get excited."

"Yeah, I should've known." Devon helped Spen climb back inside the boat, and then he got back in. They laughed and cuddled for the remainder of the ride even though they both were soaking wet.

Chasity smiled at DreStar as he pulled off down Tader's street. If her friend didn't need her, there was no doubt that she would still be kicking it with him. He made her smile and that was a very difficult task seeing that Chatt was so use to frowning. It felt good to finally have a male in her life that made her happy. She tried to hide her grin as she stood on Tader's porch, patiently waiting for her to answer the door. Once she opened it, Chatt could do nothing but shake her head. She had never seen Tader look so miserable in her entire life. Her hair was in a sloppy ponytail and she looked as if she hadn't slept for days. There was most definitely something going on with her. Chatt could only imagine what Tader had gotten herself into. She knew how wild Tader's life style was so there was really no telling. Tader had nothing but her T-shirt, panties, and socks on. "Girl get some clothes on," Chatt told her. There was no way they were gonna hold a conversation with Tader half-naked.

"This is my house," Tader argued.

"Well, I would prefer if you put some pants on, so I don't have to stare at you in your damn draws." Tader huffed, and went into her room to put on some shorts. When she returned, she found Chatt sitting on the couch. "Sit down."

"Okay Chasity, enough with the demands."

"Girl ain't nobody demanding you to do shit. I came over here to talk and that's exactly what we 'bout to do."

Tader sat on the couch, making sure not to plop down too fast. "I'm so fucked up right now."

"What's wrong with you girl? You act like you can barely stand up."

Tader sighed. "My shit hurts."

"What the hell?"

"No Chatt, not that. Do you remember the night we was all supposed to meet over Spen's?"

"Yeah, the night you played us to fuck Terrell all night."

"I wasn't with Terrell." She started getting emotional. "I was with David."

"Whaaat?!" Chatt shouted. "You left us hanging to be with that nut?"

"You think I wanted to be with him?" Tader hollered, offended.

"Shit, I would think no, but now you accepting his proposal and shit, so I'm confused Tader."

"I have no other fuckin' choice Chasity. He's got me where he wants me, and ain't shit I can do about it. That ma'fucka been raping me," she screeched, burying her face in her hands, crying like there was no tomorrow.

"It's okay," Chatt tried to comfort her.

Tader rocked back and forth wailing. "You can't tell nobody girl. If David finds out that I told you, he'll kill me."

"Well, you have to tell somebody. This nigga sexually abusing you girl. Tell Terrell."

"Terrell doesn't want shit to do with me. I told him I wanted a steady relationship and ain't shit changed."

"Well, make the changes yourself girl. You need to settle down with Terrell and leave these other men alone. You can't let David just threaten you and continue to have his way. He'll never leave you alone if you don't do something."

Tader shook her head. "I know. I'm just clueless at this point because I know his crazy ass means business."

"Well you better mean business too! Do something about this, or I will."

"No, Chatt! You ain't gettin' into this shit."

Chatt crossed her arms and spat, "It's too late. I'm

already in it."

Hearing Chatt's words, Tader grew even more frustrated than she already was. She appreciated Chatt's intentions on helping, but she didn't want her getting involved too deeply. All she was looking for was advice, not a nineteen year old body guard. She knew she would have to promise Chatt that she would handle her David problem immediately, in order for her to fall back. Only problem was; she didn't have a clue on how she was going to do so. The room was silent as Tader tried to contemplate a plan. She knew Chatt was waiting on an explanation and she planned on giving her a convincing enough one, in order to drop the subject. She thought hard for a minute, until Chatt's word's replayed in her head. *You need to settle down with Terrell and leave these other men alone.* Tader wiped the tears from her face and tried to listen to Chatt's words more clearly; and then it hit her. "I think I know what I'm gonna do," she stated.

"Well," Chatt said, awaiting her explanation.

"I'm gonna tell Terrell. He should be able to help me, like you said."

Chatt eyed her suspiciously. "That's it?"

"Don't worry about it Chatt. I'm gonna take care of it, I promise."

"I guess I'll believe you for now." She reached for her hand. "Just promise not to keep anything else from me, okay?"

"I promise." Tader hated to lie in her best friend's face, but she did what she felt she had to do.

"I have to work later on, but call me tonight, okay? And stop crying. You know that's for them weak bitches."

"I will," Tader said, releasing a dry smile. "Is Dre coming back to get you?"

"Nah, he did enough by just dropping me off. I'll catch the bus to work since your truck is busted." Chatt grinned, hoping Tader wouldn't take the joke to heart.

"That's another problem that needs to be solved," Tader mumbled, remembering that she needed to call her friend Anthony, in regards to getting another whip. She wasn't in any rush for Chatt to leave, but as soon as she did, Tader had some phone calls to make. She glanced at Chatt, as she called the bus station.

"Yes, could you tell me what time the next number seventeen, gets to Dixie and Sibenthaler, going down town?"

Tader smiled as she hung up the phone. A few hours after Chatt left, she put her plans in motion. She set up another date to meet with Anthony and was excited to see what he had waiting for her. Once she knocked out that issue, she called James and Leon, two other men that she messed with. She informed both men that she was having trouble with an ex-boyfriend and needed their help solving the problem. James told her he would handle it, while Leon just said that he would work on it. Tader figured that if she had two anonymous men going after David, her problems with him would be solved. After she completed those calls, she finally reached Terrell after several times of getting his voicemail. She didn't mention the Crispy incident, wanting to confront him about it in person. She told him that it was mandatory that he come see her tonight. She planned on asking him to move in with her, even though that's not actually what she wanted. Tader knew she needed to settle down soon, but as of now, she just wasn't ready. She considered herself too young, with too much of an exciting life ahead of her. Her intentions with asking Terrell to move in were just so that she could feel secure for the time being. Once James and Leon came through on the David issue, Tader would find a way to convince Terrell

Triple Crown Publications *presents* . . . DAMAGE

that him moving in wasn't the right idea. As much as she was feeling him, she wasn't ready to let her freedom go just yet. In her mind, she had plenty of time left to settle down with somebody. She figured the more dating she did would help her narrow it down to the right one for her, if it didn't end up being Terrell. Even though she knew that was just an excuse, she planned on doing her, regardless. Tader was Tader, and she loved her men. Once she ended her conversation with Terrell, she called Spen to see what she had been up to all day. She wanted her to know everything Chatt knew, so it didn't come off as if she was keeping secrets.

Spen answered on the first ring. "Hello?"

"Hey, girl. What you doing?"

"Girl, talking to Devon. You ain't gon' believe what my baby did for me today."

"Tell me about it," Tader requested, not really wanting to hear about it. She couldn't stand Devon, so anything he said or did didn't matter to her.

"Girl, let's just say me and you have more in common than you think."

Tader was confused. "Excuse me?"

"Tader, we're both engaged girl!" Even though Spen didn't agree with Tader accepting David's proposal, her excitement for herself, washed away her harsh feelings for the time being.

"That's great." Tader was happy for Spen, but the comment she made about her being engaged to David put her back in a shitty mood. She had to let her know about the whole situation, and it had to be as soon as possible.

"Thanks. We should go out tonight and celebrate. Frickers sound good?"

"I would love to Spen, but Terrell's coming over tonight. You know we're a little rocky right now."

Triple Crown Publications *presents* . . .   **DAMAGE**

"Hell nah Ta'Ronna, you are not bailing on me again for a nigga," Spen stated, referring to the night that Tader didn't show up at her place for drinks. "Just have Terrell pick you up, and y'all can go back to your crib and do whatever afterwards. Eight thirty sound good?"

Tader thought about the offer and agreed to it since she wanted Spen to know about her situation with David. "Okay, I guess that can work. Chatt's at work, but I'll text her and let her know. You got us on transportation, right?"

"Don't worry, Cab Spencer is on the job," Spen laughed, hanging up the phone.

4

Spen grinned, looking up at Devon as she lay on his chest. "You got plans tonight?" she asked.

"I got some work to do on this case later, but that's 'bout it."

"Don't let it stress you." She kissed his chin. "I'm sure it'll work out."

"What you got up?" Devon asked.

"I plan on going out later with the girls. You know I gotta make 'em jealous with the good news." She grinned, staring at her ring. "But if you want me to stay here with you, it's no problem baby."

"Nah, go ahead and have fun tonight. I can have you whenever I want, right?"

"You know you can. I'm gonna go get a fill in; you know I can't be flossing this bad ass ring with raggedy nails. That wouldn't be cute."

Devon nodded. "I agree."

"Oh, so you been clowning my nails on the low, huh?"

"See, what had happen was..." He laughed, running his fingers through her hair, his favorite habit.

"Yeah, I'm gon' let you slide on that one." She gave Devon a peck on the lips and got up to leave. She inhaled a deep scent of fresh air as she stepped outside. Things were going so well for her. When she arrived at Rose Nails, the place was packed making it difficult for her to find a seat in the already cramped place. She spotted an open seat close to the bathroom and made her way over before someone else took it. "Excuse me," she said, squeezing next to a woman with her back turned.

"No you're fine," Crispy stated, turning around. "Oh, hey Spencer."

Damn! Spen thought to herself. *All the bitches in the world and I had to run into this one.* "Crispy? I didn't know you were still in town."

"Yeah, I'm actually going to be here longer than I thought. I have some business to handle and it may take a while."

"Oh, okay. Have you been in touch with anyone since you've been down here?"

"Yeah, a few people. I've really been in touch with Terrell lately though."

"Really, why?" Spen asked, not seeing any reason for Crispy to be associated with Terrell. As far as she knew, he was Tader's man, or at least one of Tader's men.

"Nothing major. He's helping me make a few business moves, that's all."

Spen was a bit skeptical with Crispy's story. She was definitely gonna keep her eyes open and let Tader know to do the same. "Strictly business, huh?"

"Yeah girl, what else would it be?" Crispy asked, noticing the rock on Spen's finger. "Wow, look at that beautiful piece of jewelry you got there."

"It's the shit, ain't it?" Spen smiled, shoving her hand in Crispy's face, so that she could get a better view.

"It's beautiful girl. Must be nice to spoil yourself that way."

"Spoil myself?" Spen restated, almost offended by Crispy's comment. It pissed her off, but she managed to play it cool. She would never give Crispy the satisfaction of knowing that she had gotten to her. "No hunny, Devon proposed to me earlier today. Not that I couldn't afford it myself or anything," she added, knowing good and well she couldn't.

Crispy looked stunned. "Damn, he coming out the pockets like that?" She eyed the ring once more. "Lucky girl."

"Yeah, lucky me." Spen sat back in her seat, and impatiently waited for the next free nail tech to call her name. The wait was so long that she wanted to say fuck her nails and just go, but she knew that her need for a fill in was mandatory.

I like being in the same room with you and your girlfriend, The fact that she don't know, That really turns me on. She'll never guess in a million years, That we've got this thing going on.

Spen couldn't believe her ears, as she watched Crispy grab her cell phone from out of her purse. She didn't want to jump to immediate conclusions, but the sound of the ring tone 'You're My Little Secret' by Escape, had her mind wandering. She kept her eyes glued to Crispy, as she flipped the phone open to answer it.

"Speaking of Terrell," Crispy said, giving Spen the complete conformation that she had been looking for. "Hey Spen," she whispered, holding her hand over the phone. "I'm gonna take this outside, so let me know if my name gets called." Before Spen could open her mouth to say anything, Crispy was out the door. She went into the parking lot and leaned against her Benz, as she continued her conversation. "So what were you saying?"

"We need to talk."

"I agree, but now is not the time," Crispy snapped.

"What's with the attitude?"

"I have my reasons."

"Well I need to talk with you as soon as possible. Where are you?"

"I'm out and about. What do you want?"

"I want you to chill with the attitude," he spat. "I also want you to be expecting a call from me later on. You need to come through."

"Yeah, if you say so," Crispy said, slamming her cell phone closed. She walked back in the salon and patiently waited for her name to be called.

"Lettuce, Tomato?" Chasity asked her customer, as she worked behind the counter of her fast food job, Subway. Her feet were killing her as she decorated the sandwich with Banana Peppers and Black Olives. She topped the sub off with vinegar and oil, then wrapped it up and rung out the customer. *This shit is not worth it,* she told herself, as she walked to the back to take a seat. She looked at her phone and noticed that she had a text message from Tader.

SPEN WANTS TO GO TO Frickers TONIGHT. SHE HAS BIG NEWS, SO YOU SHOULD COME. NO IS NOT AN OPTION CHASITY, SO BE READY BY 8:15. SHE'LL BE TO GET YOU.

Chatt cleared the text message and looked at the time. It was already six twenty, and she didn't get off until ten pm. She stood up and looked at all the work she had left to do including, dishes, prep and taking the trash back, all while still handling customers. With her being the only person on the clock, it made the job even harder for her. It pissed

Triple Crown Publications presents . . . DAMAGE

her off that the manager was too cheap to pay more than one person to be on the clock at once. Her head began throbbing when she noticed a group of customers walk through the door. The five dollar foot-long special kept the place packed, non-stop.

"Can we get some service?" One of the customers yelled.

Chatt pulled herself together and walked up to the line. "Welcome to Subway, how can I help you?"

"We need about ten subs. We're throwing a party."

Before Chatt could reply, another group of customers walked in. Her headache turned into a migraine when the oven buzzer started going off. She didn't know whether to help the customers or let the bread burn. "I'll be with you in a second," she said, grabbing the oven mitts. When she went to grab the first tray, the phone started ringing, causing her to jump and drop the tray.

"I hope that's not Italian bread because that's what I'm ordering," a teenage girl said.

Chatt took the mitts off and grabbed a handful of tomatoes, throwing them in the girls face. She then grabbed a container of lettuce, and threw it at the rest of the customers. "I'm sick of this shit!" She screamed, breaking down in tears. "They don't pay me enough to serve y'all rude asses!" She grabbed her purse and left Subway, headed for the bus stop. She didn't care that she had left the store un-attended. "I'm not supposed to be living like this," she cried, walking down the street. "I'm supposed to be happy." She wiped her face and tried to pull it together, once she seen the bus coming down the street. She swiped her bus pass, and walked to the back of the empty bus. The whole ride home, Chatt thought about what she had just done. The little bit of money she made was now gone and she knew she couldn't depend on the little money Spen gave her from helping at the shop. She laughed, imagining the look that would be on her manager's face, once she got the news. Chatt couldn't stand her manager, so the thought made her smile. She looked at her reflection in the window, and noticed her Subway visor. She snatched it off her head, and then pulled her shirt over her shoulders leaving her wearing only a beater. After untying her apron, she threw everything on the floor and kicked it towards the front of the bus. She saw the look on the bus driver's face, but she didn't care how he felt. "This is my stop," she yelled, getting out of her seat. The bus driver immediately stopped, wanting Chatt to get off his bus. As she was getting off, he eyed her as if she was crazy and it pissed her off. She swung her purse across his face, then hopped off the bus and sprinted to her apartment. Once she was inside, she locked the door and headed into her room. She looked at the clock on her nightstand and it read seven thirty eight pm. She pulled out her phone to call Spen and let her know that she wasn't up for going out, but something wouldn't let her call. "Fuck it, man," she said aloud to herself. "I'm going."

Tader rushed outside when she heard Spen blow her horn. *Aw shit, time to party,* she thought to herself. She made sure she was looking extra sexy just in case she found herself a new man tonight. *Shit, a bitch need a new sponsor!* She got in the car and smiled, happy to see her girls. Chatt could tell that she was in a better mood than from earlier. "It's good to see you smiling."

"You too," Tader stated. "Dre must be laying that pipe quite well."

Chatt grinned. "I quit my job," she said, trying to change the subject. She was still uncomfortable discussing her sex life with anyone.

"What?" Spen was surprised. "When and why?"

"Like an hour before you came to get me. I couldn't handle it no more."

"But now you're jobless," Tader noted.

"Yeah, I'm fucked," she said, still grinning, "but I don't give a fuck."

"Young and dumb," Tader mumbled. She pulled out her cell phone to call Terrell and remind him to pick her up after they left Frickers. She grew frustrated when she got his voicemail twice in a row, so she decided to just leave a message.

Baby its Tader. Please don't forget to come get me later on tonight from Frickers. I'll try to call you again when I'm ready.

When Spen pulled up to a stop light, she glanced at Tader's wardrobe. "You been in Chasity's closet?" She asked, referring to her jeans and gym shoes.

"I ain't been shopping in a minute girl. I feel like I'm out doing my old shit."

"Well take your ass shopping," Spen spat. "I know dope man Terrell keep you loaded."

"Dope man Terrell been trippin'."

"So that explains why you accepted David's proposal. The dope man cut off the dope money, huh?"

"It's more to it than that," Tader muttered.

"What's your big news?" Chatt asked, once again changing the subject.

Spen held up her hand, showcasing her ring. "Devon asked me to marry him."

"That's great girl. It's about time y'all tied the knot."

SCUUURRRTT!!

Spen's heart raced as she slammed down on her brakes. She didn't realize what she was doing until it was already done. Looking at the look's on Chatt and Tader's face, she knew she was about to hear it.

"What the fuck is wrong with you?" Tader yelled once

she realized she was okay.

"I can't believe I forgot to mention this," Spen said. "I think Crispy is fucking Terrell."

Chatt was pissed. "You almost killed us to say that shit?"

"My bad, I forgot to mention it."

"Why the fuck would you say some shit like that?" Tader asked.

"Girl she was on the phone with him in the nail salon," Spen explained. "And her ring tone..."

"Their friends, Spen," Chatt interrupted.

"No Chasity, the bitch is sleeping with him."

Tader rolled her eyes. "I'll take care of it. Tonight when he picks me up, I'll handle this shit."

Chatt sat back in her seat and shook her head. Her friends were really starting to bother her.

Crispy pulled up to Spen's condo at nine on the nose. She hit the alarm on her keychain and walked to the door step, strutting in her Dolce Vita Trinity pumps, like she was on the runway. She already knew she was a bad bitch. Nobody could tell her different. She could see her reflection through the screen door and smiled liking what she saw. The Eight Sixty paneled knit tank dress that she wore looked as if it was painted to her body. If she was a lesbian she would be asking herself out. Everyone always told her that she was self-obsessed. "I totally understand why these hoes are upset," she said to herself.

"And I totally understand why ma'fucka's call you crazy sometimes." Devon opened the screen door. "Why are you talking to yourself?"

"Just telling myself how gorgeous I am," she replied, wrapping her arms around his neck. "I miss you," she said in between kisses.

"Whoa, whoa, chill out," Devon told her. "Can we get inside first?"

Crispy laughed, pushing him through the doorway. "It's so hard to be mad at you."

"Why would you be mad at me?" Devon asked, locking the front door.

Crispy pushed him against the wall, and started unbuttoning his Sean John Button up. "Why does Spencer have on one of the most beautiful rings I've ever seen?"

"Where did you see Spen?"

"At the nail salon." She threw his shirt on the floor. "I was talking to her right before you called."

Devon pushed her away. "Whaaat?!"

"Relax," Crispy said softly. "She's clueless, baby."

"How you know?"

"Because I know, Devon. She thought I was talking to Terrell the whole time." She bit her bottom lip. "I know what I'm doing."

Devon ignored her and walked into the living room. He plopped down on the couch and went into deep thought. *I gotta be more careful,* he told himself. *I could've lost her today.*

"Why are you acting so scary?" Crispy asked, sitting down next to him. "She's gonna know about us soon enough, right?"

"Yeah." He had to tell her what she wanted to hear.

"Great, because that ring has my name all over it." She kissed his lips. "You act like you don't miss me."

"I do miss you," he lied. "I miss the hell out of you."

"Then act like it." She started kissing his neck, hoping he would get in the mood.

"Good lookin' on the money."

She continued kissing him. "It's nothing, baby."

"I promise I'll get it back to you."

Triple Crown Publications presents . . . **DAMAGE**

"Don't worry about it." She grinned, about to say something sneaky. "There is one thing I want to ask you though."

Devon crossed his arms. "I'm listening."

Crispy looked him in the eye and spoke seriously. "I want you get Spencer to sell me her salon."

"I could never do that," Devon assured her.

"Why not?"

"She put too much work into that salon for me to just ask her to up and sell it."

"You mean *you* put in too much work?" she asked sarcastically. "I mean let's be honest Devon; you're basically her support system."

"Watch your mouth," Devon warned.

"Whose side are you on?"

Not yours, dumbass! Devon thought to himself. "What you want the salon for anyway?"

"The reason shouldn't matter. I want it and I want you to help me get it."

"I can't give you any guarantees," Devon told her. He really wanted to tell her that she was out of her damn mind.

"So that's it? You're not even gonna try and ask her?"

Devon rose up from the couch. "You don't realize what you're asking me to do."

"No, you're making it more than what it is. All you have to do is ask her to consider selling."

"Nah, I'm not asking her that. That's like me asking you to quit your job."

Crispy chuckled. "That's different."

"How?"

"Because I actually make money with my job. I stopped by the salon and it's obvious that Spencer isn't making what she could be."

Triple Crown Publications *presents* . . . **DAMAGE**

He remained calm as he spoke. "You don't know what the fuck she's making."

"I know she ain't doing numbers like me."

"She ain't doing business like you either," Devon snapped.

Crispy stood up and grabbed his chin. "What are you saying?"

"You know exactly what I'm saying," he replied, moving her hand away from his face. "End of discussion."

Crispy sighed. "Well if that's how you're gonna act, I guess I'll be on my way." She continued, "And about that twenty grand..."

"Hold up, Crispy," Devon stopped her mid-sentence. He knew she was about to use the money he borrowed against him and he didn't wanna hear it. *Come on D, you know how to play it. Tell her what she wants to hear.* "I'll ask her to consider it."

"Really?" Crispy was excited.

"Yeah. Just give me some time a'ight?" He tried to sound serious as he lied to her face. "You trust me?"

"You have to ask?"

"Tell me."

"I trust you, Devon."

"Well act like it, Crispy. I have to make Spen believe that I still care about her in some way." It killed him to speak those words.

Crispy still wasn't convinced. "Promise me you'll do your best to convince her."

"I promise."

She smiled, tugging on his jeans. "I believe you. Now if you just stop acting like you don't wanna touch me..."

He cut her off, "You know I wanna touch you." He pulled her in by the waist and reached his hand up her thigh. "Damn," he said, feeling her wetness. "You want me, don't you?"

"In the worst way possible," Crispy whispered.

Devon led Crispy into the guest room and laid her down on the bed. His conscious ate him alive as he crawled on top of her and spread her legs. He had to constantly remind himself that it was just business.

"You never answered my first question," Crispy remembered.

"Refresh my memory."

"Why did you give Spencer that ring in the first place?"

He couldn't tell her that he proposed because he wanted Spen to be his wife. In order for his plan to work, he had to continue feeding Crispy lies. "I have to keep her happy. Spen is smart, so one fuck up and she'll know everything."

"Well, when is she gonna know, Devon? I don't wanna share you forever."

Devon silenced Crispy's questioning by moving her thong to the side and gliding his tongue down her pussy lips. She immediately closed her eyes and prepared for the blessing that she was about to receive. Devon couldn't help but feel the guilt as it tugged at his heart. He knew that if Spen found out about him and Crispy, she would definitely leave him with no question's asked. He knew she would never understand his reasoning for sleeping with Crispy, but if the time ever came he would explain it the best way he could.

Devon and Crispy were always friends from school, but it was a certain business trip that linked the two together. Devon took a three week trip to California to work on a case he was assigned to and that was where it all began. On his second day in Cali, Devon ran into Crispy as he was walking through the hotel lobby. After a short conversation, he agreed to accompany her to coffee the following morning. He thought nothing of it until he noticed Crispy coming on to him. Although she was very tempting, Spen had Devon's heart on lock and she was the only woman who held the key. Crispy soon realized that her flirting wasn't working, and it bothered her because she was used to getting what she wanted. She knew she would have to dig deep to get inside Devon's shell. After discussing the reason to which he was in Cali, she opened up to him about her new life and new occupation. Other opinions didn't matter to Crispy, so she had no problem admitting to Devon that she was what you would call an expensive prostitute.

Devon was immediately turned off until Crispy went into detail about the money she was making. She had his full attention when she informed him that she was making close to ten grand a night. He couldn't deny the fact that he was impressed, seeing that he wasn't even raking in those kinds of numbers. Being a new attorney at a law firm was a huge accomplishment for him, but he was still financially unsatisfied. Devon was the type of person who liked to live the good life with fancy clothes and cars and live life as if he had no worries. He wanted to support his family and his own household, but soon realized that his bank account held insufficient funds. He was in need of fast money and even thought about trying the dope man lifestyle for a while, but it still wasn't enough. His family was in debt, Spen was still unhappy with the image of her salon, and he himself had past due bills creeping upon him. Devon was beyond stressed, and the thought of not being able to support the people around him, made him do things that he didn't wanna do. As Crispy went on about her lifestyle, he came up with a plan that could either make him or break him in the long run. He started going with the flow when Crispy would flirt with him. He had to make her believe that he was interested if he had any chance at running his scheme.

Whenever he had free time from his case, he spent it with

Triple Crown Publications presents ... **DAMAGE**

Crispy, making her believe that they were actually growing a genuine connection. He even went as far as calling Spen and telling her that his case had been extended, so he would have to spend an extra week in Cali. Devon continued to play the role of being interested in Crispy, but he knew he would have to go further in order to get what he was going for. On his last night in Cali, he did something that still eats at his heart today. He knew it was foolish and he knew he would regret it, but he still slept with Crispy. His conscience ate him alive every time he made love to Spen, but he ignored it by telling himself that he did it to help her, not to hurt her. Slowly but surely, Devon's plan started working. He kept in touch with Crispy once he returned back to Ohio. Every phone call they had, Crispy would make sure to ask Devon how he was doing. He always assured her that he was okay, until one day when he decided to test her feelings for him. Crispy called him one morning and they carried their usual conversation about what they had been up to. Devon went on about how his job wasn't going so well, hoping Crispy would question him about it. When she finally did, he took the opportunity he had been looking for.

He was having a hard time making ends meet, but he made it sound as if he were desperately struggling. Crispy didn't like the sound of Devon struggling one bit. She developed feelings for him over time and believed that his feelings for her were mutual, making it easy for her to help him out in his so called time of need. She ended up sending him five grand through Western Union to hold him down for the time being. He used three grand to catch up on his bills and help out his family, while giving the remaining two grand to Spen for the salon and other financial purposes. Spen wanted to be seen as an independent woman, so she always gave Devon a hard time when he would try and give her cash on the spot. He always told her that he knew she was independent, but he was her man and he wanted to help her whenever he could. He meant what he said, but he also knew that what he was doing was wrong. Crispy began sending him money on a regular and everything started coming together for him. He was supporting his family again, helping Spen out, and living the lavish lifestyle that he was used to.

    Crispy eventually began questioning Devon about their relationship, wanting to know where she stood. Devon always fed her lies about how he was gonna leave Spen for her when the time was right, even though he never planned on leaving Spen. Once he got comfortable with his financial stability, he asked Crispy to take a trip to come and see him. He planned on taking her out for dinner and explaining to her that things weren't working out for the two of them, but Crispy fought against it. She wanted to be with Devon, regardless of how much he loved Spen; but Devon knew he had to end it. He felt somewhat pathetic for tricking off a bitch for money, so he promised himself that Crispy would receive every piece of cash that she ever gave him back in due time. Devon thought that he had did the right thing until Spen came home one night in a disappointing mood. When he questioned her about it, she told him that she was thinking about closing down Hair Desire, because even with all the time and money that was put into it, her image for it never came alive. Devon knew how much Spen loved that salon so he couldn't let her close it down. As much as it pained him to do it, he called Crispy. She was more than excited to hear from him, and flew out to see him the first chance she got. Devon promised himself that this would be the last time that he messed with her. His mind set was on getting the twenty grand, and cutting her off for good.

Triple Crown Publications presents... DAMAGE

5

Spencer, Chasity, and Ta'Ronna walked inside of Frickers and the place was packed. They took the first available table for three and ordered their drinks. The tension that built between the three of them in the car was now thick enough to cut with a knife. Chatt's attitude developed when Spen damn near wrecked, just to tell them a little gossip. Tader however was pissed about the gossip that Spen had told them about. If Terrell was really sleeping with Crispy, she was gonna clean his pockets and cut his ass off. There was no way she was going to be getting played like a fool. She couldn't wait to confront his ass. If the news turned out to be true, Crispy had it coming to. Spen was too excited about her engagement to be sitting in silence. She decided to break the ice, knowing how stubborn Chatt and Tader could be. If it was up to them they wouldn't have talked all night. "My bad, okay? I shouldn't have broken the juice out like that."

"You could've got us killed," Chatt over exaggerated.

"I will beat Crispy's ass if what you told me is true," Tader stated.

"Hold on, y'all," Spen said, throwing her hands up. "Chatt you're being too damn dramatic and Tader, let's not jump to conclusions."

Tader smacked her lips. "You're the one who sounded so sure in the car. It's on and popping now."

"No, it's not. Now that I think about it, I could be wrong." Spen knew she was most likely right but she didn't want Tader tripping just in case.

"Don't try that Spen. I was always suspicious about the whole situation ever since the bitch mentioned Terrell in the salon. You ain't do shit but confirm it for me."

Chatt shook her head. "You can't just blame a person for something you don't have proof of. You *need* Terrell right now, so cussing him out should be the last thing on your mind."

"Why does she need him?" Spen asked. "She's a grown ass woman."

"You have no clue what she's going through," Chatt stated, getting irritated. She felt sorry for Tader not knowing that she had already developed a plan to bail herself out of her troubles.

Spen was confused. "Is there something I should know?"

Chatt nodded towards Tader. "You wanna tell her?"

"Tell me what?" Spen asked, getting nervous. She saw the look on Tader's face and instantly knew that she had some juice. Chatt sat in her seat shaking her head as if she were ashamed of the news that Tader was about to deliver. *Oh, Lord,* Spen thought to herself.

Tader revealed the whole story about how David showed

up at her house that night and continued the torture from there on. Even though David told her to keep her mouth shut, Tader felt as if she was now safe because she sent James and Leon after him. She anticipated the day when she would receive a phone call stating that her David problem had been taken care of. By the time she was finished talking, Spen was speechless. She couldn't even speak when the waiter approached their table. Chatt ordered her a large ice water, not wanting her to have any alcohol in her system at the time being. She had seen Spen drunk plenty of times and didn't want to see it tonight. She just wasn't in the mood.

"Well, are you gon' say something?" Tader asked.

"Shit, I don't know what to say," Spen finally spoke. "Why didn't you say something earlier girl? I knew you gettin' jumped was a bullshit lie!"

"Girl, that nigga had me scared to tell anybody! Shit, it took me a minute to finally tell y'all."

"What broke your silence?" Chatt asked.

Tader hated when Chatt asked questions that she didn't wanna answer truthfully. She couldn't tell her that she had two other men that she fooled around with going after David, so she thought of a lie. "I tell y'all everything, so I couldn't hold it in much longer. It feels good to open up."

Chatt smacked her lips, not falling for Tader's bullshit. "You're gonna do something stupid."

"Shut up, Chasity!" Tader was fed up. "You always got something to say."

Chatt rolled her eyes and ignored Tader's comment. Like usual, she was ready to go home and sleep away her frustration. She thought about how she walked out on her job earlier and silently cursed herself out. It just now hit her that she actually was jobless.

"You a'ight, girl?" Spen asked, looking at Chatt.

She laid her head down on the table. "I'ma bum."

Tader couldn't hold back her laughter. "She be trippin'," she mouthed to Spen.

"You are not a bum Chatt. You're just young and having a hard time."

"Yeah, and you ain't the only one having a hard time," Tader added. "Shit, I still ain't got a new whip."

Spen shook her head. *She'll never learn,* she thought. She looked at Chatt as she laid her head silently on the table. She didn't know what to say to lift her spirits because Chatt was like a land mine. If you stepped in the wrong area, she was sure to blow. "Chatt," she said, putting her hand on her shoulder, "cheer up, girl."

Chatt turned around so that she was facing her. "I'm okay," she assured her. "I'm just a little down in the dumps."

"Well that's not what this night is supposed to be about. We're supposed to be having fun."

"You damn right," Tader stated. "Let's have fun."

"You need to be thinking of a better plan," Chatt said, knowing whatever Tader had up her sleeve was no good.

Tader knew she was going to have to bite her tongue if she wanted to have a drama free night. She couldn't stand when Chatt acted as if she knew everything, especially with her being the youngest of the group. "Let's play pool," she suggested.

Spen smiled. "Now that's what I'm talking 'bout."

Chatt rolled her eyes, ready to smack Tader in the face. She was frustrated because she felt as if Tader wasn't taking her situation seriously. She was about to eliminate herself from the pool playing session until she seen the look on Spen's face. She knew how she would look if she backed out so she agreed to play, regardless to how she felt. "Tell us more about your engagement," she said in efforts of giving off a better attitude.

Triple Crown Publications presents . . .   **DAMAGE**

"I'll tell y'all while I'm whooping y'all asses on that pool table," Spen joked.

Crispy pulled her dress down and watched Devon walk out of the room. She got up and followed him while he went to the bathroom to brush his teeth. She could tell by the look on his face that something was bothering him and she knew exactly what it was. She rolled her eyes and became irritated with him. He would always do something and try to play the guilt role when it was over. *Why does he care about her so much?* She asked herself. In her mind, Spen had nothing on her. She felt like she had the better body, the better face and most importantly she had more bread. *Maybe it's her personality,* Crispy thought. She knew Spen was more of an upbeat person than she was but she felt like that didn't matter. While she and Devon were in California she had him smiling so in her mind her personality was the best. Crispy saw Spen as a boring person and she didn't understand how she kept Devon's attention. Her looks couldn't possibly be enough to keep him on lock down for as long as she had done. Crispy remembered all the way back to high school when Devon was still Team Spen. He was one of the finest guys in the school but wasn't checking for any other females but Spen. Usually Crispy wouldn't be attracted to such a love-sick nigga, but Devon had this certain swagger about him. The more he pushed you away, the more you wanted him. Crispy stared at him and wondered how he really felt about her. "It was only one time," she stated in a low tone.

Devon gargled a cup of Listerine before asking, "What are you talkin' 'bout?"

"Spencer," she mumbled. "I know that's who you're thinking about."

Devon walked out of the bathroom, ignoring her

Triple Crown Publications *presents...* DAMAGE

assumptions. He didn't feel like going through it with her at the time. He went in the kitchen and made a bologna sandwich with Crispy watching him the whole time. He planned on just letting her stare but after a few minutes it was really starting to get to him. "What?" He finally asked.

Crispy crossed her arms and leaned against the counter. There was so much she wanted to say to him but a lot of those things were kept in being used as a shield. "I said it was only once."

"I know, Crispy," Devon replied, her presence starting to irritate him. He didn't like her constantly reminding him of the one time they had sex because he knew she only repeated it in hopes of making him feel bad. Devon only slept with Crispy once, knowing that it would take their relationship to another level. Ever since then, he never went further than oral sex no matter how hard Crispy would try.

"You know, cheating is cheating. We've only had sex once, but oral is just as bad." Crispy smiled walking into the living room. She knew how to push somebody's buttons without trying.

"What does that have to do with anything?" Devon asked. "It's me and you, right?" He thought he had the role down pat, but what he failed to realize was that Crispy wasn't a fool. It didn't take her long to figure out that she was being used, but she never spoke on it putting her own personal plan in motion.

"Yeah, just me and you," she grinned, sitting on the couch.

Devon looked at the clock. He didn't know what time Spen was coming back but he knew he had to get rid of Crispy before then. Lord knows what would happen if she walked in on the two of them. "I'm glad you came by and we got this whole money thing understood. Like I said, I'll get it back to you, soon."

"Yeah, right," Crispy mumbled. She looked up to see if Devon heard her and by the way he was biting his sandwich, she knew he didn't hear a thing. *Slob as nigga,* she thought to herself. "You're so cute."

"So are you." *Mark ass trick,* the words playing in his mind of what he really wanted to say.

"I guess I better get going, huh?"

"Yeah. There's no telling what time Spen's coming back."

Crispy was suddenly in the mood for games. "What would you do if she walked through the door right now?"

"Aye, she had to know one day, right?"

Crispy laughed. "You would actually tell her?"

"Yeah," Devon nodded. Crispy's questioning was starting to get on his nerves. "When you headed back to Cali?"

"Soon," she informed him. "I only came down here to see you, baby."

"Well, you should head back soon. I don't want you missing out on too much work."

Crispy stood up and searched for her purse. "I'll be gone soon. Don't forget what I asked you, okay?"

"The salon," Devon stated. "I won't forget." Crispy smiled and turned to walk away, but he grabbed her arm. "You never told me why you wanted it."

She simply said, "I promise it's not that important."

Devon's suspicion level rose as he watched Crispy walk out of his house. He could sense that she had something up her sleeve, but what it was he didn't know. He knew he would have to keep his eyes on her until she returned to California or else things might get complicated. Even though he didn't on plan asking Spen to sell her salon, he was still curious as to what Crispy would do with it if she had it. A part of him felt like she just wanted it so that

Triple Crown Publications *presents* . . . DAMAGE

Spen wouldn't have it. Devon always sensed that Crispy was a little envious of Spen. It made him nervous because he didn't know how envious she was. He was scared that one day she might just confess everything to Spen without letting him know. He couldn't have that. He had to urge her to get back to California before she ruined everything.

Chatt bit into her hot wing as she watched Spen defeat Tader in pool for the fourth time. She gave up after the second time of losing and decided to just eat her food and watch. She saw the smile on Spen's face and wished that she could be just as happy. Chatt was definitely more miserable on the inside than what showed on the outside. She hated for someone to feel sorry for her, so she tried her best to come off as if she had no problems. *I wish I really didn't have any fucking problems.*

"You a'ight over here?" Spen asked, approaching the table with Tader behind her.

"Yeah, just smashing the shit out these wings. Who won?" She asked, knowing Tader got her ass whooped.

"I did." Spen sat in her seat. "You know can't nobody fuck with me on the pool table."

"Bitch please, it was pure luck," Tader joked. She looked at her cell phone and read a text message from Terrell. "My man is on his way," she smiled.

"Which one," Chatt asked, sarcastically.

"You know what, Chasity? I have had it with your smart ass mouth."

Spen sighed, shaking her head back and forth. All she wanted was a drama free night out, but with Chatt's smart mouth and Tader's attitude, it was damn near impossible. She ate her food while watching them bicker back and forth about the same old thing. Spen understood where Chatt was coming from, but she also knew that Tader was

Triple Crown Publications *presents* . . . **DAMAGE**

a grown woman who would do exactly as she pleased. She desperately wanted to tell Chatt to just drop it, but she knew that would do nothing but strike up another argument.

Chatt was determined to get her point across no matter what. Tader was her friend and she wanted nothing but the best for her, but Tader's dumb decisions pissed her off. She didn't understand how Tader could continue messing with random men, considering her current circumstances. Chatt saw the abuse her mother went through from fucking with too many men and she didn't want Tader going through that. As a friend, she felt like all she was doing was looking out for her.

"You always tryna' act like somebody's mama. You're the youngest one here, so chill out," Tader told her.

"Age ain't shit but a number," Chatt argued, "and I say what I want."

"And I do what I want." Tader grinned, knowing she won the argument. She eyed Chatt waiting for her response, but she remained silent.

"So, are y'all done bickering?" Spen asked. Neither of them said a word. "Oh, so now y'all ignoring me?"

"I'm ready to go," Chatt stated.

Tader rolled her eyes and searched for the waitress. When she finally flagged her down, she asked for a box to put her food in. She didn't have much of an appetite all of a sudden and with Terrell being on his way, she figured she would have to rush anyway. "Here," she said digging into her purse. She pulled out a fifty dollar bill and sat it on the table. "That should cover the bill, right?"

"I'll pay for it," Chatt insisted.

"With what?" Tader asked, not realizing that the words had escaped her mind and came out her mouth. "I promise I didn't mean it like that," she explained before Chatt could even respond.

Triple Crown Publications presents ... DAMAGE

"Yes you did," Chatt replied. "You always thinking you better than somebody." She grabbed the fifty and tore it in half. "What now?"

Spen's mouth dropped. "Chasity!" she screeched.

"I hope you gotta fifty in your pocket to replace that," Tader said, calmly. Chatt pissed her off but she kept her cool, not wanting to show her frustration. She knew after spending the night with Terrell that the fifty would be replaced with much more anyway, so she didn't trip.

"It's time to go," Spen said with disappointment in her tone. She grabbed her purse and stormed outside, leaving Chatt and Tader to have to deal with the bill.

"So, where ya money?" Tader asked, still remaining calm.

"Fuck you, Tader," Chatt barked, getting out of her seat. She left out and headed for Spen's car.

"I know they don't expect me to pull out another fifty," Tader said out loud. She got up and walked out right behind them, leaving the bill unpaid.

Spen rolled down her window and yelled, "I'll see you later, Tader."

Tader grinned when she saw Terrell pulling up. "Bye," she said, walking towards his truck. She got in and kissed his lips, happy to see him. "Oh, shit!" she whispered when she saw the waitress walking out side with the manager. "We gotta go, babe." Terrell put his truck in drive and rolled out.

Spen looked the waitress in the eye before pulling off as well. After she dropped Chatt off, she headed home. When she got in her house, she saw Devon asleep in their bed. She walked over to him and kissed his forehead, then took a quick shower and joined him in bed.

When Terrell pulled up to Tader's house, she was

overwhelmed with excitement. She knew she was about to get some good dick and a good amount of money all in one night. She heard her cell phone vibrate in her purse, so she pulled it out and saw that she had an unread text message from James. The text read:

TA'RONNA BABY, MISSION ACCOMPLISHED. YOU DON'T HAVE TO WORRY ABOUT THAT NIGGA ANYMORE, ITS BEEN HANDLED. NOW, THE ONLY QUESTION IS WHAT DO I GET IN RETURN, SWEETHEART?

Tader flipped her phone closed and took a deep breath. James had just given her the best news she could have ever received. She didn't text back but promised herself that she would call and thank him the first chance she got. She couldn't wait to hear what James had done to get rid of David. Although she wanted him out of her hair, she prayed that James didn't kill him. Her conscience would never let her live it down if David was dead because of orders. Tader was looking for nothing more than for someone to scare David shitless. She wanted him to leave her alone at all cost but death wasn't the answer she was looking for. David was truly a nutcase but he was also Tader's boo once upon a time and if he hadn't went crazy, he would probably still be.

"What you over there thinkin' 'bout?" Terrell asked, pulling the keys from his ignition.

"Something I ain't supposed to be thinkin' about." She smiled and got out the truck. "You coming in or you gon' sit outside all night?"

"You know I'm coming in," Terrell said, slamming his door. He hit the lock on his keychain and followed her inside. Tader took her jacket off and hung it up in the closet while Terrell made himself comfortable on the couch. He grabbed the remote and turned the TV on, positioning his feet on the coffee table. Tader walked up behind him and started massaging his shoulders. She loved the vibe that arose when Terrell was around.

"When you gon' move in Rell?"

He simply stated, "When I think you're ready."

"When you think I'm ready?" Tader restated.

"Exactly," he confirmed. "You ain't ready to be with just one nigga yet."

"Yes I am," Tader pouted. "I think your just not ready to be with one bitch..." she paused, going into deep thought.

POP!

"What the fuck?" Terrell barked when he felt Tader slap him upside the head. He turned around to face her and saw the pissed expression on her face.

"Are you fucking Crispy?" She yelled, pointing her finger in his face.

"Who the fuck is Crispy?" He asked, grabbing the back of his stinging head. If he were a woman beater, he would've slapped the dog shit out of Tader.

"Don't play dumb, Terrell. Chrisette Philips!"

"Man I ain't fucked that girl since high school! What the hell got you trippin'?"

"Word on the street is that y'all fuckin', so man up nigga. Be real, are you fucking the cunt or not?"

"You heard what I said, Tader. Yeah, I done fucked other bitches, but I ain't hit her since high school," he admitted.

Tader knew he was telling the truth. "Well, why Spen tell me y'all fucking? She ain't got no reason to lie about it."

"Don't know, don't care. You need to quit going off of what other females tell yo' ass."

Tader walked around the couch and sat on top of Terrell with her legs wrapped around his back. She lifted his chin with her hand and kissed his juicy dark lips. She felt stupid

Triple Crown Publications *presents* . . . **DAMAGE**

for slapping him without asking him about the situation first. "Rell, I love how you put me in my place when I'm out of control. I love how you tell me what's real and what ain't real. I'm ready to drop these other bitch nigga's for you, babe."

"You think you ready, huh?"

"Yeah," Tader stated, hoping he would believe her. She didn't plan on dropping any of her nigga's but she wanted to convince him that she would.

Without another word said, Rell stood up with Tader's legs still wrapped around him and carried her into the bedroom. Once inside, he threw her on the bed and said, "Show me you're ready."

Rell didn't have to say anything else. Tader was determined to make Rell believe that she wanted to make him her one and only. She gave him her pussy like she never gave it to anybody before. They fucked on the bed, the floor, the bathroom sink, and she even let him pound her in the tub. She had the best orgasm of her life, proving to Terrell that she was ready for him.

DreStar woke up to cold water dripping on his face. When he opened his eyes, he realized that it was Chatt's leaking ceiling. They had only been seeing each other for a few weeks and he already wanted to move her out of the raggedy apartment. He got up and went in the bathroom to wash his face. When he returned to the bedroom, he noticed that Chatt was awake. He saw her feeling the wet pillow with an embarrassed expression on her face. "Dre, I am so sorry," she explained.

He laughed. "Good morning, beautiful."

"Why are you laughing? This is serious!"

"It's just water Chasity, it won't kill me," he told her, taking the pillow off the bed.

"No, it's just embarrassing. I knew I should've slept on that side." She snatched the pillow from his hand and threw it on the floor. "I'm so fucking stupid," she yelled, getting out of the bed. She started pulling the covers and sheets off her bed and throwing them on the floor. "All this shit is fucking soaked!" she screamed.

"Calm down," Dre said, pulling her into his chest. He knew she was a ticking bomb ready to blow at any minute. She tried to pull away from him but he held her tight, trying to calm her down.

"Let me go!" she hollered, trying to snatch away until she realized that Dre wasn't gonna let her loose. She stood still and tried to calm herself before she had another outburst. "Please, just let me go."

"You gotta relax, ma. If you don't, you gon' mess around and have an anxiety attack." He kissed her forehead. "I don't wanna see that happen to you. You're too good of a person."

"What makes you so sure?" She questioned.

"Because, I just know." He released her from his arms.

Chatt leaned against the wall and slid down to the floor. She sighed, staring at her ceiling. As soon as she spoke with her landlord, she was gonna raise hell about the leaking roof. She looked at Dre as he stood with a blank expression. "Did I satisfy you sexually?" She asked him.

"What?" He asked, slightly laughing.

She stood up and faced him. "As long as we been kickin' it, we've only had sex once. Why is that?"

"You tell me."

Chatt shrugged her shoulders. "I don't know what to tell you."

Dre grabbed her hand and led her to the bed. "I wanna show you something." He laid flat on his back, a chill running through his body from the dampness of the mattress. "Take

Triple Crown Publications presents . . . **DAMAGE**

this off," he said, pulling on her oversized white T-shirt. She hesitated before pulling it over her head. Dre could since the nervousness in her as she stood there in only her panties. He ran his hand up her thigh and she instantly got goose bumps. "Relax," he whispered, pulling her panties down. He caressed her shaved vagina trying to loosen her up. She stumbled a little from the pressure that he was applying between her legs. "Stand up straight," he told her. She spread her legs further apart and tried to control her balance as Dre's fingers found their way into her entrance. He gripped her waist with one hand and continued to finger her with the other. "I'm gon' loosen you up, Chasity," he said as he dug deeper.

"I'm loose," she moaned, leaning forward. Even with Dre holding her waist, she still couldn't stand up straight.

He pulled his fingers out of her and let her body fall next to his. Never taking his eyes off of her, he stripped out of his boxers and stroked his erect penis. "I want you to ride me."

"But I..."

He cut her off, "Shhh. I'm gon' teach you." She took a deep breath then climbed on top of him. "The best way to do this is to take it in slowly," he advised. With slow movements, Chatt took him in as slow as she could. "There you go," Dre spoke in a low tone. Her tight pussy felt even better on his dick than from the first time. "Now ride it, ma."

Chatt closed her eyes as she began grinding her hips back and forth. Dre felt so good inside of her, but she couldn't help but ask, "Am I doing it right?"

"Perfect," he said, gripping her waist. "Just like that."

Dre's words were motivation for Chatt as she kept her eyes closed while speeding up her pace. "Damn, you feel good," the words slipped out of her mouth accidentally.

Triple Crown Publications *presents* . . . **DAMAGE**

Dre was thinking the exact same thing as he enjoyed the feeling of being inside Chasity's walls. "Open your eyes," he whispered. It took her a minute but she finally opened her eyes. "You like how that feels?"

"Yeah, yeah," Chatt moaned. "It's in my fucking stomach."

"Hell yeah, ma." He pointed to her clit. "Touch it." Chatt shook her head. "Touch it, Chasity."

She bit on her bottom lip wanting to enjoy the pleasure she was receiving. Riding dick was definitely something new for her but it was coming along so natural. Dre continued to tell her to touch her clit, so she finally took her hand and slightly rubbed on it. "Mmm," she moaned, the whole sensation feeling even better.

"Feels good, don't it?"

She shook her head up and down, rubbing her clit harder. "So fucking good."

Dre was beyond impressed with the way Chatt was riding him for the first time. He turned her around and let her ride him from the back where she continued to impress him. Giving her as much dick as he could, Chatt's pussy gripped him like a magnetic force. Dre could feel his manhood grow harder as Chatt bounced up and down on it. He could tell she was enjoying it by the sounds of her constant moaning. He never answered her question about satisfying him sexually because the first time honestly wasn't the best. In his opinion, she had improved marvelously and he knew that with much practice her sex game would be on point. "Shit," he grunted, feeling Chatt's body tense up. He knew that within seconds she would be cumming all over the place. He bent her over and got to pounding it from the back.

"Ooh, ahhhhhhhhh," she screamed, releasing her cream all over his dick. Dre gripped her waist tighter, pumping and pumping until he felt himself about to explode. "Pull out," Chatt told him. "Pull out, Dre."

As bad as he didn't want to, Dre pulled out in a nick of time. Chatt looked amazed as she watched him squirt his cum out all over the bare mattress. Dre smiled, laying back on the bed, trying to catch his breath. "Damn, girl. Where all that come from?"

She laughed. "You brought it out of me."

"Well damn, I need to bring that shit out of you more often."

"I agree," Chatt said right before another drop of water splashed her face. She forgot all about her leaking ceiling during their sex, but now the annoying problem was back on her mind.

"Don't worry about it," Dre stated, trying to keep her mood up.

"Easy for you to say. You're not the one living in this shit hole."

Dre stood up, still trying to catch his breath. "I have a surprise for you. Let's get dressed and I'll show you."

"A surprise, for me?" Chatt questioned.

"Ain't that what I just said?" He pulled her out of the bed and into the bathroom. After taking quick showers, they headed out the door and hit the highway. Chatt sat in the passenger's side looking out the window, clueless as to where she was going.

"Where are you taking me," she asked.

"Just sit back and enjoy the ride, ma."

"Here you go with the 'ma' shit," she barked. "I let you slide while we were fucking but now..."

"CHASITY!" He yelled. "Just shut up, a'ight?"

Chatt looked stunned by his outburst. She sat back in her seat and crossed her arms; making it known that she now had an attitude. Dre silently laughed to himself as he watched her pout. After a twenty minute ride, the truck finally stopped. "Close your eyes."

"For what?" Chatt asked.

"So you don't ruin the surprise."

She huffed, closing her eyes, pretending as if she were annoyed. She was actually anxious to see what the surprise Dre had for her was. She felt the truck start back up and make what seemed to be a U-turn.

"Don't open em' yet," Dre told her, coming to a complete stop. He got out the truck and walked around to open up her door for her. With her eyes still closed, he helped her out of the truck and guided her onto the side walk. "I know you been wanting a new place and I think I might have found you the perfect one. It's not the best, but I think you'll like it." He took the blind fold off of her eyes and she realized that she was standing in front of his house.

"Dre, this is your house," she stated.

"I know it is, but you're more than welcome to stay here."

"I can't stay here with you. This is your space, not mine."

"Why can't it be the both of ours?"

Chatt sighed. "We've only been at this for a few weeks and I just don't wanna mess shit up by moving too fast."

"It won't mess us up, I promise. Now I know you hate yo apartment so just pack yo shit up and move in with me."

Chatt was lost for words. She wanted to say yes but at the same time she had to know what she was getting herself into before making any decisions. This was a huge step for her and the fact that they had only been seeing each other for a few weeks made the decision even harder. "I'm sorry, but I can't right now. I just need some time to think."

"Okay." He sounded disappointed. "Take your time."

6

Spen smiled as she watched her children play in the backyard with their father. It was a beautiful sight. She walked away from the window only to finish preparing lunch for everyone. It was three turkey sandwiches; one for each her daughter her son and her husband. She sat them all on the table with a napkin beside each plate. Next she poured them each a glass of milk and sat them beside their sandwiches. She walked through her living room to the back door and stepped out on the patio to call her family inside. Her son was the first one to run to the door. She bent down and kissed his cheek as he slid by her, ready to get something in his stomach. Her daughter was next to run up, smiling from ear to ear. She was so beautiful and a spitting image of Devon's little sister Kimmy. Devon walked up behind his daughter and picked her up. They all stepped back inside the house and headed to the kitchen. Spen laughed as she watched her son gobble down his sandwich. He was a sloppy eater just like his father. Everyone else sat down at the table and began eating. Spen was the only one not eating, only taking the time to admire her beautiful family. This was everything she had ever asked for. But unfortunately for her, it was only a dream.

Spen yawned opening her eyes. Sometimes she hated when she woke up because she had to come back to reality. Lately she had been having dreams about her and Devon being married with at least two kids. She never shared her dreams with him because she knew he wasn't too fond of the idea of having kids anytime soon. Although she hated that in him, she was willing to wait for him. She knew he would be a great father and she could tell by the way he treated his nieces Kay-Kay and Krys. He was the ultimate father figure and Spen loved watching him while he was around them. She figured maybe he wanted to be married before they started their own family. She rolled over and kissed him on his shoulder. He smelled so good like he was fresh out the shower. She loved waking up to the gorgeous Devon Freeman every morning. She couldn't wait until she could officially rock his last name. "What are you doing up so early?" She asked him.

"Just over here fantasizing 'bout yo sexy ass." He turned around to kiss her lips. "You have fun last night?"

"Not really. Chasity and Tader can't get along for shit. Both of em' are really going through it right now."

"That's nothing new, right?"

Spen chuckled. "True. They stay going through some shit. Chatt quit her damn job and Tader's main dude might be fucking another bitch." She shook her head. "As a matter of fact, I think you know the bitch he might be fucking. Remember Crispy, from high school?"

Devon's heart skipped two beats. He didn't know what

to say. Hearing Crispy's name come out of Spen's mouth put him in the state of shock. He was speechless.

"Devon?" Spen asked, snapping her fingers in his face.

"My fault, baby. I'm still a little tired." He hoped she dropped the whole conversation.

"Do you remember Crispy?"

Damn, he thought to himself. He couldn't lie to her. "Yeah, I remember her."

Spen went on. "That bitch is foul. It's so obvious that she's fucking Terrell. Tader better get in her ass!"

"Tader fucking other nigga's, so why does it matter?"

Spen rose up. "It matters because Crispy is a bitch that we all know. Terrell is supposed to be Tader's main, so for him to be fucking a bitch that she knows is just wrong."

Devon folded his hands behind his head and faced the ceiling. "Your right," he agreed, feeling pathetic about himself.

"I know I'm right." She smiled. "I'm just lucky I already have the perfect relationship."

Devon couldn't face her. "Nothings perfect," he spoke, still facing the ceiling.

"I know." She laid back down putting her head on his chest. "But you have to admit that we come pretty close."

Devon felt like pure shit. Spen continued to use the perfect combination of words to overload his guilt. He knew he had to tell her about Crispy but the devil on his shoulder wouldn't allow him to do so. He knew it would be over if she ever found out about what he was doing. *You can't tell her, D,* he thought. *She'll never forgive you.* He removed his hands from behind his head and ran his fingers through her hair.

"Why do you always do that?" She asked.

"It's a habit." He continued to run his fingers through her hair as they laid in silence. He looked down and noticed that Spen had closed her eyes. "I'm sorry," he mouthed, finding himself getting emotional. He knew Spen deserved to know the truth but he just couldn't tell her. She was his heart, so if she left him he didn't know how he would survive. But the guilt of knowing that he cheated on her would forever haunt him if he didn't come forth with the truth. "Spen," he called out softly, hoping that she had fallen asleep.

"Yeah?" She answered, throwing his hopes down the drain.

Devon swallowed hard, his throat feeling drier than it ever had been. *Just tell her,* he thought. When he opened his mouth to speak, a different set of words came out than from what he had planned. "Tell me about the changes you plan on making to your salon." *Fuck!* He cursed to himself when the image of Crispy asking him to talk to Spen about selling her salon flashed through his mind. Those weren't the words that he wanted to speak and that wasn't an image that he wanted in his mind.

"Oh, goodness baby. I'm gon' do some serious changing with the money you gave me. Twenty thousand is enough for me to buy new dryers, re-paint, get the marble floor I've been dying for and maybe even redesign the girl's stations. I haven't told anybody yet, but I'm so excited, Devon."

"I know you are. I want you to do everything that you can with that money."

"Oh, trust and believe I will." She kissed his chest. "Thanks again, baby."

"It's nothing. I know it's soon, but have you thought about the wedding?"

"It hasn't left my mind," she confessed. "If it was up to me we would be getting married tonight."

He laughed. "Yeah, that would be dope." When he heard the sound of his cell phone vibrating on the dresser, he turned around and grabbed it. Crispy's name flashed across the screen making it easy for him to press the ignore button. Before he could lie back down, Crispy was ringing his phone again. Like the last time, he ignored the call only for Crispy to call right back.

"Why don't you just answer it," Spen suggested, the annoying buzzing sound starting to get on her nerves. Devon ignored her and continued to press ignore. When the phone started vibrating again, Spen reached for it. "I'll answer it since you don't want to."

He pulled it out of reach from her hands and answered it ready to cuss Crispy out. He made sure to turn the speaker volume down before he spoke. "Yeah?" He said sharply into the phone.

"Morning bay," Crispy greeted with much cheer in her tone.

Her voice really made his skin crawl as he tried to play it off. "What up, bra?"

"Bra?" She restated. "Devon, its Crispy."

"Yeah, yeah. I'm a little busy right now so why don't you hit me up another time. Today isn't my business day; you know what I'm saying?"

Crispy sighed into the phone. She knew what the deal was. "Spencer's around you, isn't she?"

"Yeah, tomorrow sounds great." He looked down at Spen to see if she was paying his conversation any attention. She just laid there with her eyes closed.

"I was just calling you because I plan on going to a few stores today to look at some new furniture for the salon. I need you to tell Spencer to let me redesign it for her."

"You're trippin', fam."

"Devon I'm serious! I need her to use that money wisely so I don't have to spend another twenty stacks on remodeling the salon once I get it. I know she'll design it all wrong!"

Devon wanted to tell her to beat it, but he knew he had to choose his words wisely with Spen right in front of him. One slip up and his secret was out. "Okay, my man. I look forward to doing business with you." He hung up the phone before she could say anything else and prayed that Spen wouldn't question him about the call.

His prayers were denied when she asked, "Who was that calling you this early?"

"Some nigga tryna' talk to me about his case. I'm not on that right now. I wanna spend some time with my future wife."

Spen couldn't help but grin. "I love the sound of that." She laid there thinking about her wedding day. In her mind everything was perfect. All she needed was to get pregnant and her life would be complete. Little did she know that her future husband was hiding something that could break them forever.

Tader woke up in Rell's arms just like she had planned. Even though she hadn't gotten him to agree to move in, she knew it wouldn't take her much longer to do so. She rose up and smiled, staring at him while he slept. Terrell was definitely your average tall, dark, and handsome. His skin tone was a dark chocolate complexion and he had thick juicy lips. Like Tader, he worked out often and it paid off. His muscular toned frame could have easily outshined any male model. "Wake up babe," Tader said in a low tone, brushing her hand across his neatly trimmed goatee.

He opened his eyes. "What time is it?"

"Time for us to be official." She tried to work it in on the low.

"Not just yet," Terrell stated while yawning.

Tader rolled her eyes and got out of the bed. Terrell's

little statement really got under her skin but she tried not to trip. She went in the bathroom and turned on the shower hoping he would ask to join her. He hadn't hit her off with any cash yet, so she figured some a.m. pussy would do the trick. "Wanna get in the shower wit' me?" She asked, stripping out of her underwear.

Terrell let out a laugh of disbelief. He knew what Tader wanted seeing this routine plenty of times. Morning pussy equaled a pocket full of money but he didn't have time to lay it down this particular morning. He had somewhere to be but he wanted to get a certain point across before he left. He hopped out of the bed and searched for his jeans. "Nah, I got somewhere to be," he replied, answering her question. Once he found his jeans, he stepped into them, then grabbed his shoes.

"Don't act like you don't wanna hit this again. You know I got that exclusive," she bragged, bending over to give him a view of her trimmed pussy.

"It ain't a hoe in the world that don't swear up and down they pussy is exclusive," he declared.

Tader's mouth dropped. "Hoe?" she questioned, his comment highly offending her. She never expected something so harsh to spill out of his mouth.

"Yeah, hoe," he simply replied. "Kind of like what you are."

"Nigga, fuck you!" She shouted, slamming the bathroom door.

Terrell laughed as he tried to open the door. "Come on, Ta'Ronna. Open the door."

"No!" she hollered. "I can't believe yo' black ass just called me a fucking hoe!"

"I'm just keeping it real wit' you. You want a nigga to be a hunnid so don't cry when I tell you how it is."

She snatched the door open. "Oh, so that's how it is? I'm

Triple Crown Publications *presents* . . . DAMAGE

a hoe to you, Terrell?"

"Yeah." He didn't cut her any slack. The truth was the truth and sometimes it was bound to hurt. He continued. "Let's keep it real, Tader. What separates you from the other hoes that I fuck with?"

"You tell me!" She barked.

"Well," he paused thinking of the best way to put it. "Ain't shit I can think of that makes you different. You fuck other nigga's then go for dey pockets just like any other bitch. Yeah, I throw money around but shit, I got money to blow."

Tader shook her head as if she didn't know what he was talking about, but she knew exactly where he was coming from. Hearing the truth about herself was hard to bare, especially coming from Terrell. "So I'm just another hoe that you're throwing money to?"

"That's how you act, so that's how I treat you." He balled up his fist, coughing into it before he went on. "Not too long ago you was crying and shit about how you wanna settle down and be in a steady relationship but here you are ready to fuck me just for some money." He had to keep it real or she would never understand. "That morning when I came over and yo' face was bruised, some nigga fucked you up, didn't he?"

Tader felt her eyes starting to water. She wanted to hold back the tears but she couldn't. At that moment she felt completely transparent because Terrell spoke as if he could see right through her. She wiped at her teary cheeks and asked, "Who told you?"

He smirked. "My street mentality."

"So you knew the whole time." She was embarrassed.

"It didn't take me long after you told me the story to put two and two together. I felt sorry for you but it was bound to happen. And on top of that, you didn't even tell

Triple Crown Publications *presents* . . . DAMAGE

me about it. I waited and waited, but you never told me. I even spent the night wit' you, giving you plenty of time to be real wit' me." He put his jacket on and grabbed his black duffel bag. "You would think a nigga fucking you up would be a wakeup call, but then again, some things never change." Tader didn't realize how much her actions had affected Terrell. When she told him she wanted to settle down, he actually took the thought into consideration. He didn't know how to be faithful but he was willing to try if she put forth effort to do the same. Once he realized that she was still on the same shit, he had to put her on Front Street.

"Rell, I wanna change," she whimpered. "I don't wanna fuck other nigga's but it's all I know. It's how I survive," she admitted.

"That's bullshit, Tader. You got a fucking job," he reminded her.

"The salon is part time," she argued. "And to be honest, I ain't making shit out that ma'fucka!"

"So you figured fucking me along with other nigga's was the only other way to get money?"

She shrugged her shoulders. "I guess."

"Well, when you stop acting like a hoe, I'll stop treatin' you like one. Until then, don't waste my time with that settling down bullshit."

"It's not bullshit Rell," she exclaimed. "I wanna settle down, I just don't know how."

He laughed although the situation didn't strike him as funny. "Well, let me know when you figure it out." With that said, he was out the door.

Tader searched for her robe and ran outside to catch him before he pulled off. She could tell that he was pissed and it had her overly confused. "Wait, Terrell," she called out. She walked up to his window. "Babe, why are you trippin'? You

Triple Crown Publications *presents* . . . **DAMAGE**

know how I do and I know how you do. I'm not trippin' on you about fucking other bitches."

"Are you serious?" he asked, getting out of his truck. He leaned against the door and crossed his arms. "I separated you, Ta'Ronna."

"What?" she asked. She had no clue where all of his emotion was coming from.

"What is that?" he asked, pointing behind her. She looked behind her and turned back around clueless. "It's a house," he stated. "A house that I bought. That's right, I came out my ma'fuckin pocket's and bought you a house, Tader." He stepped closer to her. "And that night I bumped heads wit' you at the club wasn't a coincidence. I knew yo' ass was lying the whole time and when I showed up you lied in my face again. You expected me to drop it but I was pissed."

That's why he was trippin' so hard, she thought. *He was jealous.*

Terrell continued. "Do you even understand where I'm coming from?"

"I'm trying to understand, Rell. I wanna say that I know what's got you pissed but I'm so confused. I mean you know I fucked other nigga's but now your all of a sudden trippin' on me about it."

"Because I care about yo' ass!" he shouted. "I ain't spoiling none of these other bitches like I do you. I'm lying to dey asses, but I ain't never lied to you! I'm taking 'em in and out of hotel's, but I got a fucking roof over yo' head! I'm giving them chump change but I'm keepin' yo' pockets fat." He lowered his tone. "And I don't trip about 'em having other nigga's because I don't give a fuck about them. I trip on yo ass 'cause I care."

Tader was now an emotional wreck. She didn't know what to say or how to feel. She never had a man lay out the truth to her as Terrell just did. To have a man actually care

Triple Crown Publications presents... **DAMAGE**

about her mentally was something that she never could've imagined. She knew that the bond between her and Terrell was stronger than what she had with anyone else, but she didn't realize just how strong it was to him. "I'm sorry," she finally said. "I didn't know you cared about me so much, Rell."

"You didn't know because you didn't separate me."

I did separate you, she thought. She didn't wanna sound ignorant and tell him that he was her favorite out of all the men she messed around with, so she said, "Just give me another chance. I swear I'll get it right this time," she promised.

"Why should I believe you, Ta'Ronna? Give me one good reason."

She leaned against his chest. "Because, I know how you feel now. My feelings are mutual and I wanna prove it to you."

"I hear you talking, but I ain't seen shit yet," Rell stated, raising her head up from his chest. He was sick of hearing her talk the talk and not walk the walk.

"Starting today, I belong to you and you only," she vowed. "I know you don't believe me but just give me time, Rell."

"I'll give you time," he told her, getting back in his truck. "But I'm not gon' let the clock tick out." He rolled up his window and pulled off with Tader watching him until he was out of sight. She walked back inside her house and collapsed on her bed facing the ceiling. So many thoughts were running through her head as she pictured herself being faithful to Terrell. *Can I honestly glue myself to one man?* She asked herself. The sound of her cell phone ringing snapped her out of her trance. She grabbed it and answered it without looking at the caller I.D.

"Hello?"

"Hey Ta'Ronna."

"Who is this?" she questioned.

"It's Anthony, baby."

Before Tader could get excited, her dedication to Terrell ate at her conscience. She knew this was her first test to prove to herself that she was really ready to give up her freedom. "Hey, Anthony," she replied dryly.

"We still on for today?"

Shit! Tader cursed to herself. She had completely forgotten that she was supposed to meet with Anthony later that day about her new whip. *I have to go,* she told herself. *I need transportation.* She stood up and began pacing the floor. "I'm sorry, Anthony, I can't," she finally managed to say. *Okay, Tader. You're doing good.*

"You mean to tell me I got a brand new Chrysler 300 just going to waste?"

Tader smacked the wall out of frustration. *Why did he have to go there?* She couldn't help but ask, "What color is it?"

"All white baby."

She hit the wall again and released a silent scream. She knew she had to make a choice between her loyalty to Terrell or her need for a new ride. Deep down, she knew the choice was between what she wanted to do and what she needed to do. After a few minutes of debating back and forth, she finally made a decision. "Let's meet in two hours."

"That's more like it," Anthony stated. "I'm gon' get some of that good stuff, right?"

Tader felt like shit as she replied, "Don't I always leave you satisfied?"

"I can't argue with you there. See you in a few, baby."

Tader didn't even say bye as she hung up the phone. *This is the last time,* she promised herself. After finally taking her shower, she threw on a wife beater and a pair of hip

Triple Crown Publications *presents* . . . DAMAGE

hugger jeans. As she walked through her room she glanced at a picture of Chatt, Spen, and herself, sitting on her nightstand. Thoughts of their bizarre night ran through her mind and she suddenly felt bad. She grabbed her cell phone and dialed Spen's number, ready to apologize for how she acted. Once Spen answered, she flashed over to three way Chatt in. Everyone was quiet so Tader decided to break the silence. "Hey, loves."

"Oh, now you wanna sound polite," Spen said. "Y'all ready to act right?"

Chatt blurted, "It wasn't me with the problem."

"Let's not go pointing fingers, a'ight? Both of y'all were out of control and it was very childish," Spen declared.

"Well, I'm willing to apologize," Tader stated. "It was supposed to be a fun night out and I showed my ass."

Chatt cleared her throat. She didn't wanna apologize but she knew it was only right. "I guess I'm sorry."

"Thank you ladies," Spen said. She paused for a minute then asked, "Tader, how's your little Crispy and Terrell problem coming along?"

"Everything's fine," Tader replied, sounding extra confident. She was in need of a desperate subject change before Spen asked about her David problem. "How are you and Devon?" *Damn, I had to ask about his ass!*

"We're great," Spen spoke with much cheer in her tone. "In fact, me and my baby are being lazy today so I'll talk to you hoes another time."

Chatt was the first to hang up, followed by Spen. Tader closed her phone and waited around until it was time for her to meet Anthony. When the time finally came, she left her house headed for the bus stop.

"Who was that?" Devon asked as Spen hung up her phone.

Triple Crown Publications *presents* . . . DAMAGE

"It was Chasity and Tader. They were calling to apologize, so I guess."

Devon hated when Spen spoke to Tader. She really got under his skin. "Tell that bitch Tader to stop calling you."

"Don't call her a bitch," Spen said, raising her tone. "This little feud between the two of y'all has got on my last damn nerve."

"Fuck her! She's a bad influence on you, Spen."

"What?" Spen took his comment offensively.

"I'm just saying that if you hang around the wrong person for so long, you start to become 'em."

"Spare me the bullshit, Devon. I'm a grown ass woman and I been around Tader my whole life, but I still manage to do me."

Devon shook his head. He knew there was no winning in this argument. "Whatever you say, Spen. I don't wanna bump heads on this subject anymore." He moved the cover away from his body and got out the bed. "There's places to go and money to be made."

Spen crossed her arms and leaned against the headboard. "Speaking of money, you sure have a lot of it and awfully soon." She eyed him up and down. "What's up with that?"

He tried to remain calm. He knew that one wrong sentence could expose him for his secret. "Wow, you're questioning my money now? What, did I forget to pay a bill or something?"

Spen wanted to smack him across his face. She couldn't believe that he would go there. She was always self conscience about the income she brought to the house but Devon always made her feel as if it wasn't a problem. He basically handled everything when it came to the household bills. "I can't believe you," she said, lowering her tone.

Devon knew he hit the wrong button with his comment. "I didn't mean it like that," he explained. "I'm sorry."

Triple Crown Publications presents ... DAMAGE

Spen shook her head. "If you didn't mean it like that, you wouldn't be saying you're sorry."

"Come on, baby. You know I would never go there."

"You just went there. Now I feel like it bothers you that I don't make as much as I want to." She lay back down and faced the wall. To say that her feelings were hurt would be an understatement.

Devon grabbed her arm. "Spencer," he mumbled. She ignored him. "Spencer!" He repeated, raising his voice.

She turned around. "What?"

"I swear I didn't say that to upset you. As long as we've been livin' here when have I ever made you feel like that?"

"Now." She tried to once again turn away only for Devon to turn her back around.

"I'm sorry for saying that, okay?" He kissed her cheek. "You know I'm more than proud of you, baby. What you make is more than enough."

"No it's not," she mumbled. She felt Devon crawl back into the bed and wrap his arms around her. They laid there in silence until they both drifted off to sleep.

7

As time passed, things were starting to look up for everybody. Tader and Terrell were on the right path to progressing in their relationship and Tader hadn't seen or heard from David in over six weeks. She hadn't fully let go of her sideline men, but as Terrell had requested, she separated him. It was gonna take time for her to fully give herself to one man. Terrell was aware that Tader hadn't fully let go but he knew she was trying and that's all he had asked her to do. He still had to turn away the money hungry hoes that were chasing after him. It wouldn't be easy for him either but he knew that if he tried then the task could be done.

Spen and Devon agreed that they needed to spend more time together. They wanted their love for one another to grow even stronger than it already was. With Crispy back in California, Devon was free of distractions. He didn't have to worry about Spen catching him if Crispy was out of sight. His main focus was getting back on track with his life and leaving his history with Crispy behind. Spen still hadn't touched the money that Devon gave her to fix her salon. As bad as she wanted to use it, she couldn't let herself spend the money. Lately she started feeling as if she depended on Devon for to many things so spending his twenty grand wasn't gonna come easy. She kept the money in her bottom drawer, looking at it every morning before she left the house.

Chatt finally caught a break, earning a job as a housekeeper at Miami Valley Hospital. Even though she only made nine dollars and seventy-five cents an hour, it was more than what she was used to. She still hadn't taken Dre up on his offer to move in with him but she spent almost every night at his place. They were becoming closer as each day went by and even went as far as making their relationship official. Chatt didn't know if she was happy because she never knew what the feeling of being in a good relationship was like. She constantly kept her guard up, shielding herself from any hurt that might come her way.

"I'm ready," she told Dre, grabbing her purse. DreStar dropped her off at the salon like he had been doing for the past few weeks. If she didn't catch a ride home with Spen or Tader, he picked her up. When they pulled up in front of the salon their lips met before Chatt got out and closed the door. She walked in the salon just knowing that it was going to be a good day. When she walked through the door, she noticed Tader jumping up and down with a pregnancy test in her hand. "Did I miss something?" she asked. Tader looked at Chatt smiling as if she had just won the lottery. She tossed the pregnancy test to her and she caught it right before it hit the ground. "Oh my goodness Spen! It finally happened for you, girl."

"Actually, it's Tader's test. Say hello to Terrell Jr." You could hear the sadness in Spen's tone. She was happy for Tader, but her own want for a child kept her from showing it.

Chatt refocused on the pregnancy test and all of a sudden lost her spirit. "Congratulations, Tader," she said, not really meaning it.

"Thank you." Tader was all smiles. "I just feel so blessed, I mean my life could not be better at this point. Ever since Rell has been staying with me, shit has been really looking up. I'm pregnant with my babe's child!" She snatched the test out of Chatt's hand and began staring at it like it was the child itself.

"Does Terrell know about this?" Chatt asked.

"Nope. I'm tellin' him today." She gripped the pregnancy test and disappeared into the bathroom.

Chatt rushed over to Spen's station and whispered, "What makes her so sure that the baby is Terrell's?"

"Girl, I'm glad I'm not the only one thinking that. She can't be that damn naive."

Chatt noticed Chelae trying to ear hustle on their conversation so she decided to cut it short for the time being. "We'll talk more about it later."

Spen nodded and focused her attention back to perming her client's hair. She tried her best not to stare at Tader as she walked out of the bathroom with the pregnancy test still in her hand. She appeared to be happy, but Spen knew that Tader had to know. There was a huge possibility that her baby did not belong to Terrell. She knew she was going to have to have a serious conversation with her sooner rather than later; preferably before she delivered the news to Terrell that she was pregnant. Her thoughts about Tader's pregnancy left her mind when Crispy walked through the door. A short brown skinned man followed behind her sporting a wife beater, skinny jeans, and a pair of all white flip flops. You didn't have to be a genius to realize that he was gay. Crispy approached Spen's station with a pen and note pad in her hand. Spen was more than confused. "Can I help you?" She asked, her tone with much attitude.

"Hello, Spencer. This is my assistant, Ceddy." Crispy nodded towards Ceddy, informing him to introduce himself a little more.

"Spencer is it?" He asked showcasing his feminine tone.

Spen replied sharply, "I prefer Spen."

"Okay then, Spen. My name is Ceddy and I'm an amazing home designer, so I can have this place looking fabulous!" He snapped his right hand and put his left hand on his hip before he continued. "Just call me a life saver because I'll turn this place into a miracle. You better ask about me honey 'cause I'm bad."

"Okay, what does that have to do with me?"

Crispy smiled. "Ceddy is amazing at designing shit, so I was thinking maybe he could help you redesign."

"How the hell you know she redesigning?" Tader asked, almost shouting.

Crispy stood silent as she thought to herself, *Devon didn't tell her. I bet he didn't even ask her about it with his lying ass!* Crispy knew that if she told them Devon told her all about it, then the secret about the two of them would be out for good. She wasn't ready to expose Devon just yet, so she came up with the first lie she could think of. "The little dark skin chick that works here told me," she lied, remembering Tiffany's face and name tag from her first visit to the salon.

"Well, no thanks, Crispy. I don't need your help," Spen replied sharply.

"Fine." Crispy and Ceddy headed for the door. "Don't hesitate to call me if you change your mind."

Spen didn't reply but Tader spat, "Terrell's mine, bitch!"

Crispy smirked exiting the salon. She found it funny that Tader actually thought she wanted Terrell. *If I wanted him, I would have him,* she told herself.

Crispy hit the alarm on her Benz and got in, waiting for Ceddy to hop in the passenger's seat. She put the keys in the ignition and pulled off with her mind set on one thing. She was so irritated. Things weren't going the way she planned and that didn't sit well with her. She was the type that made things happen whether they were supposed to or not. She didn't care who got fucked over in the process; just as along as she was happy. She couldn't wait to see Devon. He was really gonna get an earful from her. All she asked him to do was one thing and he couldn't come through for her on it. *All the money I've spent on his ass and this is what I get?* She thought to herself. *That ungrateful bastard!* Crispy was riding far beyond the speed limit as she turned the corners with a heavy attitude. "That bitch is going to ruin that salon," she said, turning the radio up.

Ceddy faced her. He had been around Crispy long enough to know when she was trying to hide her feelings behind her body language. She was pissed and no matter how hard she denied Ceddy saw right through her. "Crispy, you have a shit load of money. I don't understand why you just can't buy a whole new shop."

"I have my reasons."

Ceddy shook his head and sat back in his seat. Even though he and Crispy were close, he still didn't fully understand her train of thought. The two rode in silence until Crispy reached her destination. "Where are we?" Ceddy asked.

"Devon's house," Crispy replied. "Don't trip, this will only take a minute."

Ceddy rolled his eyes and shook his head. "I don't have time to be following you around while you're creeping around with some other woman's man."

"Ceddy, get your ass out the car and follow me. Damn, you always complaining!"

Ceddy ignored her comment and got out the car. He followed Crispy to the doorstep and watched her open the unlocked screen without even knocking. He followed behind her as she made her way into the living room where she found Devon sorting files from his briefcase while glancing at the television. She grabbed the remote and turned the T.V off, throwing the remote on the floor afterwards. "Aye, what the fuck?!" Devon shouted standing up. "Don't ever walk in my ma'fuckin house without knocking!" He got so close to her face that their noses touched. "What the fuck is wrong wit' you?"

"Wooh, child," Ceddy gasped. "Do you hear this man's tone of voice?"

"Get that fucking fag out of here!" Devon demanded, shoving Crispy in Ceddy's direction.

"Oh, hell no, Ms. Crispy! I will not be disrespected by this man or anybody else." Ceddy stormed out of the house feeling supremely disgusted.

Crispy stared at Devon for at least ten seconds straight before smacking him across the face. He tried to control his anger as he grabbed his right jaw. "Bitch, you better leave right now!" He warned.

"Don't ever talk to my friend like that!" She screeched. She smacked him again and yelled, "Don't ever call me a bitch again either!"

Devon grabbed both of Crispy's wrist, and rammed her into the wall causing a picture of him and Spen to fall on the ground. The glass from the frame broke and scattered all over the floor. "Look bitch," he said as he began pinning her arms against the wall. "You know I don't hit women, but if you touch me again, I swear I'ma beat yo' ma'fuckin ass!"

"Hit me then," she dared. "Since you so big and bad, hit me, Devon!"

He backed away from her and pointed to the door. "Get out."

"I care about you," she spoke softly. "Even though you used me, I still care about you."

He couldn't stand to repeat himself, but Crispy wouldn't comprehend. "Get the fuck out of here!"

"Why, Devon?" She flipped her hair over her shoulders. "Spencer ain't got shit on me, baby. I'll kill that bitch if that's what it takes to have you to myself. I really..." Before Crispy could continue her sentence, she felt a powerful blow to her face, sending her crashing down. Blood flowed from her nose like a waterfall and at that moment, she knew it was broken. Devon stood over her grabbing both sides of her collar, almost cutting off her air circulation.

"I bet not ever hear you say no shit like that again!" He barked as he began dragging her towards the door. Crispy was kicking and screaming with a mixture of blood and snot gushing from her nose. Once Devon reached the door, he released his grip from her collar causing her head to smack the ground. "Come get this bitch," he yelled out of the screen door to Ceddy.

Ceddy got out the truck and rushed towards Crispy. He tried to stand her up but she continued to sob on the floor, kicking and screaming like a three year old. Devon was disgusted as he let her free and watched her act a fool. He went back inside the house and slammed the door, not caring what her next move was. She had just pulled the last straw with him. He was done with her for good and he hoped she'd stay away on her own because he would hate to have to make her stay away.

Ceddy pulled up to the Marriot hotel and parked Crispy's Benz. He finally got her to calm down on the ride there but he knew she wasn't fully back to herself. Her nose was completely disfigured and her white T-shirt was now blood and snot stained. Ceddy got out of the driver's seat then went over to the passenger's side to help Crispy out. They walked through the hotel lobby until they reached the elevators and headed up to their floor. Once they reached their room, Ceddy went into the bathroom and came back out with a warm rag. He began wiping the blood and snot from Crispy's face while she sat on the bed looking lifeless. "Child, what has gotten into you?"

"I don't know, Ceddy. I think I want that salon so bad that I'm willing to go any mile to get it."

"Well, this Devon guy doesn't seem to give two fucks about you or plan on giving you that salon."

Crispy winced from the pain of her broken nose. "Fuck Devon! His ass is so out. He put his hands on the wrong bitch and that ma'fucka didn't even ask Spencer about selling her salon."

"I still don't understand why you want it, Crispy."

She lay back on the bed. "It was my mom's property years ago. I never told anybody but after she died, I promised myself that I would buy it and make the best use of it." Crispy's mother owned one of the most successful hair salons in the city. It was shut down years before she died, but still Crispy wanted more than anything to re-open it and keep her mother's legacy alive. "Spencer got to the property before I could."

"Why don't you ask Spencer herself? Maybe if your price

is right, she'll agree."

"Do you think my mother would be proud of me?" She asked, completely blowing his question off.

"If she agrees with classy prostitution. Hell, you make more money than half people I know, so damn if she ain't proud."

In many states, people were paying various amounts to have you exposed, seduced, and even turned out. But for the most part, people just wanted sex. Clean and safe sex that is. Jasmine Fisher ran a low down establishment that she liked to call *'Legs Open, Mouth Closed'*. She made all the phone calls and decided who she would send to whom and what type of session you would be involved in. Once that was taken care of, she would decide on a price and split your earnings with you, seventy percent while she took the remaining thirty percent. She usually sent Ceddy out when a customer wanted to expose somebody to the truth of being gay or bisexual. When introduced to Crispy, Jasmine knew her clientele would boost. With Crispy's flawless looks and shape, she figured that she could seduce just about any man. When Crispy began working, she started to get a taste of the fast money that she wanted, but soon realized that she didn't want to be a sex toy her whole life. She started putting eighty percent of her money in the bank and by the time she hit twenty-three, she had stacks on top of stacks!

Tader walked in her bedroom and collapsed on her bed tired from work. As dead as the shop was most of the time, it seemed as if she did fifty heads at once. Although her legs were aching, she was still anxious for Terrell to come home so that she could tell him the good news. She kicked her shoes off and crawled under the covers. Two hours later, she felt someone tugging on her arm. She rolled over and yawned opening her eyes. Terrell stood there looking handsome as ever. She couldn't read his facial expression as his eyes were glued to hers. *Oh shit,* she thought, thinking that he found out something he wasn't supposed to. She tried to play it off and close her eyes hoping he would believe that she had fallen back to sleep. She didn't know what he was on but she didn't feel like arguing. Terrell grabbed her arm and turned her over.

"Get up, mommy," He joked.

"Mommy?" Tader questioned.

"Yeah, mommy. I found this on the kitchen table." He revealed the pregnancy test from behind his back.

Tader was beyond relieved. Even though she wanted to tell Terrell herself, she was glad that he wasn't tripping off something else. She sat up in the bed and crossed her arms. She poked her lip out, playfully pouting. "Thanks for ruining the surprise."

"Well you the one who left the shit out on the table," he argued.

Tader stared at the test and sighed. "So, how you feel about it?"

"It's cool and all, but I need a DNA test."

"Here you go wit' that shit. I thought we were past that Rell, I mean damn."

He shrugged his shoulders. "It could be mine, but it could also be by that nigga that got you driven' round in that new Chrysler."

Tader huffed. "Whatever. If you want your stupid test, I'll give you one."

He smiled and kissed her lips. "That's all I ask."

"Yeah and after this shit I'm done proving my loyalty to you, nigga. It's either you trust me or you don't."

Terrell ignored her and sat the test on the bed. Tader shook her head and lay back down. This wasn't how she expected everything to come out. She was frustrated because Terrell didn't give her the reaction that she was looking for. She was glad that he wasn't upset about the baby, but she wished that he was confident enough in her to not want a DNA test. Earning Terrell's trust would be harder than she thought. *Why does he have to be such a smart ass?* She thought to herself. She stared at him as he sat on the edge of the bed, rolling a blunt. Tader wanted to hit it badly but she knew Terrell would object because she was pregnant. She turned over on her side and begun to pout. This pregnancy shit wasn't gonna be easy. Tader was used to being able to have a drink whenever she wanted. She sighed and closed her eyes as she inhaled the scent of Terrell's blunt. He got up and left the room leaving her even more irritated. *This is bullshit,* she thought to herself as she dozed off again.

8

"What happened to the frame for this?" Spen asked, picking up the picture of her and Devon from off of the dining room table.

"I bumped into the wall on some clumsy shit and it fell."

She placed it back down on the table and sat an envelope beside it. "You got a letter from your brother."

Devon quickly snatched up the letter anxious to hear from his brother. He was about to open it but stopped, not wanting to read it in front of Spen. Sometimes she could be on the nosey side.

"You okay?" She asked him.

"I'm stressed, baby. It's so much shit going on and I can't handle it." He pulled her close to him. "You gotta be there for me, a'ight? I need you."

"Devon?" She questioned, confused by his words and

actions. "What's going on?"

He looked her in the eyes and spoke from the heart. "I just love you, Spen. Please, don't let nobody break us, a'ight?"

Spen knew it was a problem. Devon was acting strange all of a sudden and to say it had her nervous would be an understatement. "Nobody's gonna break us," she assured him. "But if there's a problem, you need to tell me."

Tell her D, tell her, he urged himself. *She needs to know before Crispy fucks around and tells her.* After trying to find the words to confess, he couldn't do it. He wanted to tell her but he couldn't hurt her. "There is no problem, Spen. I just don't want us apart baby. You know how much I love you."

Something told her he was lying. "Yeah, I know."

"Tell me you love me," he demanded, gripping her tighter. "I need to hear it."

Spen pulled away from him. "I....I...I lov..."

"You can't tell me you love me?" He sounded like he wanted to cry. "Tell me, baby."

"You're acting strange, Devon. I don't wanna be around you while you're like this."

He tried to reach for her again but she backed away. "Ain't shit wrong wit' me," he replied, raising his voice. "I just need to hear my girl tell me she loves me."

"Well, I'm sorry," she stated, trying not to blink so that her tears wouldn't come out. "I can't tell you that right now because something's not right, Devon. Something is wrong with you and you're hiding it from me."

Devon's conscience was screaming for him to confess but he couldn't do it. He wouldn't be able to handle the hurt that it would bring Spen. The look that she would give him would crush him. The things she might say just made his heart crumble. And the things she might do were just hard to think about, the most difficult being if she ended their relationship. "I swear I'm good," he lied. "I'm not hiding anything."

Spen shook her head. "You're lying."

She left the room before he could see her break down. After grabbing her jacket and purse, she was out the door. She couldn't stand to see Devon acting that way so she had to leave.

Crispy rummaged through her purse trying to find her vibrating cell phone. She finally found it and hesitated before answering it. She wasn't in the mood or any types of lectures or any complaining about her whereabouts, but knowing that call could be important she reluctantly answered. "Hey, Jasmine."

"Crispy, I've been trying to reach you."

"Sorry, I've been super busy. What's up?"

"What's up is my customer request. When are you and Cedrick coming back to Cali?"

Crispy sighed knowing that Jasmine was calling to complain about she and Ceddy being missing from California. That's one of the exact reasons that she didn't wanna answer. "Soon, I promise. I'm almost done handling everything I need to do."

"Well, I have plenty of jobs lined up for the two of you. I need you to be down here within the next week, Crispy."

Crispy bit her lip in frustration. She knew she needed more than a week to accomplish everything she wanted to get done. "Two weeks tops," she compromised.

"One week," Jasmine stated, not accepting her compromise.

Crispy wanted to cuss her out, but she was her boss so she said, "Fine. We'll be there in a week."

"That's what I like to hear," Jasmine said. "Later Crispy."

Triple Crown Publications *presents* . . . **DAMAGE**

Ceddy walked out of the bathroom with a tooth brush in his mouth. He looked at Crispy and asked, "Jasmine needs us?"

"Ceddy, we can't go down there yet. I have shit that needs to be done."

"Well, honey listen, I need some cash. When do you plan on going back?"

Crispy smiled. "After I've damaged everybody who decided to fuck with me, we can leave." She got up and went into the bathroom and began applying her makeup.

"Child, what in the name of sexy chocolate men are you doing?" Ceddy asked.

She ignored him and continued to apply her make-up. She balled up her face looking at the huge bandage across her nose. She couldn't wait for it to heal so that she didn't have to walk around looking ridiculous. Once she was finished, she touched up her curls and asked him, "How do I look?"

Ceddy grinned. "Like trouble."

"Perfect," Crispy said, leaving the hotel room. Somebody's ass was out tonight and it felt good knowing that it wasn't gonna be hers.

Chatt grabbed a magazine off of the stool in front of her and began flipping through the pages. She was deciding if she finally wanted to get personal with the girls in the salon and reveal some of her life secrets. She was a little skeptical at first, knowing that the salon was gossip central. She wanted anything she said to be kept inside the salon and not spread on the streets to everybody and their momma. *Fuck it,* she told herself. She had some juice she wanted to share and she knew just about every female in the salon would be thirsty to hear it. "You guys, I have something to tell you," she said.

"Oh, snap. What's up," Chelae asked. Chatt was the quietest person in the salon so when she spoke up damn near everybody listened waiting to hear something juicy.

"Girl, you so damn nosy," Tader blurted. "Chatt, what you gotta tell us?"

Chatt laughed. Tader was just as nosey as Chelae was. "Not that y'all need to know, but Dre has been teaching me a lot of new things."

"Like what girl?" Spen asked. Everyone in the salon focused on Chatt.

"I mean like sexually." She smiled, feeling awkward. "It's like he's a sex teacher and he wants me to know everything about how to turn a man out. I love it!"

"Ooooh girl!" Tader shouted. "Ain't nothing like a man that knows what he's doing to teach me some thangs."

"Now I actually understand what y'all be talking about when I hear y'all talking about y'all sex lives."

"Get it girl," Spen chimed in. "I'm proud of you."

"Bitch alert!" Tader said, referring to Crispy pulling up outside.

"Now what this hoe want, damn? I'm not letting her ass redesign for me!" Spen barked.

Crispy walked through the door with a yellow sun dress and white sandals on her feet. Everybody in the salon had their eyes glued on her. Crispy loved the attention she got. It made her feel good to have a room full of females staring her down because in her mind they were all jealous and envious because she was the shit. She stared at Kimmy, Devon's little sister as she sat in Spen's station. She wondered if Kimmy remembered her from the one time she spotted her with Devon. Kimmy wasn't the sharpest tool in the box so Crispy figured that she didn't remember. She cleared her throat before speaking. "Spencer, I need to speak with you."

"About?" Spen questioned.

Triple Crown Publications presents . . . DAMAGE

"It would be much better if we talked in private. I have some personal things to discuss with you."

"Well, I'm busy."

Crispy eyes the clock on the wall and asked, "What time do you get off?"

Spen didn't like Crispy's questioning. "Why?" She asked sharply.

"Never mind," Crispy replied. Without another word said, she was out the door. She didn't like the tone of Spen's voice and things would go completely wrong if she would've stayed any longer. *Weak bitch,* Crispy thought as she thought of another plan. If Spen didn't wanna talk things out with her in private then she was gonna bring everything out in the open. She pulled out her cell phone to make a quick call and ask Ceddy for a favor.

Meanwhile, everyone at the salon now had their eyes glued to Spen. They were all waiting on her to speak hoping they would collect some good gossip from the whole Crispy situation. But unfortunately for them, Spen was just as clueless as they were. She didn't know what the fuck Crispy wanted with her but she was itching to find out.

"What was up with that?" Chelae asked.

"I don't know," Spen answered. "There's something about her that I don't trust and I'm very anxious to find out what she has to tell me."

"Ole light skin sneaky ass bitch," Tader stated. She wanted to hop in her car, chase Crispy down, and beat her ass till she was unconscious. She couldn't stand her for nothing in this world.

"What do you think she wants to tell you?" Chatt questioned as she sat back and tried to figure the whole situation out. She knew something was up with Crispy just coming in the salon uninvited the way she did, trying to talk to Spen in private.

Triple Crown Publications *presents* . . . **DAMAGE**

"I don't have the slightest clue. I don't even communicate with her like that."

"Well, watch her," Chatt advised. "It's some shit in her closet that's bound to come out soon."

"Where do I know that chicken from?" Kimmy asked herself out loud.

"You know her?" Spen wanted to know.

"Chicken looking real familiar. I think she's Kylen's teacher."

Tader smacked her lips, trying to hold back laugher. *This bitch is so damn stupid,* she thought to herself. "Kim, I didn't know your son was in school."

Kimmy laughed with extra exaggeration. "Of course Kylen's not in school yet. He's still a baby."

"So, how can Crispy be his teacher?"

"I never said that," Kimmy replied as serious as a heart attack. She really didn't remember making the statement.

"Leave her alone," Spen demanded knowing that Tader would keep purposely picking with Kimmy. Kimmy wasn't stupid, she just wasn't the smartest.

Fucking airhead! Tader thought as she silently laughed to herself. Chatt didn't find anything funny as she sat back and thought to herself. She thought about how Crispy came in and even though Kimmy didn't know where she saw her, Chatt had a funny feeling. She hated to think negative, but something was telling her that Crispy and Devon were fooling around. She figured Kimmy must've seen Crispy with Devon before but she was still stuck on the reason Crispy stopped by. As she tried to think of another situation, she prayed her best friend wasn't getting played. She knew it would crush Spen if Devon was cheating on her; especially with Chrisette Philips.

It was eight o'clock sharp when Crispy headed to Spen's condo. After sending Ceddy to watch the salon for a few hours, he finally gave Crispy a call to inform her that Spen was finishing up her last client. Crispy pulled up in the driveway then got out and hit the lock on her key chain. She slowly walked up to the door step and rang the doorbell. In no time, Devon was at the door shirtless with a towel wrapped around his waist. It was a beautiful sight which automatically got Crispy moist. She thought about just trying to seduce Devon and then leave but the actual reason she came by would give her an even greater feeling at the end of everything. She noticed how he looked at her. It bothered her because it wasn't a look of like. It was more so a look of 'Will you get the fuck on?' She smirked staring at his chest. "Just stepping out the shower?" She asked.

"Obviously!" he barked. "What the fuck are you doing here?"

"For your information, Spencer invited me over."

Devon grabbed his forehead in frustration. His first intention was to slam the door in her face but he had to play smart. Crispy was up to something and in order for him to stop it, he had to know what it was. Most likely it had to do with Spen and seeing that they were already on rocky terms, he couldn't let Crispy add to the fire. He opened the screen door and told her to come in.

Crispy smiled. "Wow, inviting me in? Don't mind if I do." She walked in and took a seat on the living room couch. She sat her purse down on the table and flipped her hair over her shoulders. She couldn't stop staring at Devon's body. He looked so damn good with water dripping down his chest. She tried to control herself. The devil on her shoulder told her to get up and lick him dry.

"So what is it that I need to do?" Devon asked.

"What do you mean?" Crispy asked focusing her attention back to his handsome face.

"What do I have to do to get you to go back to Cali and

leave me and Spen the fuck alone?"

"Devon, the world does not revolve around your ass! You decided that you wanted to leave me over something stupid, so now it's time for your ass to get left!"

Devon had to hold himself back from slapping the shit out of Crispy. "You're really starting to get on my last damn nerve girl! When will you understand that the only type of connection we ever had was just sexual?"

"It was more than that and you know it."

"Look, if this is about your money, I'll have it all back to you by the end of this month. Until then, let's call it truce, a'ight?"

"Truce my ass," she smirked. She knew Devon was terrified of her exposing the truth about them. To see him trying to grace her good side made her feel as if she was back in control. She loved the feeling of being on top.

"Look bitch," Devon hollered, the word bitch slipping out by accident. "I'm tryna' make things right, a'ight. I don't have all day so work wit' me, damn."

"Where do you have to be?" Crispy questioned.

Devon was getting impatient. He didn't know what time Spen would be home so he had to get rid of Crispy fast. He figured that he would have to deal with whatever plan she had up her sleeve another time and another place. "I ain't got time for this shit," he stated. "Get out."

"Here you go with that," Crispy said rolling her eyes. "I'm not going anywhere."

Devon started to get paranoid thinking about Spen showing up. "Don't make me drag yo ass outta here again," he threatened balling up his fist. He was losing his mind. He looked through the living room blinds and his heart immediately dropped. "SHIIIT!!" he shouted as he saw Spen pulling up. He knew there was no explaining himself out of this one. *Why the fuck you let her in here?* He cursed to

Triple Crown Publications *presents* . . . **DAMAGE**

himself, pacing the living room floor.

"Stop it!" Crispy yelled when he grabbed her arm and attempted to drag her in another room.

When he heard Spen's car door shut, he let go of Crispy's arm and rushed to the screen door. He couldn't read her facial expression as she approached the door. "Baby," he stated in a low tone. Spen ignored him and tried to brush past him but he blocked her path.

"You know, I seen Crispy riding in that same Benz earlier. What is it doing here?" She asked, hoping his response would correct her assumptions. Devon was silent. He didn't know what to tell her. "Move," Spen said trying to get past him. When he didn't answer her question, she knew her assumptions had to be true. "Is that the reason you were acting so strange?" She punched his chest. "Is it?" Her heart sank in her stomach when Crispy walked up behind Devon completely naked.

"Hey, Spencer," she said smiling.

Devon covered his eyes. "Baby, I swear I didn't touch her!"

By now Spen's eyes were raining bullets as she put two and two together. Crispy was but naked and Devon was basically naked too except for the towel around his waist. "This bitch told me she had some shit to discuss with me and you been acting strange as hell lately. I can't believe you!" She shouted pushing her way through the screen door. She looked at Crispy and as an instant reflex she swung on her. Crispy wailed out in pain as her nose felt like it had just been re-broken. She wanted to fight back, but her pain was too unbearable. Spen looked at Devon as he shook his head searching for the right words to say. Catching him off guard, she went across his face next. She tried to swing again but he grabbed her arms.

"Spen, please just listen to me for a minute."

Triple Crown Publications presents . . . **DAMAGE**

"NO!!" she screamed, trying to free her arms. "You fucking this bitch in our house? How could you?!"

"I didn't fuck her!" He shouted. "She took her dress off trying to be funny." He pinned her against the wall. "I swear I would never do no shit like that, baby. I wouldn't do that."

"He's lying," Crispy screeched. "He fucked me plenty of times and promised to give me your salon. He even took the twenty-grand that he gave to you out of my account!"

"Shut up, bitch!" Devon yelled. He looked at Spen who was completely heart broken. "I only fucked her once," he admitted. "But it wasn't in our crib baby, I swear!"

"That doesn't make it any better," Spen whispered, unable to scream anymore. The pain from her heart literally took a toll on her strength. "What makes you think you can just give her my salon? It's mine, Devon, mine!"

"It wasn't like that," he told her. "You know I wouldn't do that, Spen."

Spen didn't believe him. "So she's lying?"

Devon closed his eyes and took a deep breath. He knew he had to be honest. "I told her I would ask you to consider selling it," he confessed. "But I never asked you because I..."

"Oh, God!" Spen cried, cutting him off. To hear him speak those words crushed her heart even more. She started feeling as if everything was a complete lie. The engagement, her salon, and all of the years she spent of her life with Devon felt like a total waste. Besides Tader and Chatt, all Spen had was Devon and her salon to keep her happy. Now that they both were down the drain, she didn't know where to go or what to do. "I wanted to have a baby by your ass," she whimpered. "I wanted to marry you, Devon."

"You're still gonna have my baby and marry me," he stated with confidence. "Don't let this lying bitch break us,

Spen."

As the two of them went back and forth, they never noticed that Crispy had left the room. When she returned, she had her dress back on and she was carrying a small black device in her hand. She looked at Devon. "Tell her the truth, Devon. Tell her how you promised me the salon and promised to leave her ass! And tell her how the whole engagement was fake as shit."

If Spen had the strength, she would have went across Crispy's face again. Devon still had her pinned up against the wall and she didn't want to fight him anymore. "Please, get off of me," she said softly.

"I need you to believe me, Spen. I would never give her your salon, baby! And when I proposed to you, I did it because I wanted to be with you for the rest of my life and I still do!" He looked her in the eye hoping she would believe him. "I never planned on leaving you, I swear on my life, baby." He tried to kiss her but she turned away. "I love you, Spencer."

Spen wanted to believe him so bad. For some reason she felt his pain as he spoke those words. The love and emotion that they had been lacking for the past few days was now written all over his face. Crispy saw it in Spen's eyes that she was on the verge of believing him. "Spencer," she shouted, grabbing her attention. She held up the black device that she held in her hand and to Devon's surprise, it was a voice recorder. Crispy hit play and stood confident as she let Spen listen in on a past conversation between her and Devon.

"Why are you acting so scary? She's gonna know about us soon enough, right?"

"Yeah."

"Great, because that ring has my name all over it. You act like you don't miss me."

Triple Crown Publications presents... DAMAGE

"I do miss you. I miss the hell out of you."
"Then act like it."
"Good lookin' on the money."
"It's nothing, bay."
"I promise I'll get it back to you."
"Don't worry about it. There is one thing I want to ask you though."
"I'm listening."
"I want you to get Spencer to sell me her salon."
"I'll ask her to consider it."
"Really?"
"Yeah. Just give me some time a'ight? You trust me?"
"You have to ask?"
"Tell me."
"I trust you, Devon."
"Well act like it, Crispy. I have to make Spen believe that I still care about her in some way."
"Promise me you'll do your best to convince her."
"I promise."
"I believe you. Now if you just stop acting like you don't wanna touch me..."
"You know I wanna touch you. Damn, you want me, don't you?"
"In the worst way possible. You never answered my first question."
"Refresh my memory."
"Why did you give Spencer that ring in the first place?"
"I have to keep her happy. Spen is smart, so one fuck up and she'll know everything."

She hit stop on the tape recorder and smiled knowing she had won the battle. Devon released Spen and rushed over to Crispy ramming her against the wall with his hand around her neck. "She erased a bunch of shit," he shouted. "I swear it didn't go down like that!" He looked at Crispy as he tightened his grip on her neck. He knew she couldn't breathe and he didn't care if she collapsed right at that very moment. He couldn't believe that Crispy had fixed the conversation to make it seem as if he just turned against Spen completely. Even if it wasn't to the fullest, he defended her but he knew Spen would never believe him. "Fuck," he hollered as Crispy started digging her fingernails into his face. With his free hand, he grabbed her broken nose and started to squeeze on it until he felt something move out of place. Crispy tried to scream but nothing would come out. She knew Devon was about to choke her ass to death until she saw Spen flying out the door. Almost to her breaking point, she managed to point to the door trying to show Devon that Spen had left. He released his hand from Crispy's neck and ran outside after her, still wearing nothing but a towel around his waist.

Spen's emotions were running high as she got in her car and drove away. When she was finally at a point where she could look Devon in the eye, Crispy played the tape that sent her over the edge. She felt like Devon had literally grabbed her heart out of her chest and stomped on it until it exploded. "He...he...he didn't even wanna marry me fa'real," she cried aloud to herself. "My salon is all I have and he thought he could just give it to her!" She looked in her rearview mirror and noticed that Devon was following behind her. She stepped on the gas, trying to leave his ass in the dust. But it didn't work. He was still right behind her with every turn she made. She finally gave up and continued towards her destination. She pulled up to the salon, hopped out of her car, and went to her trunk. Once she got what she needed, she walked inside and locked the door behind her. Devon came scurrying around the corner almost hitting a parked car. He parked his truck and got out

Triple Crown Publications presents . . . DAMAGE

in a rush to get inside the salon. When he tried to open the door, he noticed that it was locked.

"Open the door, baby," he yelled, banging on the glass. "Open it!"

Spen walked to the door where she and Devon held eye contact. "I hate you!" she shouted. "I hate you, Devon!"

"Baby, I love you! Crispy is a lying bitch and you got the story all wrong. She twisted the shit."

"I didn't twist anything," Crispy stated, rolling her window down. After she finally got herself together, she was trailing right behind Devon without him even noticing her.

"You knew this salon meant everything to me and you were gonna ask me to sell it to her," Spen cried. "This all I have!"

"I never had intentions on really asking you, baby," Devon exclaimed.

"After all this, you're still gonna lie in my face? I heard the shit for myself, Devon!" She looked at Crispy as she sat in her Benz with a smirk on her face.

"That's right, Spencer. Enjoy the salon while you have it, girl." Crispy rolled her window back up and smiled, ignoring the pain from her nose.

"Please, bitch!" Spen barked. "You'll never have this ma'fucka either!" Spen went to the back of the salon and returned with a gas can in her hand. "Ahhhhhhhhh!" She screamed as she started pouring the gas all over the place. She was losing her mind and didn't even realize what she was doing as she sat in her station and lit a match. "You see this?" She asked, looking at Devon as he pounded on the doors. "Once I drop it, it's over."

"Baby, no!" Devon shouted. "Don't do this! Please, think about what you're doing Spen." He started kicking the door but he knew it was no use. The glass was far too thick to be broken down that easily. "NOOOO!" he yelled when Spen threw the match to the back of the salon. *Think, think, think, D!* It seemed as if his mind blanked out as he watched the flames rise through the salon.

Crispy jumped out of her car and started banging on the glass right along with Devon. "Spencer, what are you doing?" she yelled. She could care less if Spen burned in the fire but she didn't want her to burn the salon down with her.

Devon was losing it and he wracked his brain trying to think of a way to get inside the salon. Finally something came to him so he ran back to his truck, the towel falling from his waist, leaving him now naked. He didn't care about the towel. The only thing on his mind was getting Spen out the salon alive. He grabbed his .45 from under the seat and ran back to the doors. After firing five shots, the glass finally shattered.

Ding...ding...ding!

The sounds of the fire alarms had fire trucks immediately turning the corners. Devon kicked through the shattered glass and tried to maneuver through the fire. Spen was choking on the smoke, trying to breathe. By the time Devon finally got to her, she had already passed out. He scooped her up in his arms looking towards the exit for a clear way out. "Fuck," he whispered, noticing that there was no clear path. He started choking on the smoke and soon it became too much for him to inhale. The last thing he remembered before he passed out was a dozen fire trucks surrounding the salon.

"I can't believe she did this," Crispy whined, drowning herself in her own tears. She watched as the firefighters stormed in the salon attempting to put the flames out. "This was my mother's salon. This was supposed to be mine and now look at it," she sobbed.

Triple Crown Publications presents... **DAMAGE**

9

Chasity and Ta'Ronna fled off the elevators searching for Spen's room number. "I think they said it was Room 308," Chatt said. "There it is right there." They rushed inside the room and found a nurse standing beside Spen's bed. "Is she okay?" Chatt asked, looking at Spen as she slept. She was so worried about her best friend. God forbid something ever happening to the person she was closest to in her life. She and Tader had a thick bond as well but not as thick as she and Spen's.

"She's fine," the nurse assured them. "The results from her blood test look great. We're just waiting for her x-rays to come back to see how her lungs and heart are doing. The doctor also wants to look for signs of infection like pneumonia or look for collapsed lungs, just to be safe."

Chatt looked confused. All she heard was collapsed lungs. That was enough to make her believe that Spen was dying.

"What are all the test for?"

"Well, she passed out from inhaling too much smoke from the fire. Smoke itself can contain products that don't cause direct harm to a person, but they take up the space that's needed for oxygen. We needed to check for anything possible."

"Oh, hell," Tader mumbled. She didn't understand a thing the nurse was saying. "When she gon' wake up?"

"She actually just went back to sleep not too long ago. Give her a few hours and she should wake up. Her voice may be a little hoarse for a while, but that's completely normal under the circumstances."

Chatt took a seat. "Well, we're gonna wait till she wakes up."

"That's fine." She grabbed her clip board and smiled. "You ladies let me know if you need anything."

Chatt nodded and gave her a fake smile in return. "Will do."

Tader sighed, pulling up a chair. She and Chatt sat in silence with their eyes glued to Spen as she slept peacefully. Tader shook her head thinking about everything that had happened. "I bet Devon's ass is the one to blame for everything."

"We don't know that yet," Chatt disagreed. "Don't start pointing fingers until you know the story." Chatt prayed that Tader was wrong. She hoped Devon wasn't the one to blame even though she had a feeling in her gut that he was.

Tader rolled her eyes. She didn't feel like going back and forth with Chatt at the time so she just kept her thoughts to herself. After sitting in silence for so long, they both eventually drifted off to sleep. The sound of Spen's voice woke them up after about an hour nap. "I'm almost out of Ice Chips," Spen whined, shaking her cup.

The nurse laughed. "Don't worry, hun. "I'll get you more."

Triple Crown Publications presents . . . **DAMAGE**

"Spen!" Chatt shouted, relieved that she had awaken.

"Shhh," Spen told her. "Why are you yelling?"

"I'm just happy that..." Chatt stopped in mid-sentence when she saw a short man with grey hair walk into the room.

"You must be Spencer," he said, walking towards Spen's bed. She didn't say anything. "I'm Detective Morrison. I'm here on account of an arson investigation."

"Oh, shit," Tader mumbled.

Crispy pushed down the handle and entered her hotel room. She sat on the bed and began to cry all over again. Everything she had planned was now down the drain. She couldn't believe that Spen had actually sat the salon on fire. If she would've known her actions would be that severe, she would've never exposed the truth about she and Devon's relationship. *That was so stupid of me,* she told herself. The image of the flames inside the salon wouldn't leave her mind. It was a horrible sight, one that Crispy couldn't get out of her mind.

Ceddy turned over in is bed to face her. "What is it Ms. Crispy? She didn't leave Devon like you planned?"

Crispy shook her head while still letting the tears flow. "Ceddy she ruined it for me. She burned down my mom's salon!"

"She wouldn't!" Ceddy screeched, placing his hand on his heart.

"Yes she would! That bitch ruined my life plan! Now what am I supposed to do?" Crispy asked wiping her teary eyes. "I can't be a slut forever."

"Buy another salon," Ceddy suggested.

"Ceddy, that was my mom's property, okay? I'm not buying another place because I wanted that one!" Crispy was beyond hurt when she watched Spen burn down her mother's salon. She had to seek revenge on her and soon in order to make herself feel better. She thought long and hard about how she could ruin Spen's life, and that's when it came to her. She grabbed her cell phone and called Jasmine. She answered after the first two rings.

"This is Jas."

"Hey Jasmine, it's Crispy. I know me and Ceddy were supposed to fly down but I've found something for you."

"And what might that be?" Jasmine questioned.

"There's this gorgeous woman who just lost her only income. She's flawless Jasmine, so I know she'll do you some good."

Jasmine laughed. "That's not how I recruit my employees, Crispy."

"I know, but this is serious paper Jas. This girl is young, sexy, and beautiful. You have to hear me out."

Jasmine grabbed her pen and notepad before asking, "What's her location?"

"Ohio."

"Ohio?" Jasmine restated.

"Yeah," Crispy confirmed. "Is that a problem?"

"Not necessarily." Jasmine opened her laptop. "That's quite a coincidence."

"How so?" Crispy questioned. She sat up straight on the bed and grabbed the notepad that was on the dresser next to her. She knew Jasmine was about to feed her some information so she wanted to be prepared.

"I usually don't recruit the women for this business because my strong points are the men. You said Ohio, correct?"

"Yeah, that's actually where me and Ceddy are now."

"Well, I'll tell you what. My brother recruits the finest young women and if this woman is as bad as you're making her out to be, he'll take it from there."

"Great," Crispy stated. "Who is he?"

Triple Crown Publications *presents* . . . **DAMAGE**

"He keeps a low profile so I want you to do the same once I give you this information. He's known as DreStar and he just so happens to stay in Ohio."

Crispy was more than excited. She felt as if God had answered her prayers right on the spot. "This is so great," she cheered. "What's his work ethic?"

Jasmine smirked. "He's excellent at finding young girls that'll do this business some good. Once he finds them, he teaches them everything that they're lacking sexually. It's like a training process to get them ready for this business. You wouldn't know because you came into this whole thing an entire different way."

"Well, I'm ready for whatever," Crispy assured her. "How can I get in contact with him?"

"I'll have him get in contact with you, Crispy, but I'm serious when I say he means business."

"So do I."

"We'll see," Jasmine stated before ending the call. Crispy smiled.

Spen couldn't hide her nervousness as she and Detective Morrison held eye contact. She didn't have a clue what was on his mind but she knew she was in trouble. She didn't think about the consequences of her actions while she was purposely burning down the salon, but now she wished she would've thought twice. After several moments of silence, the detective finally spoke. "Spencer, I had a chance to speak with Mr. Freeman earlier and he fed me some well needed information."

"He did?" Spen questioned, not knowing what to think. Devon could've told the detective an entire different story than from the actual one.

"Yes, he did; and now that he's come clean about starting the fire, I need to ask you a few questions that may or may not affect what he will be charged with."

Spen couldn't believe that Devon took the blame for her mistake. "What is he being charged with?"

"Well, as if now he's being charged with second degree arson. That's a Class four felony."

What the hell does that mean? She thought to herself. "That's not that bad right?"

The detective took a seat. "Let me give you a run down. If convicted of a Class four felony, Mr. Freeman could get a minimum sentence of 18 months, a presumptive sentence of 30 months, or a maximum sentence of thirty-six months in prison, depending on the circumstances."

Tader loved every minute of listening to the detective talk about what charges Devon could be facing. He could've gotten life for all she cared. Spen on the other hand felt bad. She had to ask herself if she was willing to let Devon do the time for a crime that she committed. "So, what do you need me for?"

"I just need to ask you a few questions about the fire." He pulled a piece of paper out of his jacket followed by a pen. "Was there anyone else present during the time the crime was being committed?"

Spen remembered Crispy being there, but she couldn't tell the detective because she knew Crispy saw everything that had happened. "No, only Devon and I were present."

Detective Morrison looked as if he didn't believe her. "Alright," he stated, writing something down on the piece of paper. "Now, is there any reason that Mr. Freeman would want to physically harm you?"

Spen was so confused. She didn't have a clue if the information she was sharing with the detective would make or break her. She prayed that she didn't slip and end up saying the wrong thing. "No, there isn't any reason he would want to harm me."

"So he just set the building on fire with you inside for no apparent reason?"

"You know what," she paused, pointing towards the door. "I have to ask you to leave."

"Spencer, I understand that for some reason you're trying to protect Mr. Freeman, but in order for me to help him, I need you to cooperate with me. I'm only asking for the truth."

"I told you the truth," she exclaimed. "He doesn't belong in jail, okay. This whole thing is just a big misunderstanding."

Detective Morrison stood to his feet and folded the piece of paper up. After placing it back in his jacket, he walked towards Spen's bed. "I'm gonna take the information you gave me, as well as Mr. Freeman's information and see what I can do."

"Please don't send him to jail," Spen begged. "He's not a criminal."

He nodded. "Mr. Freeman may be eligible to be placed on probation for up to three years instead of being sent to prison. As a term of probation, the court could impose some jail time, up to one year. They will more than likely look at the circumstances surrounding the offense and his history to determine the appropriate sentence."

Spen sighed, knowing there was no telling what the future held for Devon. A part of her felt extra guilty for not telling the detective that she was the one responsible for the fire. Letting Devon take the blame was awful, but for some reason she couldn't find it in herself to tell the truth. She only hoped that he didn't get any jail time because she knew it wouldn't be right. After Detective Morrison left, Chatt and Tader stayed for a couple more hours. Spen laid back down and tried to clear her mind from everything that was happening. *How did it get to this?* She asked herself.

10

Tader walked inside her house and found Terrell sitting on the couch counting money. She took her jacket off and sat next to him. It bothered her that he didn't even acknowledge her presence. "Wow, dope got you paid like this?" She asked. He ignored her and continued to count the money. Tader's first instinct was to slap him upside the head but she let it go and tried again. "Babe, I lost my job last night," She said, scooting closer to him.

"What you mean you lost it?" He questioned, confused. "Yo friend fired you?"

"Nah, she fired the damn salon, literally."

He finally looked up. "Word?"

Tader laughed. "Hell yeah. All over a cheating ass nigga."

Terrell gathered all his money and threw it in a duffel bag. He got up, walked in the kitchen and pulled a carton of juice out of the refrigerator. Without grabbing a cup, he opened the juice and drunk it straight. "Wassup with that test?" He asked nonchalantly.

Got damn nigga! Tader thought to herself. *The baby is yours so just shut the fuck up about it.* "What you mean wassup wit' it?"

"When are you gettin' it?" He stated more clearly.

Tader huffed. Terrell and this whole DNA test was starting to drive her nuts. "I'll get it this weekend, okay?"

"What you salty for? You should want it just as bad as I do."

She got up and joined him in the kitchen. "I know for a fact that this baby is yours." She pointed to her stomach. "The timing and everything is right, Rell. I haven't been with anybody else."

Terrell faced her. "You haven't been wit' nobody else?" He restated.

"No, I haven't. How are we gon' start trusting each other if you always doubting me?"

He shrugged his shoulders. "You tell me."

"You gotta trust me, Terrell. I trust you," she stated. "I can't go on knowing that you don't trust me."

Terrell was silent for a moment. He wanted to trust her but he knew he couldn't, at least not at the time. "I'll work on it."

Tader rolled her eyes frustrated. "That's not good enough. I want you to prove it since I have to prove it to you."

He sighed. "Go change your clothes."

"Why?" She questioned.

"I'ma take you somewhere that's gon' cut all the games. Now go get dressed like I said."

Tader smiled as she went to change her clothes like Terrell told her to. She knew if she pressured him enough about trusting her, then that would buy her more time from taking the DNA test. Tader wasn't confused at all to who her baby's father was. She knew it wasn't David's or Terrell's, but she would never tell anyone. If she played her cards right, she planned on getting away with having Anthony's baby and claiming it as Terrell's.

Chatt walked in Dre's house and took off her jacket. She found him in his bedroom on his laptop. She walked in and sat on his bed waiting for him to finish whatever he was doing. It took him about ten minutes to finally look up. She wondered what was so important that it took him so long to acknowledge her presence. "What are you doing?" She asked curiously.

He stared at her for a moment before speaking. "Just checking some important e-mails. Where you been?"

"At the hospital. My girl Spen is in some crazy shit."

Dre closed his laptop and joined her on the bed. "What happened?"

"She found out that her man was cheating, so she handled it in her own insane type of way."

Dre laughed. "You talkin' bout that one lawyer dude?"

Chatt nodded and crossed her arms. "Unbelievable, right?"

"Maybe, maybe not. He could've had a reason for doing what he did. Niggas don't cheat for no reason."

Chatt stood up and shook her head. "That's a bunch of bullshit Dre! Nigga's cheat because they're stupid and don't realize when a bitch trying to be good to them." She rolled her eyes. "Y'all just don't understand how hard it is for us to be faithful! Niggas want us just like bitches want y'all, but we hold our ground and stay true to one bitch nigga!"

Dre smiled. "Well, then I guess that makes y'all the stupid ones, right?" Chatt huffed, storming out of the room. She hated when people didn't take her seriously. Dre followed

Triple Crown Publications presents... DAMAGE

behind her laughing. He had gotten use to her mood swings and was at the point to where he knew how to handle them. "It was a joke," he stated, following her downstairs into the living room.

She sat on the couch and began to pout. She blocked Dre out as he tried to explain the reasoning for his comment. They hadn't been in conversation for over twenty minutes and he already made her mad. Feeling her cell phone vibrate, she grabbed it from out of her pocket. The caller I.D. displayed an unknown number. "Hello," Chatt said, answering the call.

"This is a call from an inmate at the Montgomery County Correctional Facility. Please Press one to except the charges or press two to decline."

Curious to find out who was calling her from a jail facility, Chatt accepted the call. "Chasity?" a female voice spoke.

"Yeah, this is Chasity. Who is this?"

"This is your mother."

Chatt grew silent. She hadn't spoken to her mother in over a year, so to hear her voice put her in shock. "Shawan?" She finally asked.

"Yes, baby. It's me."

"Well, what do you want?" Chatt asked sharply.

"I need your help, Chasity. Mommy's in trouble and she needs you."

Chatt looked at the phone as if she could see her mother's face. "Why the hell are you talking to me like I'm three?" She put the phone back to her ear. "And it's funny how you only reach out to me when you need something. How the fuck did you get my number anyway?"

"Chasity, please," Shawan screeched. "We haven't had the best past, but I really would like to make a better future for us."

Triple Crown Publications presents ... **DAMAGE**

"Oh, really?" Chatt asked in a sarcastic tone. "How do you plan on doing that?"

Shawan sighed. "I honestly don't know. But baby, once I get out of here, I'm gonna try."

"Well, what do you need me for?"

"I need you to help me get out of here. I don't belong in jail, Chasity."

"What you wanna get out for? So you can run back to the nearest crack house?" Chatt showed no remorse as she spoke to her mother. It pissed her off that she only called her when she needed something.

"I'm clean," Shawan stated. "I haven't done that stuff for over six months now."

"Bye, Shawan."

"No, wait," Shawan yelled, trying to stop Chatt before she hung up the phone.

"I don't have any money, a'ight."

"It's only three grand. I swear I'll get it back to you, Chasity. Just help me, please."

"Fuck you, Shawan," Chatt replied, hanging up the phone. She shoved it back in her pocket and went into deep thought. She felt Dre staring at her but she pretended not to notice him. Her mind was somewhere else and she didn't wanna focus on him at the time. Shawan really hurt her feelings by calling her only because she needed something. She could've called to say hello, how are you, or anything, but she only called because she was in trouble. *Does she really want to change our future?* Chatt asked herself. It would make her more than happy to see that her mother wanted to make a change with herself. She closed her eyes and thought about her father. *I wonder where his drunk ass is.*

"You a'ight?" Dre finally asked.

Chatt opened her eyes. "Yeah."

"That was your mom?"

"She wants my help. After all this time, she calls me because she wants me to help her."

Dre grew quiet. He knew Chatt would blow if he shared his honest opinion about the situation. He looked at the time and noticed that it was time for him to break out. "I have to go," he said, rising up from the couch. He kissed her cheek and headed back upstairs. When he came back down, he gave her another kiss before heading out the door. Chatt watched him through the window as he got in his truck and pulled off. Once he was gone, she started to think of her mother again. Her heart told her to help her, but her conscience said fuck her. *Even if I wanted to help her, I couldn't,* she thought to herself. *I'm broke.*

A flash back of Dre digging into his closet ran through her mind. He was always in that closet coming out with a handful of money, but Chatt never understood where it came from. She had checked the closet plenty of times being nosy, but never found anything. She took a deep breath before heading up the stairs towards the closet. *It has to be something,* she told herself as she opened the door. She scanned the closet seeing nothing but the same old rags and towels. She got frustrated not being able to find anything. *Where the fuck is it?* She thought as began moving the towels to the side. She saw nothing there but worn out wallpaper in the back of each shelf.

She started stacking the towels back up neatly when she had an instant thought. She took a closer look at the wallpaper on the second shelve, and noticed that it had been ripped a couple of times. She reached towards the back of the shelf and pulled on the already torn wallpaper. Once she had it completely pulled back, she saw a wooden drawer. She pulled it opened, and there it was. "Damn," she said out loud. "He's paid like a ma'fucka!" She gazed at the money in awe before thinking about what her next move was. The words *Yes & No* played in her mind as she debated on whether she wanted to take what wasn't hers.

Just call and ask him, she told herself. *But what do I say; hey Dre, I went through your closet and found your money, so can I have some?* She shook her head, feeling stupid about arguing back and forth with herself. *Where is all this money coming from anyway?* She hesitated before grabbing a wad of money. She counted ten one hundred dollar bills, so she figured there was a thousand in each wad. After grabbing two more, she closed the drawer and pulled the wallpaper back over it. "Lord please forgive me," she prayed, "for I am not a thief, but a loving daughter." She knew she had to come up with a quick way to replace the money she took before Dre found out about it. It was so much in the drawer, she hoped that he wouldn't even notice. *I hope she honestly wants to change,* Chatt thought as she headed to the bus stop, thinking about bailing her mother out.

Terrell and Tader pulled up to an old blue house in Fair Bourne, Ohio. The house had a garden surrounding the front porch with colorful flowers blooming everywhere. Exactly seven cats roamed through the yard, scaring the shit out of Tader as she got out of Terrell's truck. "Babe, who lives here?" she asked.

"My mama," Terrell stated.

Tader was ready to shit bricks. "Rell, I can't meet her! I'm not ready."

"You'll neva' be ready for something like this." Tader didn't know just how serious Terrell's statement was. He was a true mama's boy and he knew his mother didn't play games. She would go to hell and back for her son. He grabbed her hand and led her towards the front door. "Just relax and be yourself."

Tader was wearing an all-white V-neck sweater, black leggings, and a pair of white suede boots. Her hair was pinned up into a bun and she had on a pair of diamond stud earrings with the matching necklace. Before they could reach the doorstep, Terrell's mother was flying out the door with open arms. She was a short light skinned woman which surprised Tader because Terrell was so dark. She had shoulder length pretty brown curls and a nice toned body, although her arms looked as if she lifted too many weights. *Damn, is this chick a fuckin' boxer or something?* Tader joked to herself. She could tell that she worked out on a daily and she smiled, thinking they had one thing already in common. "Oh, my baby, I've missed your black ass!" Terrell's mother said, wrapping her arms around him.

Terrell smiled. "It hasn't been that long, ma."

"Oh, honey, let's get inside before we start any type of conversation." They all walked inside and took a seat on the couch. The house had a huge scent that smelled like a mixture of cigarettes and liquor. The living room was filled with pictures of her family on the walls and Tader smiled, looking at a picture of Terrell when he was younger.

"Now, who is this beautiful young lady you have here with you?" Terrell's mother asked.

"This is Ta'Ronna," Terrell introduced.

Tader's face displayed a fake smile. "Hi."

"Hi," Terrell's mother replied, giving her hand out. "I'm Terrell's mother, of course, but you can call me, Momma Lee."

"Nice to meet you, Momma Lee," Tader said. The woman had a strong grip. "I'm Ta'Ronna, like he said, but everyone calls me Tader."

"Well, the pleasure's all mine, Tader."

Terrell glanced at his mother, trying to read her vibe. Her face was blank making it hard for him to read it. "I'm thinkin' bout gettin' serious wit' her, ma."

Momma Lee never took her eyes off of Tader as she spoke. "How long have you two been seeing each other?"

"It's been..."

"I'm talking to Ta'Ronna," Momma Lee interrupted.

Tader was nervous. "We've been at it for a while now."

"What's a while?"

Bitch, why you so damn nosy? Tader thought to herself. "We've been messing around since high school."

"Messing *around?*" Momma Lee restated.

"You know, ma," Terrell chimed in. "We been back and forth but ain't decided to get serious until now."

Momma Lee looked at Terrell and shook her head. "Neither one you are ready to settle down."

Terrell laughed. "How you know, ma?"

"Cause I know, baby." She looked at Tader. "You know, I'm very over-protective of my son. I have a good eye when it comes to something or someone that's not right for him."

"Well, I hope you can see that I'm right for him."

Momma Lee laughed. "You know, Ta'Ronna, I'm not sure if I see that. Why are you so nervous?"

"I'm not nervous. I'm very calm." She looked at Terrell. "Will you tell her that I'm calm, babe."

"You don't need to tell my son what to tell me, honey." She smiled. "He knows how to speak for himself."

Tader started to feel uncomfortable. She could sense that Momma Lee wasn't feeling her, but at the same time, she didn't care. She wanted to be with her son, so she didn't care for other opinions. She faced the ground, breaking eye contact with Momma Lee. Terrell laughed inside, placing his hand on Tader's upper thigh. "You ain't gotta be so nervous," he told her.

"I'm not nervous," she replied.

Momma Lee rose up from the couch and said, "Terrell,

let me speak with you for a minute."

Terrell kissed Tader's cheek. "I'll be right back." He got up and followed his mother into her bedroom. He watched her light a cigarette and sit on her bed. "Wassup, ma?"

She took a puff on the cigarette. "Why did you bring her here?"

"Your approval, of course." He smiled. "You know how to read a woman and determine if she's right for me or not."

"Well, baby, I don't have to read this girl to know that she's not right for you."

"What's wrong with her?"

Momma Lee looked surprised by his question. "I don't know if it's just in front of me, but the girl is definitely putting on an act." She shook her head. "I don't trust her. You know I don't play games when it comes to my son. Where are her parents?"

"From what I know, they stay in Brooklyn. She only speaks wit' 'em from time to time."

"And why is that?"

Terrell shrugged his shoulders. "I guess she ain't too cool wit' 'em. She said her life was moving at a pace they couldn't handle."

"Bullshit," Momma Lee replied, rolling her eyes. "She's a liar and I know it."

"It's unfortunate that you feel that way because I really like this girl. Ain't nothing she can do to change your opinion?"

Momma Lee blew smoke from her mouth. "No."

"Come on, Leona. Don't leave me hanging."

"I done told you about calling me by my first name, boy. Now I said, no. I don't trust this girl one bit and she will get you into some things you don't wanna be in, Terrell. You know what I'll do to her if she gets you in trouble."

Triple Crown Publications *presents* . . . **DAMAGE**

"I felt that way at first, too. But listen ma, I done broke this girl down. She's changed tremendously since I first met her."

"The child is not yours, Terrell. If you let that girl trap you, I'll cut your manhood off and you'll never be able to have any kids that actually belong to you."

Terrell looked completely shocked with his mother's statement. But it wasn't the part about chopping his manhood off that had him shook. "Ma, how you know she's pregnant? She ain't even showing."

Momma Lee took the last puff on her cigarette then tossed it in the ashtray on her nightstand. "Son, you know good and well not to sleep on me. That girl is trying to trap you and you better not let it happen!" She grinned, something evil. "Now, if you don't take my advice and kick her to the curb, you'll regret it, Terrell. And if she fucks you over, she'll be hearing from me. End of discussion."

Terrell sat on the bed and sighed. His mother's opinion meant everything to him, so it was hard for him to hear that she wasn't feeling Tader. *Maybe she just ain't ready,* he thought.

11

DreStar exhaled deeply as he lay back on his bed, feeling great from the nut he just got off. He had been watching pornos and jacking off all day. He looked at it as a treat to himself for finding two new lovely girls for Legs Open Mouth Closed. They were thick, beautiful, and going to make him hella' money. Money made him happy like nothing else could. After lying down for a few more moments he got up and took a shower. Once he got fresh he hopped in his whip to make a few runs. Remembering that Jasmine had asked him to check into something, he pulled his Nextel out of his pocket and flipped it open followed by a piece of paper with a number written down on it. He dialed the number and after two rings, a female answered. "Hello?"

"Yeah, it's Dre, who dis?"

"Oh, hey, Dre. My name is Crispy; I work for your

sister."

"I see. What's yo' approach?"

"Well, I told Jasmine that I found someone new for you guys. I think you should check her out."

Dre laughed. "Employee's don't scout other employees. That's my job."

"Yeah, Jasmine told me that. Look, if you see this girl, you'll fall in love with her. I know you mean business, so just trust me."

"Let's meet."

"Now?" Crispy questioned.

"Yeah," Dre confirmed. "Where are you?"

"For now I'm staying at the Double Tree, downtown. I'm in room 204."

"I'll be there in 'bout half an hour. Keep a lookout for me."

"Okay, great." Crispy hung up her phone and begun straitening her hotel room up. She hopped in the shower and slipped on a grey wife beater and a pair of black jeans. She pinned her hair up and let her long curly ponytail hang. When she came out of the bathroom, she noticed that Ceddy was awake. "Hey sleepy head!" She giggled a little. "Bout time you got up." Ceddy rolled his eyes and got out the bed. "Ceddy, when are you gon' stop the morning attitude shit?"

Ceddy grabbed his Baby Phat purse and took out a pack of Newport's. He then grabbed his lighter from off the dresser and headed outside. "Ms. Crispy, I'll be on a plane to Cali this weekend. I'm dead broke and need to make some ends soon."

"You see now boo, I've been thinking about you lately and found a way for us to make some cash." She grabbed a cigarette from the pack of Newport's Ceddy had in his hand.

Triple Crown Publications presents... **DAMAGE**

"What did you have in mind?" Ceddy asked.

"Jasmine hooked me up with her little brother. He's gonna be here soon, that's why I was cleaning up."

"Well, why didn't you say something before? Let me go take a smoke and I'll be back to get dressed!"

"Damn boo, why you so excited?" Crispy asked.

"Honey, we have a man about to arrive! How could I not be?"

They both stepped outside to take a few puffs on their cigarette's. When they returned to their room, Ceddy put on his favorite blue skinny jeans and a white T-shirt that read 'Taste Me' across the front. He slid his manicured toes into a pair of white flip flops and sprayed oil sheen over his s-curl. Within the next fifteen minutes, DreStar was knocking at the hotel door. "He's here Ms. Crispy, go answer it," Ceddy said, positioning himself on the bed. He had his legs crossed and his right hand sitting on his knee. His back was slightly arched and he tooted his glossy lips.

Crispy smiled, opening the door to let DreStar in. "What up, ma?" He greeted her.

"Hey, nice to meet you." Crispy gave out her hand. "Let's get down to business."

When Spen opened her eyes, her room was filled with balloons and flowers. There was a card sitting on her food tray next to her ice chips. She grabbed the card and opened it, only to find a letter from Devon inside. The letter read:

> Spen,
> Sorry I haven't been to see you yet. I'm in the mix of getting this whole salon shit situated. I have some people from my job helping me out with this whole thing, so I'm hoping everything will be straight. I know you think the only reason I took the blame was to suck up to you. I promise that's not the reason. I

took the blame for it because I deserve whatever time they were gon' give you. I love you so much, baby and it kills me knowing that I'm the reason we failed. My mom always told me to accept my wrongs like a man, and that's exactly what I'm gon' do. I cheated on you, Spen and there's no excuse for what I did. I know you'll never believe me, but I never had feelings for Crispy. I made her believe that I did so I could get money off of her. Pathetic, right? Yeah, I know. I only had sex with her once and that's the truth. I hated every minute of it and I felt like shit afterwards. You deserve so much better, baby. You deserve better than me. If it's the last thing I do, I promise I'm gon' buy you another salon. Your dreams don't go unnoticed in my eyes. Like I said before, I'm so sorry, and I love you and always will. I hope one day you can forgive me for all the pain that I've caused you. I swear I didn't mean to hurt you, and I would give anything to make the time go back.

 Love,
 Devon

Spen wanted to cry as she closed the card. She glanced at the colorful balloons that read 'I'm sorry' and 'Get Well Soon' on them. She wanted to forgive Devon so bad, but how could she? He had broken her heart by cheating on her with another woman for money. Spen just didn't understand why he would cheat on her. She felt as if she gave her all to him and he just threw it away over some light skinned pussy. She knew no matter what he did to her, her feelings for him wouldn't just fade overnight. He was her rock and she knew deep down he loved her as well; but when a female throws free pussy up in a man's face, eighty percent of them are bound to take it. It just crushed her that Devon had to be a part of that percentage. She sighed and lay back on her bed waiting for the nurse to come tell her when she could be released.

Terrell gave his mother a kiss on the cheek before heading out the door. "I'll be out here to see you more often, ma. Take care of yo' self."

"Oh, don't you worry about me baby." She looked at Tader. "That's your main focus."

Tader gave her a fake smile. "Nice meeting you, Momma Lee. Hopefully we can see each other more often." She gave her a hug and then got in Terrell's truck. Momma Lee watched them as they pulled off and she didn't take her eyes off of them until they became invisible. "She don't like me," Tader stated, sitting back in her seat.

"Give it some time," Terrell told her. "She gotta get to know you a lil' more."

Tader rolled her eyes. "I don't think I'm the type to bring home to your mom."

Terrell laughed. "Chill out, girl. Like I said, give it time. But I do advise you not to fuck with her, though. Mom is crazy." He laughed to himself, but Tader didn't find anything funny. They pulled up to a stoplight and Tader could feel a pair of eyes staring down her back. True enough when she glanced at the car to their right side, the eyes of David were looking directly at her. She could feel the sweat build up over her forehead, as it seemed to take the red light forever to change. When it finally did, she watched David stomp down on his gas pedal like he was Jeff Gordon in a NASCAR race. "Fuckin' stupid ass nigga," Terrell shouted. "He gon' get his self killed driving like that."

Tader remained silent as she listened to Rell shout. She closed her eyes and swallowed a big gulp of saliva down her throat. She was scared shitless. "Just drive, babe," she said in a shaky voice.

"I am driving. I just hate when dumbass people drive like

Triple Crown Publications presents . . . **DAMAGE**

they ain't got no sense." Tader kept quiet for the remainder of the ride. When they arrived at her house, Terrell told her that he had a few things to do. She gave him a kiss, then went inside and ran her some warm bath water, soaking for three hours straight. She washed herself then got out, and threw a towel around her body. When she opened the bathroom door, she felt a force snatch it back from her. She thought to herself, *What the fuck?* She looked towards the bottom of the door and spotted a shadow, but before she could make a move someone had swung the door open hitting her in the face. She fell to the ground, bumping her head on the toilet. Her head was spinning and she couldn't see straight. When she finally lifted her head from the ground, she found herself looking at three Davids. She was breathing hard, and she stuttered through her words. "You, you, you, you're a triplet?" she asked finally getting her speech together.

"Hell nah, you dumb bitch," David barked. "Snap out of it, hoe!" She couldn't get herself together. She tried to stand up but slid right back on the floor. Her towel eventually came off, exposing her naked body. "Are you drunk bitch?" David asked. She watched him pull out his .9 millimeter and point it directly at her chest. "Any last words?" he asked.

She closed her eyes and spoke softly, "Tell Rell I love him and that..."

Boom! Boom! Boom!

The gun went off before she could finish. Her head was still spinning and she could feel her body surrounded by her own blood. She opened her eyes to realize that it was her now cold water that her body was surrounded by. She placed her hand on her heart. *Thank goodness it was just a dream*, she thought, taking deep breaths. She had a bad habit of falling asleep in the tub, but she knew that would be the last time.

Triple Crown Publications presents . . . **DAMAGE**

12

Chatt sat across from Shawan feeling awkward. She didn't know what to say or do. All she did was constantly shake her head not knowing what to think. She thought that if she and her mother ever reunited, it would be special. They sat in silence until Shawan finally spoke. "This is a nice place you got," she complimented, looking around Dre's house.

"I told you this isn't my place," Chatt snapped.

"I'm sorry. It slipped my mind again."

Chatt was more than disgusted as she stared at Shawan. Her clothes were filthy and she looked about ninety pounds. "You need to sit down," she told her.

Shawan took a seat, but continued to look around. It was very hard for her to keep still. "How long do I have to sit right here?"

"Until Dre gets here." Chatt was becoming annoyed

with her mother.

"Is he your boyfriend?"

"Yes," Chatt replied sharply.

Shawan smiled. "You want me to meet him?"

"No," Chatt confessed. "I have to explain to him that you're the reason I stole from him." Chatt's conscience wouldn't leave her alone about taking the money from Dre. As soon as he arrived back at home, she planned on telling him everything. *She wasn't even worth stealing for,* she thought to herself.

"You stole from him?" Shawan asked, looking surprised.

"Yes, I did," Chatt stated standing up. "Actually, I borrowed it because I'm gonna give it back." She shook her head in disgust. "I took that money to help you."

"Thank you," Shawan said, standing up to give her a hug.

Chatt pushed her away, covering her nose with her hand. She couldn't ignore the foul stench that Shawan carried. "You need a shower."

"I know," Shawan admitted. She sat back down on the couch and laid her head back. Chatt grabbed the T.V remote and flipped through the channels. She continued to glance at Shawan until she noticed her doze off. Chatt couldn't believe that her mother was the same old fiend. She sounded so different during their phone call, and Chatt now regretted even answering the call. *Some things never change,* she thought. She looked at the clock and wondered where Dre was. She was ready to confess to him that she had stolen from him and accept her consequences. She called him to see where he was, but his phone went straight to voicemail. After waiting another thirty minutes, she found herself dozing off as well. She tried to fight it, but once her head hit the arm of the loveseat, she was out for good.

Triple Crown Publications *presents* . . . **DAMAGE**

When Chatt opened her eyes, she saw nothing. She rose from the loveseat and stood up, trying to find a light switch but she found more than that within the next few steps. Someone swung an empty beer bottle across her face causing her to fall forward to the ground. Her head was throbbing and she felt as if she couldn't move. She rolled over on her back wiping the blood from her lip that the beer bottle had caused. The cuts in her face were quickly starting to burn. She tried to raise up, but caught a fist in her mouth, causing her lip to gush out more blood. "Fuck," she cried out in pain sucking her swollen lip. The attacker grabbed her by the collar of her shirt so that they were face to face. With the house still pitch black, she was still unable to see who it was. Chatt was never scared of anything but right now she feared for her life. She didn't know what the fuck was going on.

"Dumb bitch!" The attacker whispered before throwing her back on the floor. He hit the light switch to reveal his self, and when Chatt realized who he was, her body cringed.

"Why, Dre?" she asked attempting to lift up off of the floor. "What the fuck did I do to you?"

"You put yo hands where they didn't belong." His eyes were red as he continued. "You stole from me, you sneaky ass bitch."

"Look, I swear..." Chatt was cut off by Dre's fist going into her jaw.

"Fifteen stacks!" He hollered. "You got me for fifteen fucking stacks!"

"I only took three," Chatt confessed, whimpering in pain. She wanted to get up and knock the shit out of him, but with nothing to protect herself with, she couldn't do it.

Dre sat on the couch staring at Chatt as she laid on

the floor. "I can't believe you got me for fifteen stacks." He turned up his nose. "Why the fuck my couch smell like piss?"

"Oh, my God," Chatt whispered under her breath. She looked around the living room curious to where Shawan was. That's when it hit her. *As soon as I dozed off,* she thought. *How could I be so stupid?* Chatt shook her head looking around the messy house. She knew Shawan had searched the house up and down until she found something worth taking. "I didn't do all of this," she muttered. "My mom did."

Dre stood up and hollered, "You had a crack head in my house?"

"She didn't have nowhere else to go," Chatt snapped. She was confused when she saw Dre burst out with laughter. "What the fuck is so funny?"

"Yo dumb ass!" he yelled out. "You are so fucking stupid, that it makes no sense." He stood over her and crossed his arms. "Let me tell you something, Chasity. I'm not a good dude, a'ight? I pick up little dumb bitches like yourself and take advantage of 'em."

Chatt shook her head in disbelief. She couldn't believe that she let another nigga take advantage of her. "I should've known," she mumbled. "You were too good to be true."

Dre smiled. "You're a beautiful person, Chasity." He caressed her cheek. "I shouldn't have done you like this, but when I first saw you, I saw money stacking up. You could bring in so much paper for me, baby." He wiped at the blood on her lip. "Now that you've stolen from me, I guess it's safe to say that you owe me."

She smacked his hand away from her face. "I don't owe you shit."

He gripped her jaws and replied, "You owe me fifteen fucking stacks, and you're gonna get it to me." He brushed his hand over her body. "Niggas will pay the ultimate price just to touch you."

Chatt felt so stupid. She was disgusted with herself and even more disgusted with Dre. "You fucking bastard," she cried. "I knew you didn't like me for me."

"Chill out with the name calling," he told her. "I don't know why you're acting stupid. You think I taught you all that sexual shit for the fun of it?" He bit his bottom lip. "Nah, let me take that back, that shit was fun. I got yo sex game on point so you could turn out just about any nigga." He lifted her chin so they could see eye to eye. "Don't act like you don't need this money. Once you pay me back, the rest is yours."

Chatt continued to shake her head back and forth in disbelief. "Why did you ask me to move in if you weren't feeling me?"

Dre laughed once again before replying, "I got sick of seeing that beat down ass place you call home. I mean I know you gotta fake it till you make it, but damn!"

Gathering all her strength, Chatt lifted her leg and kicked Dre in his nuts as hard as she could. She watched him fall back on the floor and scream like a little bitch. "You will never get shit from me," she screeched. She slowly rose up from the floor and walked towards the door. She was so through with Dre and she couldn't deny the fact that he hurt her feelings when he revealed his truthful intentions. She finally found herself falling for someone, but like always, it would never work. She hated that she had put her trust in such a cruel person. How could she not read between the lines? She turned the door knob to open the door and suddenly crashed into the screen, caused by Dre charging at her. Gripping her by her hair, he swung her against the wall and watched her fall to the floor.

"Have you lost your fucking mind?" He asked, hovering

over her.

"Fuck you!" She screamed, spitting the blood from her lip in his face.

"You little bitch," he hollered, wiping his face. "You gon' pay for that." He reached down to grab her arms, but had a hard time with Chatt swinging from every direction. He continued to wrestle with her until he finally had her under his control. Chatt felt the burning sensation of carpet as Dre drug her across the living room into his cramped closet. She tried her hardest to put up a fight against him closing the door, but he was too strong for her. He forced the door shut and locked it from the outside. "You're gonna get me my money," he assured her. He walked off smiling as he listened to the sounds of Chatt kicking and screaming.

Tader woke up happy as can be. She had her man sleeping beside her and it felt good. Even though she didn't earn brownie points with his mother, she was slowly locking him down in her own way. She tapped his shoulder. "Babe, get up."

He opened his eyes and looked at the clock. It read eight a.m. "Girl, do you see the time?"

"Yes, it's time for you to get up."

He rose up. "Where my breakfast at?"

Tader smiled. "I'm on it." She got out the bed and went to brush her teeth. She then went into the kitchen and turned on the stove. She sat six slices of bacon in the skillet, then walked into her living room. "Oh, shit," she whispered, placing her hand over her heart. She could have sworn she saw David sitting on her couch. She took a deep breath and walked back into the kitchen. She grabbed a fork to flip the bacon with. "Aghh!" she screamed when Terrell approached her from behind.

He laughed. "I didn't mean to scare you." She turned

back around and continued to flip the bacon. Terrell sat her phone on the counter. "It was ringing a minute ago," he told her.

She snatched it up quick, hoping it wasn't one of her sideline men calling. She searched through her missed calls and noticed that it was Spen who had called. She highlighted her number and pressed send to call her back. Spen answered on the second ring. "Hey, girl," she spoke dryly.

"Wassup, mama?"

Spen sighed into the phone. "Where y'all been?"

"I'm sorry, girl. I've been with Rell, but I don't know about Chatt. You okay?"

"I get released today, but I don't have a ride."

"Oh, you know I got you," Tader assured her. "Where you going?"

"I don't know," Spen stated.

"Have you heard from Devon?" Tader hoped her reply was no.

"He sent me a card, flowers, and a ton of balloons." Spen got quiet for a moment. "I love him, Tader."

Tader rolled her eyes and shook her head. "Spen, the man is a lying ass cheater! Him and Crispy had us both fooled, thinking she was messing with my man, when in reality she was fucking yours."

Spen closed her eyes and let a tear roll down her cheek. "You're right," she muttered. "I wanna forgive him so bad."

"Hell, no!" Tader barked. "He does not get forgiven for this shit."

Spen sighed, sitting up in her bed. She wished Chatt would've called her back before Tader did, because she knew she would've understood her more. "Just come and get me," she said.

Triple Crown Publications presents . . . DAMAGE

"I'll be there as soon as I can." Tader hung up the phone and shook her head. She turned to Terrell and said, "Spen is actually thinking about forgiving her cheating ass nigga."

Terrell leaned against the counter. "What's wrong with that?"

Tader looked shocked by his comment. "What's wrong with it is that he cheated on her!" She rolled her eyes. "And to make matters worse, he did it for money."

Terrell laughed, although he didn't crack a smile. "People make mistakes."

"Well, fucking a bitch for money is an unforgivable mistake," she replied, becoming annoyed with Terrell's point of view.

"So you're saying I shouldn't forgive you?"

Tader was stuck on stupid. "What?" She asked.

"Are you saying I shouldn't forgive you?" He restated. "You were in the same situation that he's in now."

No, I wasn't! Tader thought to herself. *I never belonged to your ass, so don't play me.* "Whatever, Terrell."

"Don't get mad," he told her. "Just listen to where I'm coming from. Where would most people be without second chances?"

Blah, blah, blah. Tader didn't wanna hear it. "You're right," she said, trying to easily drop the subject.

Terrell kissed her neck. "I know I'm right."

Tader hated biting her tongue, but in this situation, she figured she had to. She didn't wanna argue with Terrell, so she let him believe that she heard where he was coming from.

Chatt listened to her stomach growl for what seemed like the thousandth time. She felt like she was on the verge of starving, from not having anything to eat in over two days. Her muscles were stiff from being cramped in Dre's coat closet for so long. When she inhaled, a foul aroma

Triple Crown Publications presents... DAMAGE

entered her nostrils, causing her to cough. She knew the stench was from her body odor. She had to use the bathroom on herself when she had to pee. She got nervous as she heard someone turning the knob from the outside of the door, but she was excited at the same time, thinking she would finally be free. When the door swung open, she covered her eyes, not being used to so much light. When she finally looked up, Dre was standing there, his facial expression showing no remorse. He gripped her arm, and pulled her out of the closet. Chatt wanted to scream when she saw her mother laid on the couch naked with a tray of cocaine next to her. Her eyes were closed as if she were passed out. Chatt turned to Dre infuriated with him. "What did you do to her?"

Dre released a devilish grin. "The question is, what I am going to do to her."

Chatt's body cringed. "Why are you being like this?"

"Because you're not cooperating." He walked towards her mother. "It took some time, but I finally found her. But guess what? She didn't have my money." He spit on her. "Worthless bitch probably got robbed right after she took my shit."

Chatt stood to her feet. *I'm gonna kill this ma'fucka*, she thought to herself.

"Don't even try it," Dre told her, noticing the deadly look in her eyes. He knew Chatt was crazy and would do anything her mind came up with. He removed a switch blade from his pocket, and held it to Shawan's neck. "Her fate is in your hands. If you decide to act right, I'll leave her alone."

Chatt shook her head in disbelief. She didn't know who the person was that stood before her. His whole persona had changed completely. "This is between me and you. Why do you have to bring her in it?"

"She brought herself into this shit. Now it's your choice, Chasity. What's it gon' be?"

Chatt looked at Shawan. She wanted to tell Dre to go fuck himself, but she couldn't give up on her mother. "I'm not gon' let you kill her," she stated, her eyes starting to water.

Dre grinned, something evil. "Wise choice. You're about to bring me some serious cash, baby." He put the knife back in his pocket. "I want you to go shower up. I'll have you something to eat when you come back down." He watched her drag herself upstairs, tears pouring from her eyes. He knew she was more so pissed then sad and he reminded himself that he would have to pay close attention to her. He knew Chatt wasn't gonna sit back and take this situation lightly, so he planned on keeping both his eyes open. "By the way," he yelled up the stairs, "I called your job to let them know you'll no longer be working there." He smiled, thinking about the money he saw in his future.

13

Chatt spread the red lipstick across her lips and rubbed them together. She looked at her reflection in the bathroom mirror and didn't like what she saw. Her hair was flat ironed straight down her shoulders, and she wore a set of silver hoops so big that they could have been bracelets. She had caked up dark makeup on her eyes and cheap blush on her cheeks. She could barely breathe in the skin tight black dress she was wearing, and her black knee high boots were two sizes too small. "You look beautiful," Dre said, putting his arms around her waist. He put his chin over her shoulder and joined her in staring at her reflection. He placed his finger in one of the holes in her fish net stockings. "You're so sexy, baby," he whispered in her ear. She stared at him through the mirror, but he couldn't make out her expression. He kissed her neck and caressed her breast. "I wanna have you to myself one last time." He led her into his bedroom and laid her on his bed. He crawled on top of her and spread her legs. He lifted the dress up over her hips, and removed the black thong she had on. He began kissing her thighs until he made his way to her prize. He opened her with both his index fingers and slid his tongue in side.

Chatt had to hold herself back from squeezing her legs together, and choking the shit out of him. Every time she had a crazy thought about hurting him, her mother's life flashed through her mind. Even though she didn't wanna believe it, she knew Dre would kill her. He was a sick man and Chatt couldn't believe she didn't see the truth about him from the start. She wanted someone to like her for who she was so bad, that she was blinded by the obvious. "I hate you," she cried out.

Dre ignored her and continued to eat her pussy like he was starving. He ate her till she came all over his mouth, and slurped every drop of it. He then pulled her down by her waist so that they were face to face. He tried to kiss her but she turned away. "Don't try to fight me," he told her. "You'll never win." He laid flat on his back and pulled her on top of him. Dre had made Chatt a dick riding expert. Out of all the girls he trained, she had a natural talent for riding him. He liked to call her the monster of dick riding. Her pussy felt so good to him that he had second thoughts about sending her out to other people but he knew she was his ultimate money maker. He wanted to shout out loud as she rode him. Nobody body had ever gave him the tingling sensation that she did. "Damn," he panted as he came inside her. He was glad that Chatt faithfully took her birth control because if she didn't, he would've had her pregnant by now. He sent her into the bathroom to freshen up. "Okay, let me explain how things are gon' work." He waited until she came back in the bedroom before stating the rest so that he knew she was paying attention.

She sat on the bed and crossed her legs. "I'm listening."

"Good. Now this lady's name is Felicia. She's twenty-one and thinks her boyfriend is playing her. His name is Kilo, and he's twenty-five. She's paying three grand to catch this nigga in the act."

Chatt looked confused. "Who pays three grand for something that might not even be true?"

"A dumb bitch," Dre stated. "But that's the catch. Your job is to make the nigga fuck you, therefore if he hasn't cheated before, he did now."

"So, basically you're beating these people out of their money?"

"Take it how you want it."

Chatt was lost. "So, what if he hasn't cheated until now?"

"It doesn't matter! The fact that he's willing to fuck you says that he don't care about the bitch no way."

Chatt shook her head in disgust. "So, what if he turns me down? I mean, what if he doesn't wanna cheat on his girl?"

Dre became annoyed with Chatt's questioning. "Look Chasity, that's their problem, okay? Besides, do you think she would be willing to pay that much if she wasn't sure that he was cheating?"

Chatt smacked her lips. "I guess not."

"Exactly. Now she said he'll be at that bar Gator's around eight o'clock to kick it with his friends. All you have to do is get his attention an invite him to the telly with you. Once you're in, go in the bathroom to call and give me word."

"What if I can't get him to go in with me?"

Dre sighed. "Look at yourself, Chasity. That nigga gon' go! When you call and give me word, I'll let Felicia know that's it clear to bust his ass!"

Triple Crown Publications *presents* . . . **DAMAGE**

"And then what?" Chatt questioned. "She just bust in on us?"

Dre smiled. "Yeah, so move fast when you're in there." He sensed the nervousness in her eyes. "It'll be fine," he said touching her arm. "Most of my girls are nervous their first time."

She smacked his hand away from her. "This is bullshit."

"It could be much worse," Dre stated. "I started you off with this kind of work because it's simple. I could've easily placed you in the prostitution section of the game, but I'm sure you'd prefer something else." He kissed her shoulder. "I'm looking out for you, baby."

Chatt wanted to go in his mouth so bad. Everything he said to her at this point was pure bullshit. "Why can't you just find somebody else?"

He ignored her question. "Look, the room is already paid for. I put the key in your purse, along with the rest of your protection."

Chatt eyes grew wide. "Protection?" she questioned. "He's not a killer, is he?"

Dre gripped the temples of his forehead out of frustration. "No, Chasity. I put condoms and a knife in there, just in case. You can never be too safe." He handed her a picture of Kilo so that she could easily identify him once she got to the bar. In Chatt's eyes, Kilo was gorgeous. He had smooth brown skin to match his brown eyes, and a head full of hair that was braided into singles. He had a slight gap between his two front teeth, but he was so cute that you barely noticed. He had nice muscular arms and from the picture, and he looked as if he had a nice height on him. Dre noticed her studying the picture. "Quit staring at his picture and go seduce his ass." He was excited to see how she was gonna do for her first time. He hoped she decided to act right or he would have to punish her again. He grabbed her hand. "And remember Chasity, your mother's fate is in your hands. Don't fuck this up."

Kilo sat at the bar with his friends, sipping on his drink. "I'm real sick of her attitude, man. She bitch every day about how she just know I'm playing her and shit." He took another sip of his drink.

"Damn, Kilo, she's on that now?" His friend asked.

"Hell, yeah, man. I don't know what it is that got her ass all suspicious and shit, but I can't deal with her no more."

"Hang in there Lo," another one of his friends advised. "Shit ain't easy with these broads now-a-days."

Kilo shook his head. "I don't understand how shit got to this point."

Chatt spotted Kilo immediately when she walked through the door. He was the finest one of his three friends. She noticed them having a serious talk around the bar and decided to go take a seat close to them. She was so nervous, and the fact that Kilo was fine, made it even worse. "Can I get you anything?" the bartender asked.

Chatt jumped because she caught her off guard. "Umm, what would you suggest?" She felt a little embarrassed because it was obvious that she didn't know too much about liquor. She pulled out her fake I.D, and sat it next to her. The bartender glanced at it, but paid it no mind. Chatt felt stupid. She put it back in her purse and looked away.

The bartender slightly laughed. "It depends on how you wanna feel."

Chatt glanced over at Kilo. "Something sexy, but not too strong."

"You trying to steal somebody's attention?"

Chatt turned back around towards her. "Something like that."

Triple Crown Publications presents . . . DAMAGE

The bartender smiled. "I'm Meesha."

Chatt shook her hand. "Hi Meesha. I'm Chatt."

Meesha looked at her carefully. She could tell that Chatt was a young girl, but she wondered why she was dressed like a hooker. In their few seconds of talking, Meesha could tell that Chatt was a laid back, shy kind of girl. She decided to whip her up one of her favorites. She went to the back and came back with a glass in her hand. She sat it in front of Chatt. "I think you'll like this, Chatt."

Chatt gave her a half smile. "What is it?"

"A Bacardi Limon Mojito."

Chatt picked up the glass. "Well, it looks good."

Meesha chuckled. "Go ahead and try it."

Chatt took a sip of the Mojito and to her surprise, she actually liked it. She smiled at Meesha as she walked away to fulfill another order. Twenty minutes had passed and she still hadn't gotten Kilo's attention. *Damnit, I gotta do something,* she thought to herself. She decided to do some exotic dancing on the dance floor. She removed her jacket and sat it on the back of her chair. *Okay girls.* She lifted her breast. *Time to work.* Chatt walked slowly and seductively by Kilo and his friends, but the next thing she knew, her legs were in the air and the back of her head was hitting the ground. She looked next to her and put her hands over her face in embarrassment when she spotted the 'Caution Wet Floor' sign. She heard the voices of Kilo and his friends bursting out with laughter, and at that moment she swore she could have died from embarrassment.

"You a'ight, lil mama?"

Chatt removed her hands from her face and realized that Kilo was standing in front of her with his hand held out. She thought to herself, *Damn I have to bust my ass to finally get this nigga's attention?* She took his hand and he helped lift her off the floor. "Thanks," she said. "I guess I didn't see the sign."

He laughed once more. "Yeah, well we all have our moments, right?"

She smiled. "Yeah, I guess." She turned away and walked back towards her seat at the bar.

"I didn't get your name," Kilo stated, following Chatt back to her seat.

She sat down before responding, "I'm, Chatt. You?"

"Kilo." They shook hands. "So, you here alone, tonight?"

"Yeah, my date cancelled on me. What about you?" she asked, knowing exactly who he was with.

He took a seat next to her. "I'm here with a few of my brothers."

"Handle that Lo!" Kilo's friend yelled.

Chatt shot him and evil look that told him she wasn't anything to be handled.

"Don't mind him," Kilo stated, noticing her evil eye. "That nigga drunk."

Chatt noticed that time was moving fast, so she had to speed up her process. "It's no problem," she assured him. "You come here often?"

Kilo nodded. "This place helps me clear my mind."

"You going through something?"

"I just don't understand the typical female mind. I mean, my girl steady accusing me of cheating and shit, for no damn reason." He shook his head in disbelief.

Chatt could tell that this situation had him frustrated. "Well, have you ever cheated, or gave her a reason to believe so?"

"Man, I ain't never cheated on that girl. All I did was try da' be a good nigga to her ass, and this is the shit she got me putting up with."

"Do you love her?" Chatt asked, repositioning herself in her seat.

Kilo glared at her with a look of confusion on his face. "I used to love her."

Chatt saw the emotion in his eyes. "You still do."

He shook his head. "Nah, not anymore. Love don't love no man."

Chatt nodded in agreement. "Love don't love no woman, neither."

Kilo laughed, thinking about everything he and Felicia had been going through for the past few weeks. "It all started crashing down when she got on some jealousy type shit. I think she just scared that I'm gon' end up cheating on her or have a baby by another female." He faced the ground. "But what she fails to realize is that I don't want these hoes out here. I may talk to other females, but it never goes any further than that."

Chatt studied him carefully. "So, you're a one woman man?"

He nodded. "For now. If she keeps accusing me and shit, I'm gon' end up being a single man."

Chatt touched his hand. "Don't give up on her."

Kilo sighed, looking at Chatt's hand as it rested on his. He didn't even know this girl, yet here he was telling her about his relationship. "I'll try not to," he told her.

An hour passed, and Chatt found herself lost in conversation with Kilo. Her cell phone had been vibrating, but she was so in tuned in Kilo, that she didn't pay it any mind. She finally decided to take a bathroom break and return the missed calls. She walked in the bathroom and took the last empty stall. "Fuck!" she hollered, realizing that Dre had called eight times. She was hesitant about returning his call, but she knew it had to be done.

"Where the fuck have you been?" Dre barked, answering his phone. His tone of voice let Chatt know that he wasn't happy.

"I got caught up in conversation," Chatt admitted.

Dre stared at his phone as if he could see Chatt's face through it. "Chasity, get it together! You ain't getting paid to know the nigga's life story! Now you already behind schedule so get on the fucking job. Felicia is waiting, and so am I." He hung up before she could respond.

Chatt closed her phone and sighed. She wished Shawan would've never called her that day. Now she was in a situation where there was no room for mistakes. She exited the stall and washed her hands. As she washed, she thought of how she would ask Kilo to her room. She didn't wanna trap him but if she didn't, that would be her ass and she knew it. Kilo didn't deserve to be set up the way Felicia had planned. He was a good guy caught up in a bad situation. Chatt wanted to confess everything to him, but couldn't find it in her gut to do so.

Crispy puffed on her cigarette, while watching Spen get out of Tader's car. She had been watching them ever since Spen was released from the hospital. She watched Tader turn off the ignition and get out the car as well. She had a look on her face that spoke all types of cocky volumes. "Ta'Ronna thinks she's the shit," Crispy said, turning to Ceddy in the passengers' seat.

Ceddy smirked. "True, but I must admit that the bitch got back." He stared at Tader's oversized butt as she walked by in skin-tight jeans.

Crispy smiled. "You know what the best part is?"

"What?" Ceddy questioned.

"She's a money hungry ass bitch. Always has been, always will be."

Ceddy shook his head. "Something's telling me you wanna be the one to feed her."

"I can hear the bitch's stomach growling from here."

Crispy watched Tader and Spen walk inside the hotel. She and Ceddy waited patiently for one of them to return back outside. After about twenty minutes, Tader was walking out the doors. Crispy took a deep breath, then opened her car door. "I'll be right back," she told Ceddy.

"Handle your bizz', Ms. Crispy."

Crispy trotted across the parking lot towards Tader's car. She wanted to catch her before she pulled off. She watched Tader get in her car and strap her seatbelt. She knocked on the window and smiled. "Hey, Ta'Ronna. Can we talk for a sec?"

Tader rolled her window down. "Bitch," she said, that being the first word that came to her mind. "What you want?"

Crispy ignored her insult. "I wanna talk with you for a minute."

"What the fuck could we possibly have to talk about?"

Crispy smiled. "Six stacks, which could possibly be yours."

Tader sat back in her seat. "I'm listening."

Crispy nodded towards the passenger seat. "May I?"

"Yes, bitch, damn," Tader said, reaching over to open her passengers' side door.

Crispy got in the car and crossed her legs. The scent of her *Pure Seduction* perfume flowed heavily through the car. She turned to Tader, flipping her hair over her shoulders. "How you been, Ta'Ronna?"

"Good," Tader stated, sharply. "Now what's good with this money?"

Money hungry bitch, Crispy thought to herself. "I need you to help me do something."

"I wish you would stop beatin' around the damn bush."

"Fine." Crispy retrieved six thousand dollars cash

Triple Crown Publications presents... DAMAGE

from her purse and sat it on her lap. She knew big faces was Tader's weakness. "You know, that was my mother's property that Spencer burned down."

Tader eyed the money on Crispy's lap. "You wanna tell me why I should care?"

"You should care because she also burned down your only income."

Tader was two seconds from going across Crispy's face. "Bitch, don't worry about my damn income. You know what, get out my damn car!"

"Chill, Ta'Ronna. I wanna make you a deal." She gathered the money from her lap. "I'll give you this now, if you agree to help me."

"Help you do what?"

Crispy grinned viciously. "You're helping me get revenge. My mother worked hard while she had that shop and Spencer thinks she can just get away with burning it down."

Tader laughed. "You're asking me to turn on Spen for you?" She clapped her hands. "Hilarity, Crispy."

"You're not turning on her. All I want you to do is get her to have a drink."

"Bullshit," Tader spat. "You're offering me six stacks to get Spen to have a damn drink?"

Crispy nodded and said, "Yeah. Of course there's a catch though."

"It's too much money for there not to be." Tader crossed her arms. "So, what is it?"

"It's a pill. I want you to put it in her drink, make sure she sips every drop, and then I'll take it from there."

Tader never took her eyes off the money. "You can't pay me enough to do some shit like that."

Crispy asked, "You need a better price?"

"No, bitch! I'm not settin' her up for you to do who

knows what. Shit, you might kill her for all I know."

Crispy shook her head in her defense. "Whoa, slow your roll, girl. I'm not a killer."

Tader rolled her eyes. She couldn't deny the fact that she would've love to have the money Crispy was offering her, but the job was way too much of a scandalous task. She looked at the clock on her radio and decided that it was time to go. "I got somewhere to be," she told Crispy. She reached over her and opened the passenger's side door.

"Ta'Ronna, just hear me out. All you have to do is drop the pill in her drink, and then it's over. She'll never know it was you or anything."

Tader was silent for a moment. She looked at the money Crispy had in her hand and sighed. It had been a long time since she went on a priceless shopping spree, and she had to admit that the money was calling her name. Terrell had been holding out on her lately, and she desperately missed her big faces. She put her keys in her ignition and looked at Crispy. "It's time for me to go."

Crispy sucked her teeth, then got out the car. She was pissed that Tader didn't agree to help her, and she knew Tader would warn Spen that she was out to get her. *Maybe the bitch is finally full,* Crispy thought to herself as she walked back to her Benz. *Or maybe she's looking for a five course meal.* Crispy smiled as she turned around and jogged back towards Tader's car. "Ta'Ronna!" she shouted, trying to catch her as she pulled off. Tader slowed down, but her car never stopped moving. Crispy finally stopped jogging and shouted, "How does twelve stacks sound?"

Chatt walked to Dre's door step more paranoid than ever. She knew he wouldn't be happy with her because he never received his confirmation call. She enjoyed herself with Kilo, and wasn't able to set him up. He had grown on her. It was something about his personality that separated him from other men she knew. Before leaving the bar, she made sure Kilo had her number, and she told him to stay in touch. That was very unusual for her seeing that she had just been played. But Kilo had something about him that just made her unable to resist. She had to put him in the back of her mind as she waited for the torture she was sure she was about to endure.

Ding-dong!

She rang the doorbell hoping that Dre wouldn't leave her outside. She had to ring it a few more times before he finally answered. He opened the door with a look of disappointment on his face. Chatt was nervous but ready for whatever he was up to. "Dre, let me explain before you say anything," she stated. He ignored her and walked upstairs to his bedroom. Chatt followed behind him searching for her mother. She prayed like hell that Dre didn't do anything to her. If he did, things were gonna get ugly. She didn't care that she didn't get the job done on her part. "Where's Shawan?" she asked, her tone filled with nervousness.

Dre turned around to face her. He could kill her for messing up his money. "Don't worry about where the fuck she is." He clenched his jaw. "I wanna slap the shit out of you so bad right now."

Try me, ma'fucka! Chatt thought. She had had enough of Dre's ignorant comments. "Where the fuck is my mom?" She asked, looking around the room.

Dre laughed. "I told you not to mess this up, didn't I?"

Chatt grew worried. "Where is she?" she shouted.

"Lower your voice," Dre told her, putting his finger to her lips. She smacked his hand away, pissing him off. "I see you still actin' up," he said as he back handed the shit out of her. Her tiny body went falling to the floor. Dre shook his head as he scooped her up and carried her back downstairs.

Triple Crown Publications *presents . . .* **DAMAGE**

Chatt hated that he was so much stronger than her. That was his only advantage over her but she didn't care as she tried to defend herself anyway. Dre was becoming extremely irritated as she pounded his back with her fist. She was acting like a little brat who was upset because she couldn't have any candy. He carried her through the living room all the way to the coat closet. "You must like it in here," he said, as he threw her in and locked the door. Of course she pounded on the door threatening to break it down. Dre shook his head realizing how much of a handful she was. He never had as much trouble with any girl as he did with Chatt. All the other girls gave in easily to anything he ever persuaded them to do, but Chatt was different. If she didn't wanna do it, he had to force her or use something against her to try and make her cooperate. He walked away from the closet thinking about how he could get her to calm down and stop fighting him. Until she decided to act right, he planned on making the closet her permanent home.

14

Terrell glanced out of the window over the stove in the kitchen. He noticed an unfamiliar vehicle pull into the driveway, while making his famous egg and cheese omelet. "Who is this pulling up?" he asked Tader, as she sat on the couch in the living room.

Tader pulled the curtains back to see who Terrell was talking about. "I don't know who that is," she answered. She fled off to her bedroom to slip on some sweats. Usually, she walks around the house in her underwear, but seeing that they had an uninvited guest, she had to change. As she pulled her t-shirt over her head, she heard slight commotion coming from her living room. She opened her bedroom door and walked down the hallway to see what the noise was about. Her heart sank in her stomach when she saw David standing in her kitchen with his 9 pointed at Terrell's chest. She pinched herself to make sure it wasn't another dream, and unfortunately, it wasn't.

David smiled at her. "Come on out," he told her. Tader glanced at Terrell's gun as it rested on the living room table. David followed her eyes. "Your boyfriend didn't make it and neither will you." He started laughing. "Speaking of boyfriends, when the last time you talked to yo' boy, James?"

Tader thought about the text she had gotten from James, telling her that her David problem had been handled. She never sent him a text back to thank him, and now she was happy she didn't because the problem obviously wasn't solved. She tried to play it cool. "I don't know what you're talking about."

"Oh, I get it. You're playing the dumb game." His smile faded. "Well, let me remind you how things went down. You sent that nigga to kill me, but it didn't work. I killed him, then sent you a confirmation text from his phone. Although you didn't hit me back, I'm sure you got it."

Tader was shaking uncontrollably. "I swear I didn't tell him to kill you. You know I wouldn't do that," she explained.

"I thought you wouldn't do me like that either," David replied, shaking his head. "Especially after you accepted my proposal and shit."

Terrell was on fire. He wanted to charge at David so bad that he didn't know what to do. He kept thinking about how his gun was resting fully loaded on the living room table. If only he had brought it in the kitchen with him. He looked at Tader. "You accepted his proposal?" he asked, his tone low and nonchalant.

Tader and David held eye contact. She knew what she had to say in order to keep him from blowing up. "Yes," she muttered, still looking into David's eyes. She finally looked away and noticed that Terrell's anger had risen. She prayed like hell that he didn't try to do anything stupid or David would blow his brains out.

"So, have you been playin' me all this time?" Terrell asked. "And you wanted me to believe that you had my seed inside you?"

David's eyes lit up. "You let this nigga get you pregnant?" His finger locked tighter on the trigger of his gun.

Tader was scared as shit. "It's not even his," she cried. Her eyes were raining bullets.

Terrell shook his head in disbelief. He was so convinced that Tader was changing, but here she was converting back to her old ways. He felt so stupid for not reading between the lines. He knew there was a reason she kept dodging the DNA test, but he never pressured her about it. "My momma was right," he stated.

"I'm sorry," Tader sobbed. "I didn't mean for it to come out like this."

"Well, it's out now," David spoke. "So, who's the father?"

Tader fell to the floor, wailing. "This dude named Anthony," she confessed.

Terrell felt so betrayed. All the things that he and Tader had talked about were now down the drain. Everything she told him was now bullshit in his mind and forever would be. He would never believe another word she said. "I don't know what made me believe that I could turn a hoe into a housewife."

David chuckled. "Me either, bra." He glanced at Tader. "I want you to have an abortion by this weekend. If you don't choose to do it the right way, we'll handle it my way." He faced Terrell. "And you nigga; don't try and come after me," he kept the gun facing Terrell as he began walking backwards towards the door before finishing his words, "because I know where your mother stays. Ask Tader. She saw me out there when the two of you decided to take a visit." He laughed, then slammed the door shut.

Tader's heart crumbled. She looked at Terrell, but didn't know where to begin. "I'm so sorry," she managed to mumble.

Terrell walked towards her and stood over her. "You brought my mother into this shit?" He asked with his tone filled with anger. Before Tader got the chance to reply, Terrell struck her across the face.

Tader grabbed her jaw and cried out in pain. "I swear I didn't know he was following us."

"Well, why the fuck you ain't tell me when you found out?" Terrell shouted. He held himself back from going across her face again.

"I didn't know what to say," she cried. "I didn't know how to tell you."

Terrell shook his head. "You one scandalous ass bitch." He walked off and grabbed a few of his things, including his gun, before heading towards the front door.

"Please don't leave," Tader begged.

Terrell faced her. "My mother's in danger because of you. You think I'm just gon' sit around and wait for that nigga to do some crazy shit to her?"

That crazy bitch can handle herself, Tader thought to herself, remembering how aggressive Momma Lee was. She stood up. "You can't leave me here by myself!" she shouted. "David's gon' take advantage of this situation, Rell. He's the reason I asked you to move in here with me in the first place!"

Terrell laughed out of anger. "You deserve everything that nigga does to you," he said, before he walked out the door. Tader crawled up in a corner and cried her eyes out. She knew her future with Terrell was down the drain and so was her future child.

Triple Crown Publications presents . . . DAMAGE

Spen lay back on her hotel bed, facing the ceiling. She wanted to go back to sleep, but all she could do was toss and turn. Devon weighed heavily on her mind. She hadn't heard from him since she was in the hospital, and she was starting to worry. She also hadn't heard from her girl Chatt, which also worried her. She tried to close her eyes and clear her mind, but it wasn't working. She wanted Devon. She needed him. Nobody would be able to make her feel better but him. She looked at the ring on her finger and started to tear up. Through everything she had been through throughout the last few days, she never took the ring off her finger.

She didn't want to. She wanted to keep it on forever. It was special to her. She was snapped away from her thoughts by the sound of the hotel phone ringing. She knew it was Tader because she was the only one who knew where she was. She picked up the phone, not really wanting to talk. "Hello?"

"I need somebody to talk to," Tader said, dryly into the phone.

"What's wrong?" Spen questioned.

Tader sighed, heavily. "Me and Rell are over."

Spen shook her head. She knew it wouldn't be long before Terrell left Tader, but she never spoke about it. "I'm sorry, girl. What happened?"

"Last night, David showed up. I thought I took care of his ass," she cried.

"What do you mean took care of him?" Spen asked. "What did you do, Tader?"

"I didn't mean for shit to happen like this. Rell is gone and now I'm by myself. He didn't even leave me no money."

Spen shook her head. She knew Tader was more so upset about her money being cut off, more than her love for Terrell. "You'll be, okay."

"No I won't, Spen. I don't have anything, now."

"Girl, you have me and Chasity. Most of all, you have yourself. You gotta be strong, or you won't make it. Hell, you see what I've been through."

Tader replied, "You're right. You know what I need?"

"What?" Spen questioned.

"A ma'fuckin drink."

"No you don't," Spen exclaimed. She couldn't believe Tader just said that. "I want my god child perfectly healthy."

Tader was silent. She wasn't expecting Spen's comment. She thought about David's threat from the night before. She didn't know what she was gonna do. "Get dressed," she told Spen. "I'm coming to see you."

Crispy's excitement was on overload as she sat in the hotel parking lot, waiting for Tader. She anxiously tapped her nails against the stirring wheel, looking out the window. She had been waiting for about twenty minutes now. Usually she would've been frustrated, but she was too excited to be in a bad mood. She prayed that Tader didn't back out on her. She was her only connection to get close to Spen. Crispy was itching to make Spen pay for burning down her mother's property. She wanted revenge so bad, she could taste it. She was highly disappointed when Dre denied her request to recruit Spen with *Legs Open, Mouth Closed*. Dre had already spotted Spen when he found Chatt. He informed Crispy that he didn't go after Spen because she didn't fit the image of the business. But Crispy wasn't hearing that. If she couldn't get Spen in the business, then she would find another way to deal with her. She felt as if tearing her and Devon apart wasn't enough. She wanted Spen to feel the same feeling that she felt while she watched her mother's salon burn down.

Triple Crown Publications presents... **DAMAGE**

She was snapped out of her thoughts when she saw Tader pull into the hotel parking lot. Her heart started pounding fast. She was overly excited. While Tader parked her car, Crispy gathered a few of her things. She got out of her Benz and walked towards Tader's Chrysler. She knocked on the window and waited for Tader to look up. Tader ignored her and looked straight ahead. Crispy waited patiently for Tader to clear her mind. She knew asking her to turn on her friend would eventually take a toll on her. Tader finally looked up. She unlocked her door for Crispy to get in the passenger's seat. Crispy got in and smiled. She was ready to get the show on the road. She looked at Tader and saw that she still had a shitty vibe. She shook her head and reached into her purse. She hoped a check written out for twelve thousand dollars would brighten Tader's mood. Crispy sat the check on Tader's lap. Tader looked down at it and sighed. Half of her didn't wanna take it, but the other half of her told a different story. "You bet not hurt my girl," she stated, picking up the check.

Crispy grinned. "I promise to be nice."

Tader shook her head. "Just tell me what I need to do so I can get out of here."

Crispy dug in her purse again. This time she pulled out a plastic bag with a small white tablet inside. She handed it to Tader. "That's your main objective."

Tader grabbed the bag and studied the pill. "What is it?" she asked.

"Rohypnol."

"Ro, what?" Tader questioned.

Crispy laughed. "Rohypnol. All you have to do is slip it into her drink, wait about twenty minutes, then call me in."

Tader sucked her teeth. "I'm going to hell for this shit."

"Good," Crispy replied. "Now I don't have to be alone."

"I'm coming," Spen yelled as she slightly sprinted to her hotel room door. She opened it and found Tader standing there with a bottle of Cabernet Sauvignon in her hands. Spen snatched the bottle away from her. "What did I tell your hard headed ass," she nagged, seriously.

Tader walked inside the room. She was nervous. "It's not for me." She smiled dryly. "It's for you."

Spen sat on the bed. "Lord knows I need it."

"We all need a damn drink," Tader stated. "Lucky for you, you're not pregnant."

Spen was quiet. She looked at the bottle of wine, then at the plastic cups that sat on the table next to the coffee maker. "Have you spoke to Chatt?" she asked, getting up to grab a cup.

Tader shook her head. "Nah. You know me and her been bumpin' heads, lately."

"Y'all so childish," Spen declared. "I've never seen two grown women fight like the two of you do."

Tader rolled her eyes. She hated when Spen nagged about her and Chatt's relationship. "How long you plan on staying here?"

Spen sighed. "I don't know. I'm just not ready to go back home."

"Still no word from Devon?"

"Nope."

"Figures."

Spen poured the wine into her cup. She brought the cup to her lips but then stopped. "Let me go get some ice." She went into the bathroom and grabbed the ice bucket, then left the room.

Tader glanced at Spen's cup. She knew that now was the perfect time to plant the pill. She pulled the plastic bag from out of her jacket and grabbed the pill from inside. She walked over to the table where Spen's drink sat. Her hands were shaking as she held the pill over the cup. "Three, two, one," she counted down, before dropping the pill into the cup. A chill ran through her body as she walked away and sat on the bed.

Spen came back into the room with a bucket full of ice. After dropping a few cubes in her cup, she finally took a sip. "You know, I would probably be in jail if it wasn't for Devon."

Tader couldn't help but stare at the cup as Spen continued to drink. "Good thing he did what he did," she replied, shakily.

Spen took another sip of her drink. "Yeah, he had my back."

"Let's not forget his wrongs."

"Yeah, he fucked up."

"Big time." Spen shook her head while downing her drink. Tader's guilt began to build up slowly but surely. "Slow down," she told Spen, pulling the cup from her lips.

Spen snatched the cup back from her. "Uh-un, girl. I'm going through a lot."

Tader swallowed hard. "I know you are." She listened to Spen go on about Devon for the next fifteen minutes while she downed the rest of her drink. Tader didn't hear anything Spen was saying, but only the guilt song that played over and over in her head. The song never ended, but she managed to block it out for the time being. She looked at Spen when she noticed that she had finally stopped talking. "What's wrong?" She asked. "You ran out of Devon memories?" Spen didn't say anything. Her eyes hung low. Tader tried snapping her fingers in her face. "Spen....Hello?" Spen was still silent. Tader took the cup from her hand. It was completely empty. She knew the pill was starting to take effect.

Triple Crown Publications *presents* . . . DAMAGE

Tader grabbed her hand. "Spen?" She got no answer. "Spen," she called out again. Still no answer.

"Come on, come on," Crispy whispered, as she impatiently waited for the elevator to reach the third floor. Once it reached the floor, she rushed off in a hurry to Spen's room. She smiled thinking about all the things she wanted to do. She knocked on the door and waited for Tader to answer. Tader opened the door facing the ground. She knew she had just committed the ultimate betrayal towards her best friend. There was no way she wanted to be in the room when Crispy did whatever she planned on doing. She already felt bad enough but there was no turning back now. Spen had already taken the pill and she had already spent some of the money that Crispy had given her. Tader felt horrible true enough, but if she could do it all over again she more than likely would make the same decision. Money was her weakness so rather it was Spen, Chatt or anyone else she was close to, she would give in for the paper. She just couldn't help herself. She didn't say anything as she walked past Crispy headed towards the elevator. She wanted to get out in a hurry just in case anybody was watching. Crispy felt great walking into Spen's room. Spen was laid on the bed with her eyes shut. She had no control over her movements. Crispy sat her things down and stood in front of the bed. *Now how did I get this wonderful opportunity?* She asked herself. *It's amazing what money can buy.* As Crispy stared at Spen, she wondered how Devon would feel if he knew her current situation. Her plan was to ruin them and she was gonna do everything she could to make that plan go through. With Spen completely out of it, there was no way she would be able to explain herself once she finally woke up and knew the truth about what was going on.

Triple Crown Publications presents . . . DAMAGE

Crispy crawled on top of her and kissed her forehead. "I'm gonna take good care of you, Spencer."

There were two knocks on the door, grabbing Crispy's attention. She crawled off of Spen and headed to the door. Looking through the peep hole, she smiled, opening the door for her camera man. He walked in carrying all of his equipment. "What a lovely girl," he said, looking at Spen, passed out on the bed. He began setting up his equipment while Crispy stripped out of her clothes.

"I'm so excited," she explained, standing in nothing but her underwear. She walked over to the bed and turned Spen onto her back. "She has a beautiful shape," she said, slapping Spen's butt.

"I'll be the judge of that," the camera man stated. After screwing his camera on the tri-pod, he walked toward the bed, pulling his shirt over his head. "You wanna do the honors, or should I?" He asked, nodding towards Spen.

Crispy smiled. "We can do it together."

The two began taking Spen's clothes off, while discussing everything they planned on doing. Crispy wanted Spen in every position possible. Once they had her completely naked, Crispy laid next to her, brushing her hair out of her face. "What a beautiful sight," the camera man stated as he took in the sight of two beautiful women. He hit record on his camera and smiled. Out of all the films he made, he was sure this one would be his favorite. Crispy kissed Spen's chin, trailing down to her stomach. *Smile for the camera, Spencer,* she thought to herself.

Spen rolled over on her side and yawned. She blinked a few times before opening her eyes. When she finally adjusted them with the light, she stared at the ceiling for a moment. Slightly raising up, she felt soreness between her legs. *What the hell?* She thought to herself. She looked down at her naked body and shook her head, confused. *I don't remember going to sleep naked.* Scooting to the edge of the bed, she noticed her clothes in a pile in the corner of the room. "What's going on?" She asked herself outloud. She shut her eyes and tried to recall what happened the night before; but all she could remember was having a drink with Tader. *Maybe she knows somthing,* Spen thought, going for the phone. As she listened to Tader's line ring, her body shivered from disgust. She started scratching her arms and stomach, feeling nasty all over. When she heard Tader's voicemail pick up, she slammed the phone down, frustrated. Before she made anymore moves, she had to take a shower. She went in the bathroom and turned the water on full blast. Stepping inside, she stood under the water covering her face with her hands. *Please tell me I'm just panicking,* she thought. *Tell me I just got drunk and fell asleep.* She removed her hands and let the water splash down her face. She prayed like hell that no funny business had gone down. After she finished her shower, she got dressed and tried to call Tader back. Still no answer. She picked the phone back up and dialed the service desk.

"Front desk, how may I help you?" A lady questioned, in a cheery tone.

"Hi, this is Spencer Brooks, Room 304. This is gonna sound kind of weird, but I need to know if anybody stopped by the front desk lastnight looking for me or asking for my room number."

"Well, Ms. Brooks, I happened to be here lastnight, and I don't recall anyone stopping in, questioning for you or your room number."

Spen took a deep breath and shook her head. *Okay, I'm really trippin'.* "Oh, okay. Thanks."

"No problem. Everything alright?"

"Yeah, yeah," Spen quickly answered. "Everythings cool.

I was just curious, that's all."

"Glad to hear that, Ms. Brooks. Enjoy the rest of your stay with us, and have a great day."

"You do the same," Spen replied, hanging up the phone. She stared into space for a minute. Although now, she was somewhat at ease, she still wasn't convinced that she had too many glasses of wine and dozed off. Something else happened and she knew it. She just didn't know what.

15

Ceddy shook his head as he closed his cell phone. He tossed it in his purse, then crossed his legs. "Ms. Crispy is officially crazy."

Dre handed him an envelope. "What she up to now?"

"She had Spencer alone in her hotel room."

Dre smiled. "We should've stopped by."

Ceddy put the envelope in his purse. "No, I'm sure Ms. Crispy wanted the child to herself. Lord knows what she did."

Dre laughed. "I'm sure it wasn't that bad."

Ceddy nodded. "Honey, you don't know what that child is capable of. I've seen her get down and dirty plenty of times."

The both of them grew quiet when Chatt walked in the room. She looked tired and worn out. Dre grabbed her hand and pulled her close to him. He kissed her arm. "You feel okay?"

Chatt snatched her arm away. "I'm sick, Dre. I need to see a doctor."

Ceddy looked concerned. "What's the matter, hun?"

Chatt ignored him. She looked at Dre. "I need some medical attention."

He looked her up and down and shook his head. "You'll be a'ight."

"No I won't."

"Yes you will."

Chatt sighed and started walking out of the room. She was so irritated. She really did feel sick but she felt even more stupid thinking that Dre would actually care. She was about to step out of his room when he called out for her.

"Wait a minute," he said waving for her to come back over to him.

She turned around and crossed her arms. "What?"

"We've been doing good lately. Let's not get back on the wrong path, okay?" He spoke as if he hadn't been putting her through hell lately. Chatt rolled her eyes blowing off everything he was saying. She knew he was trying to act as if he wasn't an asshole because he had company. *He is so full of shit,* she thought to herself.

Dre pointed to his top dresser. "There's your phone. I want you call and let your friends know that you're okay."

Chatt hurried and grabbed her phone before Dre changed his mind. She damn near tripped trying to get to it. She felt like Dre having company wasn't so bad after all.

He grabbed her wrist before she left the room. "No funny business, a'ight? You play by my rules and I promise to let you see your mother next week."

"Okay," Chatt replied, pulling her wrist from his grip. She left the room and flew down the steps. She was so happy that he had a chance to call out. The first person she called was Spen, but got no answer. She then tried Tader and also got no answer. That did nothing but channel her anger. *Where the fuck are they?* She asked herself. She closed her phone and sat it on her lap hoping one of them would soon call her back. She looked at the screen door as it was wide open, blowing in fresh air. Chatt wanted badly to just run like the wind. *Be patient,* she told herself. She didn't plan on going anywhere until she saw her mother. Once she found where Shawan was, she planned on leaving Dre and taking Shawan with her. She didn't know how she was gonna pull it off, but she knew for sure that she wasn't gonna sit around and be mistreated by him for the rest of her life. It just wasn't gonna happen. Chatt wanted Dre dead. She didn't want him hurt or broke down, she wanted him long gone. He didn't realize how much he had hurt her with doing what he did. He broke her heart, although she would never let him know it.

Her phone started ringing and her heart jumped, thinking it might be Spen or Tader. She flipped it open. "Hello?"

An unfamiliar voice spoke into the phone. "Yeah, is this Chatt?"

"Umm, yeah. Who is this?"

"It's Kilo. I hope you remember me."

Chatt was quiet for a moment. Of course she remembered Kilo. She honestly didn't expect him to call her. "Yes, I remember you," she finally replied.

"Good," Kilo stated. "I thought you were gon' forget about me."

"Of course, not." Chatt got up and looked up the stairs to see if Dre's door was open. She knew he would flip out if he found out she was talking to Kilo. She continued talking when she saw that his door was shut. "I didn't think you were gon' call me."

"I had to call you. I tried calling you a few times before today, but I kept getting the voicemail. The conversation we had at the bar never left my mind. You were so easy to talk to."

Chatt tried to smile, but her mouth continued to frown. "You were easy to talk to, too."

"You think so? I thought I was gettin' on your nerves, going on about my problems."

Chatt looked up the stairs again. "No, it was cool. How did things work out?" Kilo grew quiet. Chatt immediately knew what happened. She hated to ask, but she wanted to know. "So, who finally broke it off?"

Kilo sighed into the phone. "I did."

"I'm sorry. I'm sure it was for the best, right?"

"Only time will tell. I got a feeling that I did the right thing, though."

"I'm sure you did." There was an awkward silence. Chatt didn't know what to say.

Kilo finally spoke up. "Did you ever figure out why your date cancelled on you?"

Chatt was confused. She didn't have a clue what he was talking about. "What date?"

Kilo laughed. "You said you were alone at the bar because your date cancelled on you."

Chatt instantly remembered telling him the lie. She felt stupid. She knew she had to cover this one up fast. "Oh, yeah. He wasn't feeling too well."

"That's too bad. A little cough would've never stopped me from going on a date with you." Chatt was quiet. Kilo's constant flirting was cute, but she wasn't in the mood for it at the time. She had way too much shit on her plate. She looked up the stairs, once again. She was so paranoid. Dre's door was still shut. Chatt focused back on the phone call. She still didn't know what to say. She was happy when Kilo

Triple Crown Publications *presents* . . . **DAMAGE**

spoke up. "So, when will I get the opportunity to take you out?" he asked.

Chatt sighed. She wanted to say today. Hell, anything thing that could get her away from DreStar sounded good. But she knew she had to wait it out. Besides, Kilo was a nice guy and all, but she didn't want to get herself into that again. Once upon a time, Dre seemed like a nice guy too, but Chatt saw where that led. "I'm sorry. I can't date right now."

"Oh." Kilo felt shitted on. "I hope you're not in a relationship."

"No, but you just got out of one. I think you should give yourself some time to think about what it is that you want."

Kilo could do nothing but agree. "You're right."

"Yeah, probably." She looked at the time. It was getting late and she wanted to try and get in touch with her girls once more before the day was over. "I have to go," she told Kilo.

He didn't want to, but he let her go. "Okay, Chatt. You mind if I call you some other time?"

Chatt smiled dryly. Kilo was so cute. Too bad she couldn't trust him. "Yeah, you can call me some other time."

"Okay, bet."

Chatt stared at her phone before hanging up. She tried her girls again, but like the first time, she got no answer. She was starting to worry. She hadn't talked to them in a while. Something in the back of her mind told her that something was wrong. She wanted to clear her mind from the negative thoughts. She jotted up the stairs to run her some bath water. She couldn't ignore the high pitched sounds that were coming from Dre's bedroom. She tiptoed to his door so that she could get a better hearing. Putting her ear to the door, she couldn't believe what she was

Triple Crown Publications presents... DAMAGE

hearing.

Chatt didn't give a fuck. She knew it couldn't be what she thought it was, so she opened the door to see what was going down. Instantly, her mouth dropped. She was so disgusted when she saw Dre with his manhood half way up Ceddy's ass. She immediately shut the door and tried not to throw up in her mouth at the sight of what she had just seen. She was beyond shocked. She would've never thought that she was sleeping with a homosexual.

"You better start knocking first, bitch!" Dre yelled, from his room.

Chatt ignored him and went into the bathroom. She got in the tub and closed her eyes. That was some sick shit that she just witnessed. She was overly disgusted. She felt her stomach turn in the wrong direction. Once she got out the tub, she ended up throwing up in the toilet, thinking about the nasty sight. She was so grossed out. After she left the bathroom, she went to lie down. She had no problem falling asleep, seeing that there was nothing for her to be awake for.

It had been two weeks since Tader had an abortion. She felt as if she was lost between worlds, back at square one. Terrell had walked out of her life the minute she told him she went through with the abortion. David returned with his torturing ways. She hadn't spoken with her girls in a while and money was very short for her. Her conscience continued to eat at her mind with the thought of setting Spen up with Crispy. She knew she was wrong. A true friend would have never done anything like that. She shook the thought and tried to constantly tell herself that she needed the money. Spen burned down her only place of employment, so she had to do what she had to do.

She prayed Spen didn't remember anything that had

happened. If she did, Tader knew their friendship would be over. No questions asked. Spen would dismiss her with the quickness. Tader was starting to feel lonely. She didn't have anybody. Besides other men that she messed around with, she was in it for herself. She needed somebody to talk to. Anybody. She wished her friends were there with her. Tader didn't want to lose her girls, even though there was a chance that she might have already lost one. She had to know where Spen's head was. Despite how nervous she was, she called her. When Spen picked up the phone, Tader grew even more nervous. "Hey," she said, shakily.

"Hey, Tader. Where you been?"
"I've been at home. Where you been?"
"I finally came home, too."

Tader was a little relieved. She figured if Spen hadn't mentioned the situation yet, then she probably didn't remember. She tried to keep her cool and go with the flow. She hoped she didn't sound too nervous. "I'm glad you went home. Is Devon there?"

"No, I still haven't heard from him. I'm worried sick, man."

Tader rolled her eyes. "I'm sure he's a'ight."

"I sure hope so, girl. I hope my baby's not in too much trouble."

Tader was far past annoyed. She had no clue why she even asked about Devon, knowing Spen was gonna go on forever. She didn't feel like hearing her whine about him so she changed the subject. "I miss you, girl. You and Chatt."

"Girl, I miss you too. I got a missed call from Chatt a while ago, but no word ever since. I'm worried about her, too."

"I'm sure she's fine. She has a new man in her life, so that's probably why she's been M.I.A for a minute."

Triple Crown Publications presents . . . DAMAGE

Spen shook her head. "That's not like Chasity. You know we're her only family. There's no reason why we shouldn't have heard from her again."

"You're right. How about we all meet up tomorrow. I'll try to get in touch with Chatt to see what's up wit' her."

"That sounds okay. But, how about you and I meet up a tad bit earlier?"

"Um, sure," Tader replied hesitantly. "Might I ask why?"

"I need to talk to you about something and I want the conversation to be held in person."

Fuck! Tader cursed to herself. "Okay, that's cool."

"Okay then. See you soon."

Tader knew she was ass out as she hung up the phone. *She knows!* she thought. *I'm so fucked!* She buried her face in her hands and thought about what she was gonna do. If she bailed, she knew she would look guilty, so she decided to keep things as planned. *I'm gon' need one hell of a lie to save my ass this time!*

Chatt sat on Dre's couch, rocking back and forth. She kept her eyes glued to the door. She was expecting him to walk in with her mother any minute now. This was the day she was waiting for. The day she planned on leaving. She finally looked away from the door to take a peek at the clock. It read eight minutes after seven p.m. Dre should've been back by now. Chatt was growing impatient. She felt like something was wrong. She didn't want to think negative, but she couldn't help herself. She got up from the couch and went into the kitchen. After pouring herself a glass of cold water, she took big gulps and sat at the kitchen table. Time was flying. Still no Dre, nor Shawan. Just when Chatt was about to call DreStar's cell, she heard him pulling up. She rushed towards the living room, her heart pounding threw her chest. She heard the screen door open, then Dre walked in. She looked behind him to see if Shawan was there, but she saw no sight of her. She looked at Dre. He tried to avoid her eye contact. Chatt walked towards him and slightly shoved him. She knew he was about to feed her some bullshit. She hated him. It took everything in her not to punch the shit out of him as he stood before her.

"She's not ready," Dre stated.

Chatt didn't say anything. She shook her head, her eyes starting to water. She shoved him again, this time with much more force. He let her pound his chest until the blows started becoming too aggressive for him. He grabbed her wrist. Chatt started to cry as she looked up at him. She felt like he wasn't being fair. She was so ready to leave that she wanted to just forget about her mother. She couldn't do it. Her conscience wouldn't allow her to. "Why do you keep doing this to me?" she asked. "You keep fucking playing me!"

He still held her wrist. "I'm not doing anything. She's not ready for you to see her yet, Chasity."

Chatt pulled away from him and shook her head. She didn't know what to do. "You're not playing fair. I'm cooperating for you, but you're steady playing me."

"I'm not playing you. I know you don't wanna see your mother while she's like this." He lifted her chin. "Trust me. And by the way, I do appreciate your cooperation."

"I wanna see her!" Chatt yelled. "If you want me to fucking cooperate, let me see my mom."

Dre nodded. "Next week, I promise."

"No, fuck that!" Chatt screamed, shoving Dre once more. This time the force in her shove sent him back against the wall. Chatt expected him to fire back at her, but he didn't. She was somewhat relieved because she was tired of fighting with him. It was all they did for the past few weeks.

Triple Crown Publications presents . . . DAMAGE

"Come here," he told her. He could tell she was nervous. He walked up on her and grabbed her hand. "I want you to spend some time with your friends tomorrow. They been calling you and earlier you got a text saying they wanna have lunch." He looked her in the eye. "Can I trust you enough to let you go?"

Chatt sighed and pulled her hand away from him. She hated when he touched her. It really bothered her skin. "Yeah," she replied wiping at her teary face. She was tired. Seeing her girls was exactly what she needed. She had been worried about them and she knew they were worried about her as well.

"I think I can trust you too."

Chatt walked away headed back into the kitchen. She knew DreStar was being a smart ass. He knew Chatt wasn't going to do anything to jeopardize her chances at seeing her mother. Chatt hated that he held Shawan as bait and she couldn't wait until the day came where she took her and her mother away from him. Only time would tell when she would be able to break free. Until then she was gonna try her hardest to play it cool. She didn't want DreStar having a clue that soon enough she was gonna get ghost on his ass.

16

The next day came quickly for Tader. She was so anxious to catch up with her girls and see how everyone was doing. But on the other hand, she was nervous as shit about talking to Spen. They decided to meet at Roosters. Spen arrived first, followed by Tader. "Glad you could make it," Spen said with a hint of a smile.

Tader flashed her a fake smile in return. "Of course. You know I missed you."

"Missed you too, girl." They found a table near the back and took a seat. "How you been?"

Tader shrugged her shoulders. "I can't complain."

Spen nodded, clearing her throat. "That's great. I wanna ask you something,"

"Go ahead," Tader replied, with confidence. She already had her plan in motion if Spen decided to accuse her of something. *Deny! Deny! Deny!*

"Do you remember that night you came to my room with a bottle of wine?"

Oh, shit, Tader! Get ready. "Yeah, the night you got hella' drunk, why?"

"Oh, so I was drunk?"

"Girl, you were so gone! Devon really had you upset, so I don't blame you."

Spen faced the ground and lowered her voice. "I was just asking because the next day I woke up feeling kind of weird. I wasn't myself at all."

Tader laughed. "It's called a hangover, Spen. I watched you get fucked up, but I didn't let you do anything crazy."

"Are you sure that's all I did, because when I woke up, I—"

"I'm positive," Tader assured her. "You're just trippin', girl."

Spen immediately jumped up when she saw Chatt walk in. She hugged her like she hadn't seen her in years. Tader just watched. There was still tension between her and Chatt. Spen didn't wanna let go, but Chatt backed away from her embrace. She missed Spen, but she had to back away or they would've hugged all night.

Tader was quiet. She was happy to see her friends, but soon enough she had to face reality. It was only a matter of time before Spen found out about what really happened. What's done in the dark, always comes to light. Spen and Chatt finally sat down. Nobody said anything. They all stared at each other waiting for somebody to strike up a conversation. The waiter came to their table, breaking the silence. They got quiet again until she returned with their drinks. Spen was the first to speak. "So, what's the deal with you guys?"

Tader looked at Chatt. She wanted her to speak before she started going on about her own life. Chatt didn't say anything so Tader spoke up. "My life has been horrible."

Chatt took a sip of her virgin Strawberry Daiquiri. She couldn't put her finger on it, but something wasn't right with Tader. She was acting funny and Chatt couldn't take her attention away from it. She wanted to know what was up. "Why has your life been horrible?" She asked, not really caring.

Tader laughed. "Wow, for a minute there, I thought you forgot how to talk."

Chatt didn't find anything funny. "You gonna answer my question or not?"

"Come on, Chatt. Calm down," Spen said, placing her hand on Chatt's shoulder.

"No, it's cool," Tader assured. "I have no problem telling you why my life has been horrible. First off, Rell left me. David's ass is back and I had an abortion. I'm broke and can't wait to drink my ass off."

Spen placed her hand over her heart. "You had an abortion?"

Tader nodded. "It was either that or let David have his way with me. I chose the safe route."

Chatt couldn't help but become irritated with the smirk Tader had on her face. She didn't understand how Tader could be taking the situation as a joke. She wanted to keep quiet, but she couldn't bite her tongue any longer. "Why are you acting like this shit isn't serious? You just killed your child because some nigga told you to!"

Spen shook her head. She knew where this conversation was headed. Lately, Chatt and Tader could never be around each other without bumping heads at least once.

"What do you expect me to be doing?" Tader asked. "You know how crazy David's ass is."

Chatt shook her head. "How long you gon' let that nigga take advantage of yo dumbass?"

Triple Crown Publications presents . . . DAMAGE

Tader's mouth dropped. "Bitch, just as long as you let DreStar take advantage of you!"

Chatt almost choked on her Daiquiri. "You don't know what the fuck you're talking about."

"Girl please," Tader replied, putting her hand up as if she were saying talk to the hand. "I heard all about you and your dick riding skills."

Chatt sucked her teeth. She didn't know how Tader found out, but she was going to get to the bottom of it. "What the fuck are you talking about, Tader? Tell me what you know."

Tader took a sip of her drink. "I don't have to tell you shit. Just know that I know about your new life style."

Chatt grabbed the drink out of Tader's hand and slammed it down on their table. "You don't know shit."

"I'm sure Crispy wouldn't lie."

Spen's eyes lit up. Hearing Crispy's name just sat her on fire. "Tader, what the fuck are you doing communicating with that bitch?"

Tader lied quickly. "I ran into her and we chatted it up for a minute."

Chatt was looking right through Tader. There was something about her and her story that just wasn't adding up. "Crispy don't know shit about me, so I know you're lying."

Tader smiled, evilly. "Crispy works for the same nasty ass company DreStar's got you working for. It's titled *Legs Open Mouth Closed* I believe."

Chatt stood up and got in her face. "How do you know all that shit? Are you working for L.O.M.C too?"

Tader laughed. "Girl bye. I'm way too classy to be doing some shit like that."

Chatt's eyes widened. "Since when? You done fucked every nigga in the city so how classy do you think you

Triple Crown Publications *presents* . . .   DAMAGE

are?"

Spen was so embarrassed with her friends behavior. She was also upset with what she was hearing. "You know what, it's time to go."

"You damn right it is," Tader said standing up. She looked Chatt up and down before walking out to her car. She didn't need this shit right now. All she was trying to do was spend some time with her girls, but like she figured, things went sour. Tader couldn't stand Chatt sometimes. She was one of her best friends, but lately they had been going at it like cats and dogs. Tader had a feeling that Chatt knew more than she was supposed to. She wasn't sure if it was a guilty conscience but she could sense that someone was on to her. She shook her head and told herself that she was just trippin'. *What the hell?* She thought as she walked to the back of the parking lot and saw Terrell's mother leaning against her car. She dug in her purse searching for her pocket knife. She knew this lady was crazy and there was no telling what she was up to. Once she found her knife, she gripped it holding her hand in her purse. She didn't wanna Momma Lee to see that she had a weapon just in case this was a friendly visit.

Momma Lee smiled when she noticed her coming. "Hi, Ta'Ronna."

"Hey," Tader replied feeling uneasy. "What are you doing here and why are you all on my car?"

"Oh, I'm sorry," Momma Lee stated rising up off the car. "I hope I didn't do any damage."

"Yeah, me either," Tader snapped back. She was so bothered with Momma Lee's presence and she wanted to know what the fuck she was doing there. "Are you gon' tell me why you're here?"

"I came to see you. We need to talk."

"Nah, I have to go." Tader walked around to the driver's

side of her car and got in. She put the keys in the ignition and rolled down her window. "How did you know where I was?" She asked curiously.

Momma Lee walked up to the window and bent down. She looked inside the car surveying every detail she possibly could. "This is nice. Did my son purchase this for you?"

"Look lady, me and your son are going through it right now. If you came to talk about our relationship then you can beat it because I'm not about to be crying to my man's mom for advice."

"You are very rude, Ta'Ronna."

"How did you know where I was?" Tader asked again, blowing off Momma Lee's statement.

"That's not important." She reached in the car and ran her hand down the side of Tader's face. "What's going on with you and Terrell?"

"Oh, hell no!" Tader exclaimed. "Bitch, get yo hand out my fuckin' car and step back so I can go!"

"Watch your tone," Momma Lee ordered. She grabbed Tader's chin and turned her face in her direction so quickly that Tader was thrown off guard for a minute. She looked into Momma Lee's evil eyes as she felt her long nails sinking into her cheeks. "Now listen here, honey! My son told me about your ass. I know all about the guy that showed up at your place causing all that drama. Do you understand that my son could've been killed?" Tader was speechless as she was unable to free herself from Momma Lee's gaze. She was in shock with the whole situation. Momma Lee released her face and shook her head. "I told him not to fuck with you. Now he has to constantly look over his shoulder until he finds that man and kills him before he gets to him first."

"You are a fucking crazy ass psycho," Tader stated putting her car in drive.

"No sweetheart, I'm afraid you haven't seen that side of me yet. But let that guy touch my son, and you'll be very familiar with it."

"I have no fucking control over what his crazy ass does!"

"Well I advise you to find some fucking control or it's me you'll have to deal with!"

Tader's mouth widened in surprise. *Who this bitch think she is?* She thought as she rolled her window up and drove off. She looked in her rearview mirror and saw that Momma Lee was still staring at her. *This bitch done went nuts!*

Chatt faced Spen as they sat in silence. She knew she ruined the day but she didn't care. Tader had gotten on her last nerve and she was gonna confront her under any circumstances. Something was off and Chatt felt it. "I'm sorry," she said.

"Don't be." Spen stared at her for a second before asking, "What's L.O.M.C?"

Chatt sighed. She didn't wanna lie to Spen so she kept it real and told the truth. "It stands for *Legs Open Mouth Closed.*"

"What is that?"

Chatt sat back down. "A low down cheating ass company, beating people out of their money."

Spen sat back down also. "And Dre has you working for this so called company?"

"It's only temporary," Chatt muttered.

Spen grabbed her hand. "Chasity, what happened to your other job?"

"I quit."

"So you're happy working for Dre?"

Chatt was starting to get bothered. "I told you it's only temporary. It's a lot of shit going on that you don't know about, Spen."

"Well, tell me."

"I can't," Chatt answered, fighting back tears. "But what I can't tell you to do is watch out for Tader. She's hiding something and I know it. Why would her and Crispy be having a conversation about me? They shouldn't even be speaking."

Spen had to agree with her there. Tader and Crispy were never the best of friends so for them to be speaking was odd. "Something's definitely fishy about that."

"I know it is," Chatt replied. "I'm keeping my eyes on that bitch."

Spen shook her head. So many things were falling apart. She scooted closer to Chatt and gave her another hug. Chatt was her little sister and she loved her to death. She wished things could've just gone back to how they used to be. "Are you gonna be okay?"

Chatt forced a slight smile. "Yeah, I'll be okay. I'll try to call you more often."

"Are you sure?" Spen questioned, raising an eyebrow. "Because if Dre is..."

"Dre's not doing anything," Chatt said, cutting her off. "Relax, Spen. Everything's cool." She tried not to, but she had to lie.

"Okay girl." Spen kissed her cheek. "Call me if you need anything."

Chatt's smile faded. "I will."

Spen walked inside her condo and threw her keys on the counter. She poured herself a glass of water and sighed deeply. She didn't know what to do or where to go. She felt like her life was slowly coming to an end. She was depressed. She had no way to pay her bills and barely had enough money to put in her gas tank. She walked into the

Triple Crown Publications presents... **DAMAGE**

living room and plopped down on the couch. She stared at the blank TV for about an hour before finally turning it on. Over one thousand channels, yet she couldn't find anything she was interested in watching. She threw the remote across the room.

"What that remote do to you?"

Spen froze. She turned around and slowly looked up. Standing there in his John Varvatos silk-cotton polo, looking excessively handsome, Devon looked back at her. They held eye contact for what seemed like forever. Neither of them said anything. Devon smiled, walking towards her. He sat down next to her. Spen instantly got goose bumps. She couldn't take her eyes off of him and it was the same with him. He touched her face and she released the breath that she was holding. His fingers traveled down her left cheek. Next, they brushed over her lips, where he stopped and kissed her.

Spen closed her eyes. A kiss from Devon seemed to be all she needed at the moment. It felt so right. His lips were warm and soft like they always were. Devon pulled away from the kiss and stared at her. He missed her. He wanted to speak but words weren't needed at this particular moment. He grabbed her hand and led her upstairs into their bedroom. Spen couldn't keep her hands off of him. She wanted him. She daydreamed about this moment for so long and now it was finally happening. She was in the arms of her man. The sexy scent of his cologne filled her nostrils. She gripped the collar of his shirt as he backed her up against the wall. His lips tasted so sweet.

"You love me?" Devon asked, his tone just above a whisper.

"You know I do," Spen answered. "Never stopped."

Spen's words were music to Devon's ears. No other words were spoken between the two as they made love

Triple Crown Publications presents . . . DAMAGE

for hours. Everything they had been through in the past was put on hold for this moment in time. They were in love and enjoying each other as if they had no problems. Spen gave herself to Devon like she had never done before. This was her man and her moment. Nothing else mattered. It blew her mind when she felt Devon let off inside her. That was something he had never done in all their time of being together. She didn't know whether to be happy or sad. Devon leaned down and kissed her forehead. "I love you too," he said, turning over on his back.

Spen snuggled up close to him and laid her head on his chest. "I was worried about you."

Devon touched her hair. It had been a while since he ran his fingers through it. "I didn't mean to worry you."

"What's been going on?"

"A couple people from my job pulled a few strings and got my case dismissed."

Spen breathed a sigh of relief. "Thank God. I thought you would get life or something."

Devon chuckled. "The offense wasn't that serious, baby."

"I'm just glad it's over. Thank you, Devon."

"Thanks for what?" He questioned.

"For taking the blame for my mistake. You didn't have to do that."

"I told you why I did it. You don't have to thank me. I should be thanking you."

Spen sighed, heavily. Everything was rushing back to her at once. She closed her eyes and tried to shake the thoughts, but they continued to flood her mind. The image of Crispy walking behind Devon naked popped up. She was pissed all over again. She rose up from his chest and stood up.

Devon already knew what the deal was. Crispy continued

to flood his mind, just as she did Spen's. She was like a disease eating at their minds. "Don't let her win, baby. This is what she wants."

"Why did you have to mess around with her? You messed everything up, Devon." She shook her head. "You fucked it all up."

Devon stood up and walked towards her. "I know and I'm sorry. I'm not making any excuses for what I did."

Spen started to pout. She wanted to forgive Devon badly, but she was terrified of getting her heart broken again. It was painful enough the first time. She didn't know if she could trust Devon anymore. "This is painful for me, Devon. It's like I love you, but I hate you."

"I hate that you feel that way and hate is a strong word."

Spen backed away from him. "I can't help how I feel. I want us back together but I know it's not right."

"It is right," Devon argued. "Any other way would be wrong."

Spen was silent. She wished that the situation was as easy as Devon made it sound. It was far more complicated than that. He just didn't get it. "I think we need some time apart to clear our heads."

Devon grew frustrated. "We've had plenty of time apart. I can't be away from you any longer."

His words made her melt. She knew he was speaking his true feelings. "I don't wanna be away from you either, but I need more time, Devon."

Devon chewed on his bottom lip. "Okay," he agreed. "The last thing I wanna do is rush you."

Spen watched him slip back into his clothes and pick up a few of his things. Once he was done, he walked back towards her and pecked her lips. When he turned to walk away, Spen grabbed his arm. "Where are you going?"

He shrugged his shoulders. "Somewhere, so that you can have your space."

"But I don't..."

"Shhh," Devon interrupted. "Don't worry. I won't go too far. If you need me, don't hesitate to call, a'ight?"

Spen was so confused. She didn't want him to leave, but for some reason she wanted to be alone. "Devon, you live here, too. You don't have to leave if you don't want to."

He smiled kissing her lips again. "I want you to take as much time as you need. Like I said, I won't be far."

Spen watched Devon walk out the room, wondering where he was going. After a long shower, she got back in the bed and slept all night, dreaming of Devon.

DreStar sat low-key at the bar keeping a tight gaze on his next target. The young woman he was watching seductively swerved her hips to the music, not even noticing that he was watching her. He got up and slowly started walking towards her. He wasn't nervous. He was never nervous when recruiting new employees for L.O.M.C. He had done this too many times to be shaken up. He approached the young lady from behind and took her hand. She turned around and smiled. Dre thought she was hella' cute. Brown skin, a little skinnier than he preferred but he could work with it. The target had a blonde bob, five-four and pretty brown eyes. He smiled back at her. "You lookin' real good in dem stilettos, ma."

"Well, thank you," the young woman replied, blushing hard.

"You're welcome." He offered his hand and she flirtatiously took it. "Can I get your name?"

She was still holding his hand. "Chelae."

Dre squinted his eyes a bit. "You look so familiar, Chelae. Have we ever crossed paths?"

Still holding his hand, Chelae replied, "You're Chatt's guy. I saw you drop her off a few times when we were working at *Hair Desire*."

Dre smiled. "I thought I knew you from somewhere." He let go of her hand. "How have you been since the shop got set on fire?"

"I've been making ends meet. Spencer reached out to me a few times and apologized for her decision."

"Yeah, that was pretty selfish."

Chelae nodded and started dancing to the music again. She bent over giving Dre a clear view of her plump bottom. He smiled. He knew he had her exactly where he needed her to be. Chelae stood up straight. "I don't think Chatt would appreciate you looking down there."

Dre's smile faded. "Me and Chasity broke up a while ago. She's a good person, but we weren't right for each other."

"Well, I'm sorry to hear that. Chatt was never good with men. She always seemed to run them away."

"You're right," Dre stated, walking up behind her. He grabbed her waist and whispered in her ear, "She just couldn't handle me."

Chelae turned around and wrapped her arms around his neck. "She's a young girl. They never know what to do with grown men."

Talking with Chelae was raising Dre's ego. He hadn't lost his touch at all. He was still the smooth talker that could persuade any young girl to hop on the band wagon. He pulled her in closer to him. "Why don't you show me what to do with a grown man like me."

"You taking me home?" Chelae asked, grinning.

Dre ran his hand over his mouth. This was way too easy. Once he and Chelae were inside his truck, he easily convinced her to come to his place. He did it purposely just to get under Chatt's skin. He knew it would piss her off to see Chelae walking in with him. He hoped Chatt would be jealous. Maybe this would make her realize that if she stopped flipping out on him then her life wouldn't be so hard. Dre put the key in the lock and opened his front door. He smiled, noticing Chatt as she sat on the couch staring at the wall. That had become her favorite hobby lately.

Chelae stepped in behind Dre. She frowned when she saw Chatt. She tried to give her a fake smile and look away, but the deadly look in Chatt's eyes wouldn't let her brake the gaze. Chelae was nervous and felt awkward at the same time. She was so uncomfortable with the current situation. She was finally able to break her stare with Chatt and turn her attention towards DreStar. She stood on the tip of her toes and whispered in his ear, "What is she doing here?"

Dre laughed and whispered back over his shoulder, "She's homeless. I didn't wanna throw her on the streets, so I'm letting her stay here until she finds a new place."

Chatt laughed to herself. Dre and Chelae thought their conversation was private but Chatt heard every word. If Dre thought he was shit on her in front of her face, he had another thing coming. Chatt sat up straight on the couch and looked at Chelae. "I hope you know he's gay."

Chelae's face curled up. "Excuse me?"

"Oh, he didn't tell you?" Chatt smirked, looking at Dre. "I hope you brought lube because he likes it in the ass."

Dre grabbed Chelae's hand and led her to the steps. "Excuse me for a moment. I need to have a word with the crack baby."

Chelae slightly chuckled. "Where am I going?"

"First room on the right."

Chatt knew Dre was pissed. She didn't care though. She was pissed off her damn self and was ready for whatever he was about to do. She balled up her fist ready to swing just in case he hit her.

Triple Crown Publications presents . . . DAMAGE

"Why you gotta show out," Dre asked, walking towards her. He leaned down and got in her face. "I thought we agreed that you were gonna act right."

"Fuck you!" Chatt spat. She was tired of playing games. She pushed him out of her face and stood up. "I've had enough of this shit."

"Watch your tone," Dre warned.

"No, you watch your tone, you fucking fag!"

Dre laughed out of anger before swinging his fist across her face. Chatt's head hit the edge of the coffee table as she fell to the floor. Dre stood over her. Her tiny body was froze. He checked her wrist for a pulse. Her heart was still beating.

"Is everything okay down there?" Chelae asked from the top of the stair case.

"Yeah," Dre assured her. "I'll be up in a minute." He pulled Chatt by her right leg threw the living room into the coat closet, once again. He figured that since she was unconscious she wouldn't mind sleeping there again.

17

Crispy lit a cigarette after stepping out of her Benz. She reached back in for her jacket. The weather was starting to get chilly. Holiday season was around the corner and she was excited to get back to California. Her bags were packed and waiting at the hotel. She hoped to catch a flight within the next week. She had already done her damage in Ohio and was ready to break out before it came back to bite her in the ass. After she finished her cigarette, she strolled inside Monique's, an expensive shoe store for women. She didn't wanna leave and not take any goodies with her.

She scanned the wall of suede boots looking for something unique to take back to Cali. There were plenty of good choices. She had her mind made up when she laid her eyes on a pair of black suede knee high boots. They were to-die-for. She grabbed the boots and took a seat to try them on. The five and a half fit her petite little feet perfectly. She waved for the sales woman to come over. The sales women walked over and frowned when she saw the pair of boots Crispy had on. Crispy saw the look on her face. She hoped their wasn't a problem. All she wanted was the boots and then she would be on her way.

The sales associate pointed to another set of boots. "Why don't you try these?" She suggested.

"I don't want those," Crispy argued. "Why can't I have the ones that I have on right now?"

"I'm sorry ma'am. Those are the only pair of those boots that we have left, and they were supposed to be put on hold for a customer."

"Well, too bad. You guys should have had them stored somewhere else." Crispy took the boots off and held them in her hand. She wasn't giving them up. They were too damn cute in her opinion. She and the sales woman went back and forth until thy heard someone walk through the doors. They both looked up at the same time.

Devon's skin crawled at the sight of Crispy. He looked at the boots that she held in her hand, then at the sales woman. "Excuse me; I thought I asked you to put those on hold for me."

"I'm sorry, sir. I asked one of the other employees to do it but I guess they never got around to it."

Crispy smiled. "You're the customer that requested these boots?"

Devon ignored her. "So, wassup? Am I gettin' the boots or not?"

The sales women looked at Crispy. "Ma'am, please. This gentleman requested these boots first. I would be happy to assist you with finding another store that might have another pair."

Crispy's smile never faded. "Devon, who are you trying

to buy these for?"

Just looking at Crispy made Devon's stomach turn. He didn't wanna see her nor be around her. She disgusted him. "You know what; I'll just go to another store." He walked out not wanting to be in Crispy's presence any longer. Once he stepped outside, the air around him just felt better. He closed his eyes and took a deep breath. Just when he felt relieved, that hint of bad air crept around him again. He opened his eyes and Crispy was standing in front of him. No wonder. He brushed past her and headed for his truck. Crispy trailed behind him. Devon paid her no mind as he got in and slammed the door. Crispy reached for the door handle, and that triggered Devon's anger. "Don't touch my shit!" He barked.

Crispy didn't expect him to react the way he did. She immediately let go of the door handle. "My bad, bay."

He put his keys in the ignition. "Quit calling me that."

She flipped her hair over her shoulders. "I just came out here to tell you that you can have those boots. I saw another pair that I wanted."

"A'ight. I'll get 'em another time."

Crispy rolled her eyes. "Devon, she's waiting for you. You better get em' now or they're gonna get sold."

Devon clenched his jaw. He wanted this bitch to get out of his sight. He also wanted that particular pair of boots for Spen's upcoming birthday. He sighed hard before snatching the keys out of his ignition. He swung his door open, not caring that it bumped Crispy's arm, knocking her off balance a little. He went back inside the store and purchased the boots, then came back out to find Crispy standing against his truck. "What the fuck do you want, girl?"

"I want you to stop treating me like shit. We used to be friends at one point of time. Why can't it go back to how it used to be?"

Triple Crown Publications *presents* . . . DAMAGE

Devon got in his truck, ready to leave for real this time. "We'll never be friends," he stated with assurance. "You're a ruthless bitch and I regret the day I ever fucked with you."

Crispy's eyes lit up. She'd had enough of the insults. "You know what's better than knowing that you ate my pussy?"

"Yeah," Devon smirked. "Knowing that it'll never happen again."

Crispy smiled shaking her head. "You're wrong like usual, Devon. The best part of it is knowing that your girlfriend eats pussy better than you do." She laughed sneakily as she walked back inside the shoe store. There she was getting under somebody's skin without even trying. She knew what she was doing and she did it well. Her comment would be stuck in Devon's head until it drove him crazy enough to the point where he had to know what she was talking about. By the time he figured it out, Crispy would be long gone back to Cali.

Tader pulled into her drive way ready to go completely nuts. Terrell was now gone and so was her unborn child. Not to mention her best friends were slowly but surely fading away from her. She walked inside and flicked on the lights. All she wanted right now was a drink to make her misery go away. She wanted to clear her mind from everything that she had been through. It never slipped her mind that karma was waiting to bite her in the ass. She knew she would soon pay for what she did to Spen. She now regretted her selfish decision. Not because she felt bad, but because she knew karma was a bitch. She walked in her living room and damn near had a heart attack. She was used to David popping up on her while she was alone, but never was he inside her house while she wasn't there.

His car's not even outside, she thought to herself. Her heart started pounding fast. She didn't have a clue what he was up to this time. His back was turned to her as he sat on the couch watching television. She knew he knew that she was there because she turned the lights on. Tader was getting sick of the David shit. She didn't know when, but she had recently gotten a hold of a pistol that she planned on defending herself with. Something told her that the time was now. If she ever wanted to be free, she would have to rid his ass ASAP.

She slowly reached inside her purse and grabbed the pistol, while tip toeing to her bedroom. She was scared as shit. She had never shot a gun before and wasn't sure if she was ready to now. She wanted to prepare herself for what she looked to be the moment of truth. When she shot the gun, her aim had to be on point. One missed bullet could cost her everything. The thought alone made her even more nervous. She didn't want David dead, but she knew it was the only way she would get away from him. Her hands were shaking. What if it took more than one bullet to kill him? She wasn't sure if she could find the strength to shoot the gun twice. She wasn't a killer and didn't want to become one. But she knew she had to do what she had to do.

"Nice to see you, Tader," David said, while still facing the television.

Tader froze up because she thought that she was being sneaky. With this being a now or never situation, she stood straight and aimed the gun at David's head. "Now what nigga?" she boasted. "The tables have turned haven't they?"

David turned around to face her and when he realized that she had her pistol aimed at him he began laughing hysterically. "Go ahead and pull the trigger," he stated, while rising up from the couch, walking towards her.

Tader's hands were trembling by now. "Don't tempt me David, because I will blow your ass away!"

"Then pull the trigger bitch! Kill me just like you killed your unborn child."

David's words hit Tader hard. She was fed up with her life at that point and ending David's life seemed to feel like it would relieve her from the pain. She pulled the trigger in hopes of killing him, but no bullets released from the gun. "Come on, come on!" Tader screamed, while squeezing the trigger, but still no bullets released.

"Do you honestly think I would give you that much of an easy chance at killing me?" David asked, while watching Tader still try to make the gun fire.

She finally became fed up and threw the gun across the room. "You emptied it didn't you?" She asked as she started to cry. "You emptied my shit, didn't you?"

David laughed. "Why ask a question you already know the answer to?"

She started to sob. "How did you even know I had it?"

"I went through your purse last week. It's actually been empty for a while now, you just didn't know."

Tader felt so stupid. Here she was about to kill David; come to find out, he ended those hopes a long time ago. "David, let me ask you a question." She tried to wipe her face, but the tears were still flowing. "Did it ever even cross your mind that the baby you made me kill was yours? What if I was lying about it being Anthony's? Would you still have made me kill it?"

"Of course it came to mind," David admitted. "That's one of the reasons I had you get rid of it. I ain't having kids any time soon."

"You fucking bastard!" Tader shouted, before slapping David across his face. She sprinted to the kitchen and

Triple Crown Publications presents... **DAMAGE**

grabbed a steak knife from out of the sink.

"You gon' pay for that shit and you know it don't you?" David asked as he got his balance together. Tader stood confident with the steak knife in her hand and was ready to gut David like a fish. He whipped his nine out from the back of his jeans and pointed it in her direction. "Now, unlike yours, my shit is loaded, so drop the knife!" David demanded.

"Fuck you!" Tader screamed. David began to slowly walk towards her, causing her to get nervous. "Back the fuck up!" She warned while walking backwards from the kitchen. He continued to walk towards her making her speed up her pace to get out of the kitchen, but she found herself moving too fast and slipped in a pile of water leaking from her dish washer. The steak knife went flying across the room. David took full opportunity in grabbing her ankles and dragging her into his favorite spot, which was the basement.

"So you were gon' try and kill a nigga tonight?" He asked her while dragging her down the stairs. She couldn't even respond because she was in so much pain from her fall in the kitchen and not to mention her head hitting each step as David dragged her down the stairs. "Well, you picked the wrong night to fuck with me, Tader. I've had a rough day and all I wanted to do was fuck tonight, but you had to pull a quick one and piss me off even more!"

"I'm sorry, David," Tader whimpered, fighting through her pain. "I'll do whatever you want, just please don't hurt me."

"I'm glad to hear that from you, baby. I actually have something in mind that I need you to help me with." He dragged her to the darkest corner in the basement and once again pointed his nine at her. "Now, this is what you gon' do for me." He pulled out his cell phone and threw it at her before continuing, "Call that nigga Terrell and get

Triple Crown Publications presents . . . DAMAGE

him over here."

"I'm not calling him so you can kill him!" Tader shouted, her eyes still raining.

"You're right," David replied, walking back and forth. "You're gonna kill him."

"There's no fucking way you could ever make me do that!"

"Oh, really," David asked while cocking his nine and shoving it in her mouth. "You're gonna do what the fuck I tell you to do, or else I'll have your tonsils splattered all over these fucking walls." He jerked the gun down her throat causing her to gag a little. He then removed it from her mouth to hear her response. But to his surprise, she gave a response without speaking. She picked up his cell phone and dialed Terrell's number. David made sure the phone was on speaker.

"Who is this?" Terrell questioned, answering his phone.

"Rell, babe, it's Tader."

"What the fuck you want?" He snapped.

Tader cried silently. "I was calling to tell you that I miss you and that I want you back home with me."

Terrell chuckled. "And why is that? Is that David nigga messing with you again? Because that seems to be the only time you want me around."

David smiled, listening to the conversation. He had a feeling that Terrell was threatened by him and he loved feeling that way.

Tader continued to sob into the phone. "Rell, don't be like that, babe. I miss you so much."

"I don't have time for all this, Ta'Ronna. I got shit to handle."

"Please," she begged. "Just come and see me, Rell. I'm breaking down and I need you more than ever right now."

Terrell didn't realize how truthful Tader's statement

was. She did need him now more than ever to rescue her from David. He was her only hope.

"I don't think I'm gon' be free no time soon, so you gon' have to deal wit' your problems without me."

Tader broke down. She needed Terrell. She wasn't asking for him to be her man again, but she did want him to save her. She knew that him having no free time meant that he wasn't coming; which meant she would have to deal with her David situation alone. "Okay," she cried into the phone.

Terrell hated listening to Tader when she sounded emotional. He hated hearing her that way because no matter how hard he tried to deny it, he knew he had a soft spot for her. How else could he have put up with all her bullshit in the past? "Look, if I get a minute, I'll pop through, a'ight?"

"Rell, thank you," Tader wailed. She felt so relieved. "Thank you so much."

Terrell hung up the phone before Tader could say anything else. David snatched the phone from her hands. He didn't understand why she was so relieved. The phone call was simply to bait Terrell over and David would take it from there. If Tader expected him to be a super save a hoe, she had another thing coming.

David looked at her and began walking up the stairs. "Whenever he decides to show up, I'll let you know. Until then, make yourself comfortable." He locked the basement door making it impossible for Tader to get out. Her only hope of getting out was by breaking down the one glass window under the staircase. She grabbed one of her twelve-pound barbells and began pounding it on the glass block. Seeing how thick the glass was, it would take about half an hour of hardcore pounding to get it to bust. In the mist of her breaking the glass, David came strolling back down the stairs.

"Trying to make the perfect escape?" He questioned, while staring at the barbell in her hand. She dropped it immediately and put her hands up in her defense. He pulled out a pair of handcuffs from his back pocket and cuffed her onto the rail on the stair case. "That should keep you down until I come back."

Tader was cuffed to the stair rail for hours until she eventually fell asleep. She had been knocked out for a few hours, but was awakened by the sound of someone calling her name. "Tader," the voice shouted out once again, and she immediately knew it was Terrell.

"Rell, I'm down here," she hollered. She heard him struggling trying to open the basement door.

"What the hell are you doing in the...?"

Tader's heart dropped when Terrell stopped talking. She knew something was wrong. "Rell?" She called out but got no response. "AHHHHHH!!!" She screamed when she witnessed Terrell's body tumbling down the stairs.

David came strolling down the stairs laughing not too long after. He had on a pair of all black gloves and had her pistol that she threw across the room in his hand. He walked towards Terrell and began kicking him in the face and stomping his rib cage.

"Leave him the fuck alone!" Tader shouted while beginning to once again cry her eyes out. She watched as David beat Terrell half to death.

"Now, finish him off, Tader. I got your gun reloaded for you, baby." David walked behind her and brought out his pocket knife and positioned it at the center of her neck. He then placed the gun in her lap. "Now, blow this ma'fucka away, or I'll slit your fucking throat."

"Fuck you, David!"

David applied more pressure to her neck. "You must

Triple Crown Publications presents . . . **DAMAGE**

think I'm joking."

"I don't give a fuck. I'm not killing him."

David became frustrated with Tader, so he decided to move on to plan B. "Well, have it your way, Tader," he said while picking the gun up out of her lap. "But either way, your ass is the one going down for this man's murder."

"You can't make me kill him no matter what you do!" Tader challenged back.

"You're right. But what I can do is kill him myself with the gun that has your prints all over it. These things on my hands are called gloves." He cocked the gun and fired four bullets into Terrell's chest.

"NOOOO!!!!" Tader screamed as she stared at Terrell's dead body lying in front of her. David dropped the gun and fled up stairs. He closed the basement door and grabbed Tader's house phone. He then dialed 911 and reported a shooting at her address before making his way out the door.

Chatt's heart pounded at a heavy pace as she paced the bathroom floor. Her emotions were running wild. She refused to live with Dre any longer. Using her mother as bait to keep her around was getting old. Chatt hated to leave her mother behind but she had to go. Not only was she beyond miserable, but she also felt herself becoming sick. She didn't know what it was but she wanted to check it out just in case it was something serious. Lately, she'd been having constant headaches and an upset stomach. She had a feeling that DreStar had been putting things in her food. She wanted to murk his ass so bad. Nothing would make her happier. Dre had really crushed Chatt's heart. He played the role of being perfect so well. Chatt had never been with anybody who treated her as good as he did. Hating to admit it, she was actually falling in love with him. Luckily, she caught herself before she fell head first. Chatt was on some new shit. No more games. All or nothing. She was still young and had much more life to live. She couldn't be stuck in Dre's cruel little world any longer. She wracked her brain trying to figure out how she would get her phone from his bedroom. There was no way she could get in there and take it without DreStar seeing her. She had to put a plan together. Something smart. There was no time for mistakes. *How am I gon' do this?* Chatt asked herself. The sounds of slurping and moaning interrupted her thoughts. Chatt put her ear to the door to get a better hearing. True enough, her mind wasn't playing with her. DreStar was getting his dick sucked at that very moment.

Chatt was so pissed. DreStar was such a man whore. Anytime he could get a nut off, he was down for it. Chatt smiled thinking about the positives. She knew how Dre was when it came to his sex. If it was good enough, he lost all focus from everything else. His only focus was on getting a good nut off. Chatt wondered if she could creep into his bedroom without him noticing her. All she wanted to do was grab her phone then she would be on her way. If only it was that simple. She bit her bottom lip out of frustration. Something told her that she wouldn't get away with it. *Fuck it,* she told herself. *If he says something, I'm just gon' run.* Chatt slowly put her hand on the bathroom door and turned the knob. She walked out of the bathroom into the hallway. When she turned to walk in Dre's room, she saw a sight that she wasn't quite prepared for. There stood DreStar with his hand on the back of Shawan's head, forcing his dick down her throat. Chatt's blood boiled. Dre had pulled the last straw this time. Ready for whatever, Chatt stormed into the room and grabbed a handful of Shawan's hair yanking her away from Dre. She was so heated that she felt like she would burst open. She looked at Dre and saw that he was pissed as well but she didn't give a fuck. She was tired of him and today was the last day that he would ever torture her.

"What the fuck do you think you're doing?" Dre barked, trying to pull Shawan back towards him.

"I'm leaving, ma'fucka, and I'm taking her with me!" Chatt exclaimed.

Shawan pulled away from Chatt. "No, Chasity! He loves me."

Chatt wanted to slap the shit out of her mother for making that statement; and that's exactly what she did. Shawan went flying across the floor from the force of Chatt's slap. "This ma'fucka don't love you!" Chatt barked.

Dre rushed Chatt against the wall, pinning her wrist up. He was beyond pissed with her behavior. "Now, listen here, crack baby. I'm sick of you actin' up and shit! Don't ever fuckin' interrupt me while I'm gettin' my dick sucked."

"Fuck you, faggot ass nigga!" Chatt fired back.

"Bitch, you gon' learn to respect me."

Crack!

Chatt fell to the floor in agonizing pain. She felt like she had been hit in the jaw with a pair of brass knuckles as Dre's fist collided with her face. Tears filled her eyes. The ma'fucka just broke her jaw.

"I hope you learned you're lesson," Dre stated, standing over her laughing. He bent down and let his dick dangle in her face. "Finish what your momma started."

"No," Shawan screeched. "I wanna do it!"

As bad as it hurt Chatt to open her mouth, she opened it wide trying to ignore the pain. Dre was super excited to get his dick sucked by Chatt. That was the one thing he never had her do before. He entered her mouth slowly, ready to enjoy great pleasure. Chatt waited until he filled her mouth with as much of his dick as possible before she

Triple Crown Publications *presents . . .* DAMAGE

bit down as hard as she could.

"FUCK!!!" Dre shouted so loud, the neighbors were sure to hear him. The more he tried to pull away from Chatt, the more her teeth ripped through his meat.

"Stop it, Chasity," Shawan exclaimed, noticing the pain that Dre was in. In her mind, DreStar was her man. Seeing Chatt hurt him like that made her want to help him. She got off the floor and rushed towards Chatt. "Let him go," she said, ramming her elbow into Chatt's broken jaw.

Chatt had planned on biting until Dre's dick fell off, but the pain from her jaw wouldn't let her. She opened her mouth and watched Dre pull out with the quickness. He was breathing hard and sweating like a slave. Chatt stood up and searched for her phone. She spotted it on Dre's dresser which happened to be on the other side of the room. She looked at Dre still wincing in pain. At the current time, he wasn't paying her any attention so Chatt took the opportunity to go and grab her phone. She was so done with him.

"Dre, she took your phone!" Shawan yelled, pointing towards Chatt.

Chatt looked at her mother and shook her head. She couldn't believe what she was hearing. She was actually taking Dre's side over her own daughter's. "I been through so much bullshit for weeks now, trying to save you! The only reason I haven't left this bastard is because I was waiting to see you so I could take you with me." She wiped the tears from her face. "But you know what? I don't care anymore. You can stay here and do whatever you want."

"If you walk out that door, I promise you gon' pay," Dre warned, his voice low and crackly.

"There's nothing more you can do to me that you haven't already done," Chatt replied. "Now fuck off, you fag." She stared at Shawan for a moment longer before walking out of the room. She then jogged down the steps and opened the front door. Just when she thought there was no turning back the sound of a single gunshot made her stop dead in her tracks. Her body froze completely. "Oh God," she silently cried, hoping it wasn't too late for a prayer. "Please God, tell me it's not what I think."

"Chasity!" Dre yelled, from the top of the staircase. "Look what you made me do." He sent Shawan's body tumbling down the stairs.

"Oh my God!" Chatt wailed, dropping to her knees. Just when she thought things couldn't get worse, they did. She was staring at her mother with half her head blown off. "No, no, no," she bawled. "You killed her! Oh my God, you fucking killed her!" Chatt closed her eyes and started rocking back and forth, saying a silent prayer to the Lord.

Dre slowly walked down the steps. He kicked Shawan's dead body. "Don't cry, baby," he said, kneeling down towards Chatt. "She was gon' die anyway."

Chatt opened her watery eyes. If looks could kill, DreStar would be lying next to his maker. She stood up still looking at him. Her face was cold and deadly.

Dre could sense that she was about to blow. He started walking towards her. "Chasity, don't be stupid."

Chatt saw him coming towards her, but her mind was gone. She didn't hear a word he was saying. Her thoughts were too focused on erasing him from her life, permanently. Dre increased his pace and finally caught up with her. Her back was to the entertainment center. Dre smiled looking down at her. He couldn't help but touch her. After the pain she had just put him through with biting his manhood, he figured he deserved to do whatever he wanted to do to her. His hand ran down her face, continuing down her neck, all the way to her breast. He was becoming aroused, so he took it upon himself to rip off the wife beater that Chatt was wearing. He then bent down, kissing her stomach until he was face to face with her pussy. He pulled her shorts down and was going for her panties when he felt an extremely hot substance spill on top of his head.

"What the fuck?" he screeched, looking up.

Chatt's face was red as blood as she stood there holding a candle that she had grabbed from off of the entertainment center. Spilling the candle wax over Dre's head wasn't enough to satisfy her. Before Dre could stand up, Chatt slammed the still lit candle on the right side of his face. She then took off out the door, running in nothing but her underwear. She ran and ran until she was out of breath. She didn't wanna stop, but she had to get her wind together. She slowed down and bent over trying to get as much air as possible. Her jaw was killing her, not to mention the pounding headache she had.

As she caught her breath, an all-black Impala pulled up behind her. Chatt stood up straight and faced the car. The windows were tinted, so she couldn't see who was inside. She started walking away when someone asked, "Aye, lil mama, you need a lift?"

Chatt stopped walking and turned around. The window of the Impala was now rolled down enabling her to see the dark skinned youngin' who sat behind the wheel. Chatt wanted a ride, but she knew not to trust a stranger. This was a young boy pulling up on her while she was wearing nothing but her under clothes. She knew what he wanted and she'd be damned if she gave it to him. "No, thank you," she replied as she started walking away.

The youngin frowned, getting out of his car. Another young thug got out of the passenger's side. They both jogged, trying to catch up with Chatt before she got too far. "Hold on, baby," the dark skinned boy stated, grabbing Chatt's arm. "I know you don't wanna be walkin' out here

Triple Crown Publications presents... DAMAGE

in yo underwear. It's kind of chilly."

"I'm fine," Chatt replied sternly. She tried to yank her arm away from his grip, but he held her too tight. "Get the fuck off me," she snapped.

The youngin's friend covered Chatt's mouth and picked her up by her tiny waist. "Don't yell at us," he whispered. "We're doing you a favor."

Chatt didn't even try to fight against em'. She knew she wouldn't win. She started to feel as if failure was her fate. Nothing she did ever seemed to work in her favor. She finally freed herself from DreStar, only to be captured by two more niggas. She was tired of fighting. Whatever was going to happen would just have to happen. She felt like God wasn't on her side anymore.

18

Spen sat on her couch, looking out the window. She was depressed. She felt like her life was passing her by. Nothing she envisioned for her future was going right. No kids, no salon, and she wasn't even sure if she had a man. How did everything come to this? At one point, everything seemed well. It seemed as if everything crumbled overnight. That damn Crispy. Ever since she'd shown her face, everything started falling apart. Spen hated her. She blamed Crispy for the failure of her relationship and for the reason she set her salon on fire. She wished Crispy would have never shown her face. That bitch was straight poison.

Spen rubbed her eyes, sitting up straight on the couch. She smiled watching Devon pull into the driveway. She knew he was probably the only one who remembered. She stood up from the couch and tried to control the butterflies in her stomach. She didn't understand why she got so nervous when Devon came around. This was a new feeling that he had been giving her lately. Nervousness.

She met him at the front door with a warm smiled painted across her face. She eyed the two white boxes he was carrying. "Hey stranger."

"Stranger?" Devon questioned, pretending to be offended.

"I'm kidding, Devon." She opened the screen door and let him slide past her.

They walked into the living room where they both took seats on the couch. Devon grinned, touching Spen's thigh. "You're gettin' old, baby."

"I am not getting old," Spen replied. "I'm just maturing."

Devon scooted closer to her and kissed her forehead. "Happy birthday."

"You remembered."

"You actually thought I would forget?" Devon asked.

Spen shrugged her shoulders. "Everybody else did."

"Well, I'm not everybody else. I'm a man that loves the hell out of you and would never forget the day you were born." He picked up one of the white boxes. "I thought you might like these."

Spen took the box from his hand. "Devon, you didn't have to." *But thank God you did,* she thought to herself, excitedly. She opened the box and inside rested the suede multi strap boots that Devon purchased from Monique's. Spen loved them. She couldn't wait to get them on her feet. "These are so cute, baby. Thank you."

"You're welcome." He stared at her for a moment. "Let me take you out."

Spen was blushing hard. "I don't have anything to wear."

Triple Crown Publications presents... **DAMAGE**

"Open the second box."

Spen sat the boots down and got even more excited as she reached for the second box. She opened it and pulled out a black Adrianna Papell ruffled mock two piece halter dress.

As Devon watched her admire the dress, he removed another box from his coat pocket. This box was black and much smaller than the other ones. "Here, open this one."

Spen took the third box from his hand and took a deep breath before opening it up. She knew she was about to be breathless, seeing that the box read Tiffany & Co. on the outside. She opened it up and found herself looking at a graduated drop pendant, with round brilliant diamonds set in platinum. In the middle of the necklace rested the matching platinum studs.

"You like em'?" Devon asked, looking at Spen as she sat speechless.

"Devon, I can't believe you went out of your way for me like this. Thank you, baby. My gifts are so nice."

"I'm glad you like everything."

Spen never took her eyes off of the necklace. "Nobody shows me how much they care except you." She finally looked away from the necklace to steal a glance at the dress. "I mean, look at all of this. You gotta care for me to go all out like you did."

Devon frowned a little. "Fuck all the material shit, Spen. If that's what makes you think I care about you then you're wrong. That shit ain't got nothin' to do with it." He grabbed her hand. "You hear me?"

Spen nodded.

"Good. Now get dressed and let me finish your day off."

"Fresh meat, fresh meat!" a crowd of young college boys

cheered. They all stood surrounding Chatt as she laid on the floor passed out. The two young boys that found her walking in her underwear brought her back to their dorm room for a little fun. After injecting her with a few drugs, she was completely out of it.

"Aye, Wa'an, start the show," a dark skinned boy urged.

"Y'all already know I'm about to work this bitch," Wa'an stated as he worked his way through the crowd until he got to Chatt. He bent down and spread her legs apart. "We gon' have a good time tonight!" Wa'an stood back up and loosened his belt buckle. He stepped out of his jeans revealing his erect manhood to everyone in the room. Pulling his boxers down, he positioned himself on top of Chatt, pushing her panties to the side.

"Work, work, work!" The crowd chanted as they watched Wa'an slide himself inside Chatt. He showed no mercy as he raped her young unconscious body without a condom on. Once he was done with her, he passed her off to his friends. Over twelve nigga's went inside Chatt raw, every one of them nutting inside her. They poured bottles of liquor over her naked body, then took turns licking it off of her. Wa'an took it upon himself to try and shove a bottle of liquor up her ass. He shoved until the bottle wouldn't go in any deeper. "Now it's my turn," he said, entering her ass. The crowd was loving the show. After Wa'an got a second nut off, he stood up and spit on Chatt's tiny frame. Just about every nigga in the dorm gotta turn to do whatever they wanted to do with her.

"Yo, Wa'an, look who decided to join the party," a young boy shouted, standing by the door.

Wa'an walked off leaving his boys to have a little more fun with Chatt. He approached the door and saw his cousin walking in. "Yo, what's good, Lo?"

Kilo gave him dap and stepped further inside the dorm.

Triple Crown Publications presents . . . DAMAGE

"Shit, cuz. Heard y'all was havin' a little party in here."

Wa'an smiled. "Hell yeah, fam. We gettin' loose, cuz. Let me show you the big party favor."

Kilo followed behind Wa'an as he made his way through the thick crowd again. Kilo was greeted by many people as he maneuvered threw the crowd. When they reached the center floor, Kilo was beyond disgusted with what he was seeing. A group of niggas taking advantage of a young girl didn't sit well with him. He was so disappointed with his little cousin. "Come on, Wa'an. You know we don't get down like this."

"Man, stop trippin' Lo. We found this bitch on the street in her bra and panties, nigga. She was asking for it," Wa'an declared, turning Chatt over. She was now lying flat on her back.

Kilo stared at her taking in her face. It couldn't be who he thought it was. He stepped closer to her and confirmed his assumptions. It was definitely Chatt. His eyes scanned over the huge lump on the right side of her face, then down her badly bruised body. He took off his jacket and covered her nude body with it.

"Aw, come on cuz," Wa'an whined. At that moment, he began regretting letting Kilo come in. He knew his big cousin was uptight and he hoped that seeing a naked female would loosen him up a little bit. Unfortunately for Wa'an, Kilo was far from loosened up.

"I can't believe you, Wa'an. I can't believe none of y'all niggas," Kilo stated, shaking his head. He bent down and scooped Chatt up in his arms. "Y'all better hope she wake up or its gon' be a serious problem wit' all y'all fools."

"Yo, is that yo shorty?" A young boy asked.

Kilo gave him a look that let him know to mind his own business. "Shut this fuckin' party down, Wa'an."

Wa'an didn't want the party to be over but he knew

Triple Crown Publications presents . . . DAMAGE

better than to go against his cousin's orders. Even though Kilo was only five years older than Wa'an, the respect level between the two had been set at an early age. Wa'an looked up to Kilo, seeing that he was the only older male in his life.

"A'ight, man," Wa'an muttered. "Party over fellas."

The entire room went silent. It was easy to tell that everyone was disappointed that Kilo had come in and ended their fun. He was being looked at as the party pooper but he didn't care. His only concern was Chatt. Kilo walked outside and put Chatt in the backseat of his car. He felt sorry for her. It was obvious that she had been put through more than she could bear. He didn't wanna see her like this. He got in the driver's seat and peeled off down the street, headed towards an emergency room.

Chatt blinked a little bit before opening her eyes completely. She raised her arm and stared at the I.V in her wrist. She was so lost. The last thing she remembered was getting picked up by two young nigga's on the street. She turned her head and was surprised to see Kilo sitting in a chair, staring out the window. Out of all people, what was he doing there? She opened her mouth to speak but quickly shut it back, feeling the pain from her jaw shoot through her face. She still had that long on going headache pounding through her head. It was starting to drive her nuts. She attempted to sit up, feeling a sharp pain shoot up her back side. "Shit," she shrieked, giving up on any movement.

Kilo quickly turned around hearing Chatt's voice. He jumped up and went to her bed side. "Wassup, lil mama?"

Chatt tried to muster a smile. "Hey," she finally spoke, forcing the word out.

"I know your face is probably killing you right now. You want me to tell the doctors to give you some more pain medicine?"

Chatt nodded.

Kilo stepped out of the room for a slight second, then returned with a nurse. The nurse had a huge grin on her face. "Hey, sweetie. Glad to see that you're finally awake."

Chatt looked at Kilo then back at the nurse. What the hell was going on? She hated feeling clueless. She and Kilo held eye contact while the nurse inserted another dose of pain medicine into her I.V.

When the nurse was finished, she asked, "Alright, hun, any questions?"

Chatt's mouth was killing her but she needed to know how she got in her current situation. She didn't wanna speak with the nurse though; she wanted to talk with Kilo in private. She figured he probably knew the story better than the nurse did. "Can you give us a minute please?"

"Sure," the nurse replied. "I'm Carrie by the way, hun. If you need me don't hesitate to call."

Chatt nodded again and then Carrie left. Kilo took a seat, followed by a deep breath. "I'm so glad I found you," he said.

"Found me? Where did you find me?"

"You were drugged up at a college party. When I found you, you were in horrible condition so I brought you out here."

"Those little bastards," Chatt mumbled.

Kilo studied her carefully. "I talked to a few of them lil' nigga's at the party and they swore up and down they didn't touch your face. The doctors questioned me about it but I didn't know what to tell em'." He paused for brief second, taking another deep breath. "But the nigga's did come forth about raping you. I'm sure by now you feel the soreness down there. The doctor also said you were torn a lil' bit in your anal area." Kilo felt awkward speaking those

Triple Crown Publications presents . . . DAMAGE

words.

    Chatt shook her head. There was no doubt that she felt sore down there, not to mention the sharp pains in her ass. Damn, she had been through a lot. Flash backs of her mother's head being blown off flooded her head. She should've killed DreStar. Burning his damn face wasn't enough. Tears came rushing to her eyes. She felt bad about leaving her mother's body there. She tried to tilt her head to the side so Kilo wouldn't see her cry. She knew how easy it was for her to scare a man away. Despite her efforts, Kilo saw the tears streaming down her face.

    He stood up and went to her bedside. "Don't cry, lil' mama. Them nigga's gon' pay for what they did to you."

    Chatt was silent. Poor Kilo. If only he knew the situation was much more deeper than that.

    Crispy sipped on her whine while watching Spen and Devon engage in conversation. Hell yeah she was jealous! All she wanted to do was have a fine night out before she and Ceddy left for California. Now here she was sitting in a lovely restaurant, watching the bitch she hated have dinner with the man she hated even more. There was no way she was going to stand for this. She wouldn't be herself if she didn't pull one of her tricks out of her sleeve. She figured that since she was leaving soon, she could do whatever she wanted and get away with it. *Nobody ever considers my fucking feelings,* she thought to herself. Ceddy sat across from her shaking his head. He knew that look in her eyes too well. Crispy was up to no good. He followed her eyes and took a look at what she had been staring at. His eyes landed on Devon. Ceddy thought he was so good looking. *I might have to turn his fine ass out,* he joked to himself. He licked his lips and smirked at the thought.

    Crispy shook her head. "It'll never happen. He's got his

head way too far up Spencer's ass, Ceddy."

Ceddy rolled his eyes. He hated when Crispy could read his mind. "Stay out of my damn head, Ms. Crispy."

Crispy grinned, turning her attention back to Devon and Spen. Even she had to admit that Devon looked nice. He had a hella-fied swag. "I want his ass," she stated.

"Then go get em'," Ceddy urged.

Crispy smirked watching Spen get up and head towards the ladies room. Devon was now sitting alone. Crispy pulled out her cell phone and began scanning through pictures. "Let's have a little fun," she said sending a picture to Devon's phone. She planned on using the dirt she had another time but right now she was pissed. Jealousy and envy washed over her. Another strong feeling hit her as well but she chose to keep that one on lock. She was too strong to let feelings from her heart show on her face. She was a tough shell and it was gonna take a little more than jealously to get her to crack.

Devon felt great as he watched Spen get up and disappear into the restroom. He felt like he was slowly but surely putting the pieces back together in his relationship. All he wanted to do was be with Spen and get his life back on track. Nothing else mattered. He hoped that in due time Spen would completely forgive him and let the past be the past. And from the way she had been acting lately, Devon felt confident about the future. The waiter approached the table but Devon informed her that he wasn't ready to order yet. He wanted to wait for Spen to come back before he made his decision. The buzzing sound of his vibrating phone went off in his pocket. He reached for it and his stomach did a complete U-turn seeing Crispy's name on the screen. He silently cursed to himself for not deleting her as a contact a long time ago. He wanted to erase everything

Triple Crown Publications presents... **DAMAGE**

that had anything to do with her, so he deleted the text message, then deleted her as a contact. Before he could put his phone back in his pocket, it went off again. He sighed looking at the screen. Another text from Crispy. Staring at his phone a moment longer, Devon realized that the text was a picture message.

What the fuck? He asked himself. What could Crispy possibly be sending him a picture of? Devon braced himself before opening the message. When he saw the upsetting sight, he immediately wished he would've just ignored the text.

"Sorry I took so long. I didn't mean to keep you waiting," Spen explained as she took her seat across from him. She picked up the menu and scanned through a few salads. "I can't decide on what I want. What are you having, baby?"

Devon ignored Spen's question. His attention was stuck on the horrifying sight he was looking at on his phone. His hands started shaking as he felt his blood pressure rise. He felt like his body was about to burst open. Another storm cloud had been placed over his head but this time it was pouring down hard.

"Devon, what's wrong?" Spen asked, noticing his sudden mood change.

Devon finally looked up with bloodshot eyes. "How the fuck could you do this?" He asked through clenched teeth.

"What are you talking about?" Spen questioned. She was nervous and lost at the same time.

Devon stood up, knocking their drinks off of the table. "What, you tryna' pay me back for what I did? Is that the shit you was tryna' pull off?"

"Devon, what the fuck is wrong with you?" Spen shouted, backing away from the table. She had never seen him act like this before. His face was tomato red with veins popping out from everywhere.

Triple Crown Publications *presents* ... DAMAGE

"I thought you forgave me," Devon exclaimed, shaking his head. "That's what that bitch was talking about when I saw her the other day." He tried his best to fight the water that began to build up in his eyes. He was a grown ass man and there was no way he was gonna cry in a restaurant full of people. He wasn't soft but at the moment he felt like cushion. Every time he turned around he was walking into some straight bullshit.

"I don't know what you're talking about, Devon. What's going on?"

"Now you wanna play the innocent role?" Devon barked. His tone was way past shouting by now. "I see the shit wit' my own eyes! How the fuck could you do that?"

Spen didn't have a clue what Devon was talking about. She looked at his hand that was pointed at his cell phone, which was now on the floor. She nervously picked it up to see what had him on fire. When she saw the horrible image she was just as heated as he was.

Crispy was all smiles as she watched the scene unfold like she had planned. She knew that sending a picture to Devon's phone of Spen's head buried between her legs would send Devon to another planet. There was no way Spen could explain herself out of that one. Crispy didn't want Devon and Spen happy. If Crispy couldn't be happy, then neither would Devon and Spen. She felt like she was the only one who deserved happiness and she wouldn't stop messing with other people until she got that. A part of her still wanted Devon. Even though she claimed she didn't want him, she knew deep down that she wished she'd had him. She paid close attention to the way that he treated Spen and wished that she had somebody to care for her the same way. Her evil intentions were simply based on her unhappiness. Everybody knows that misery loves company and Crispy was no different. She wanted the perfect fairytale life like everyone one else, and wouldn't stop until she got it. Spen had Devon ever since high school, so love was never an issue for her. Crispy had only been in love twice and even though she didn't wanna admit it, Devon was one of the two men that made her love him. Before she realized that he was using her, she thought everything was as good as great. She just knew that Devon was gonna break up with Spen for her. But when she realized that she was being played for a fool, she had to bite back. She tried to shield her heart by making it seem as if she only wanted Devon for Spen's salon. She made herself believe that their relationship was nothing more than business. Unfortunately, she couldn't lie to herself forever. She couldn't help how she felt but she would never admit it.

"Ms. Crispy, what have you done?" Ceddy asked, watching Devon blow up on the other side of the restaurant.

Crispy's smile faded. "They don't deserve to be together. It's not fair that Spencer always gets the happy ending. I'm sick of it."

"Oh my," Ceddy exclaimed, placing his hand over his heart. "You love him, Chrisette, don't you?"

Crispy rolled her eyes guiltily. "Ceddy, don't be stupid."

Ceddy waved his index finger in her face. "Honey, I'm no fool. You love that man. I've never seen you try and keep two people apart like this."

Crispy downed the rest of her drink and grabbed her purse. She hoped the picture she sent to Devon's phone was enough to keep him and Spen apart for good. If not, she was gonna release the rest of her dirt until she got what she wanted. She had her eyes on the prize and failure was not an option.

Triple Crown Publications *presents* . . . **DAMAGE**

19

Spen and Devon rode home in silence. Spen had a face full of tears while Devon continued to hold his tears back. He was so hurt. He couldn't believe Spen would go as far as sleeping with Crispy to get revenge on him. No matter what Spen said, Devon wasn't hearing it. He saw the picture for himself so nothing else mattered. *How could she?* Was all he kept asking himself. He didn't even look at her as he pulled into the driveway of their condo. He stormed out of his truck, fully enraged over what was happening. He walked inside the condo and slammed the door, making his way upstairs to the bedroom. He was on fire and his feelings were beyond hurt. Spen walked in behind him, still crying her eyes out. She didn't know what to tell him because she didn't know what was going on. Looking at herself in that picture just ripped her to shreds. She wracked her brain trying to remember anything ever happening that would have led to that photo. Something told her it had to do with the day she woke up feeling disgusting. She was terrified, knowing the truth was about to unfold. She approached Devon and tried to touch his arm but he quickly pulled away from her. Spen saw that the tears that he had been trying to hold in were now streaming down his cheeks. She knew it was serious if Devon was shedding tears. He was the type of man who held back everything, including his serious emotions. Seeing him like this just hurt her even more.

"Baby, I swear I don't know what happened. I'm not lying," Spen pleaded.

"So you got yo' head deep between that bitch's legs and you don't know how it got there? Is that what you tryna' say?"

"I swear I'm not lying to you. I don't know what the fuck is going on!"

Hearing Spen say she didn't know what was going made Devon even angrier. How in the hell could she not know what was going on? The picture said everything. Devon wiped his face and tried to control his hardcore persona. "Spen, don't keep lying to me! I kept it real wit' you and told you everything, so why can't you be honest wit' me?"

"You're not listening to me!" Spen wailed, dropping to her knees. "I wouldn't do anything like that, Devon!"

Devon searched for his phone with his emotions on rage. When he found it he gripped it tightly, pulling up the image that started this whole thing. He kneeled down so he and Spen were face to face and shoved the phone in her face. "So that's not you in this picture? That's not your head deep in her pussy?"

Spen smacked the phone out of Devon's hand. "I don't know what to tell you!" She sobbed, giving up. It was indeed her in the picture but she couldn't remember anything

Triple Crown Publications *presents* . . . **DAMAGE**

like that ever happening. "I just don't know what to tell you, Devon. Yes, it's me in the picture, but I swear I don't remember doing anything like that. I wouldn't do anything like that and you should know that! If anybody, you should know, baby."

Devon sighed, shaking his head from side to side. Even though the picture spoke for itself, something in his gut was telling him to believe her. He couldn't ever recall a time when Spen lied to him so he tried his best to hear her out. She swore to him that she didn't remember anything like that ever happening so he was gonna try and believe her. "You gotta feel where I'm coming from," he said as he rocked back and forth. "All I can go on is the picture and your word for it, Spen."

"So which do you choose?" Spen asked, looking up at him.

Devon clenched his jaw, shaking his head. "I'm gon' take your word for it."

"But you don't believe me."

"I'm trying to."

"You have to," Spen pleaded. "You have to believe me."

"I said I'm trying, Spen! I mean I'm looking at you in somebody's bed doing some foul shit to a bitch that we both hate." He ran his hand down his face. "I know I can't talk, but the shit still hurts man."

Spen sat up straight and thought for a moment. She pulled away from Devon to grab his phone that she had smacked away from him. She didn't want to, but she needed to look at the picture to make sure she wasn't tripping. "Oh my God," she said aloud. "Tader, that fucking Tader! I knew she had something to do with it!"

"What?" Devon questioned.

Spen had to block Devon out for a minute. She was too busy putting two and two together in her head. As she looked at the picture, she noticed that she and Crispy were in the hotel room she was staying in. Tader was the only person who knew where she was. *She would never do anything like that,* Spen told herself. She then thought about how Chatt told her that something funny was up with Tader. She couldn't make herself believe that her friend would do her like that, but regardless of it all, she was gonna get to the bottom of it. This shit was too serious to be playing around. Hell, who knew what else went down in that hotel room?

Sitting in her dark shades and all black attire, Tader nervously tapped her fingernails against her table. She sat inside the Waffle House on Needmore waiting for her guest to arrive. When she saw a tall, muscular man walk through the doors, she braced herself for what was about to happen. She stood up and waved for the guy to come over to her table. She grew even more nervous as he approached her. When he finally made it, she took a deep breath. "You're Hitman Andrew, right?" She asked.

He nodded.

Tader went on. "Thanks for coming. Sorry if I come off as nervous, but I'm honestly a wreck right now."

Andrew nodded, again.

Tader opened her purse and pulled out a white envelope. Inside contained six thousand dollars left of the money she had received from Crispy. "Here," she said, passing the envelope to Andrew.

Andrew shoved the envelope back in her direction. "Let's discuss the terms first," he stated in a demanding tone.

Tader sighed. "It's simple. Right now my boyfriend's in a coma fighting for his life." She felt herself tearing up. "I need you to make sure he doesn't win that fight."

Andrew cleared his throat and asked, "Why do you want

him dead?"

"Because," Tader sobbed, wiping at the tears streaming down her face, "if he wakes up, he'll tell the police what happened that night. I knows he's gon' tell em' that I basically baited him over there to be shot and killed."

"But you don't know for sure if he's gonna snitch. You sure you wanna take that chance?"

"I have to!" Tader shouted. "I can't go to jail. They'll eat me alive in there."

Andrew ran his hand over his goatee. "Get me the hospital and the room number. He'll be dead by the end of the month."

Even though Tader had sat the whole thing up, it was still hard for her to hear Andrew confirm that Terrell was indeed going to die. *I gotta do what I gotta do,* she told herself as she gave Andrew the information he requested.

"Come on, come on," Spen said as she paced the floor with her phone to her ear. She had been trying to get in touch with Tader all morning. After hours of getting her voicemail, Spen wasn't giving up. She was in desperate need of a conversation with Tader and she wasn't gonna stop until she got it. Finally after calling over fifty times, Tader finally answered.

"Hello?"

"Where are you?" Spen questioned, trying to keep her rage under control. She was ready to jump through the phone and beat Tader's ass.

"I'm out and about. I can't talk right now."

"Well, Tader I need to talk to you. It's important."

Tader sighed into the phone. "What is it?"

"Devon hit me. I finally broke it off with him and I need some comfort."

"What?" Tader's eyes lit up with excitement. She couldn't

wait for the day when Spen left Devon.

"You heard what I said, Tader. I need you, girl."

Tader swallowed a gulp of saliva down her dry throat. "Give me about an hour and I'll be there."

Spen hung up the phone and looked at Devon as he sat on the couch staring into space. It was his idea to come up with the story saying that he hit her so that Tader would definitely come over and not try and back out of it. He knew Tader was a snake and would try to slither her way out of a situation if she felt like she was being targeted. He hated to have her in his house, but he and Spen both wanted answers about the picture. If Tader did have anything to do with it, Spen was gonna dismiss their friendship immediately. She thought about whooping her ass too, and she planned on it if her emotions decided to get the best of her.

Devon wanted her to whoop that ass, regardless. He felt like Tader deserved a serious ass whooping and he wanted his girl to be the one to do it. Tader had always got under his skin. He couldn't stand her since the day she tried to throw herself at him. Tader strutted into the bar on a late night, dressed like a slut. She spotted Devon sitting alone at the bar, drinking a beer. She thought he looked so handsome. In fact, he always looked handsome in her eyes. She walked over to him smiling from ear to ear. Devon gave off his usual friendly vibe. The scent of his cologne drowned Tader's nostrils. She had to have him. She ordered herself a drink and continued to talk with him. She tried to sneakily rest her hand on his upper leg but Devon quickly brushed her hand away. She tried again and this time Devon smacked her hand away. He didn't know if she was drunk or what, but she was getting out of hand. After downing the rest of his beer, Devon stood up to walk away, but in a quick motion, Tader grabbed his arm, turning him

Triple Crown Publications presents . . .   DAMAGE

around to face her. Standing on the tip of her toes, she forcefully tried to stick her tongue in his mouth but Devon fought against her. He pushed her away with a force so strong that she fell backwards, flipping over the bar into the bartender's station. Tader was beyond furious. She couldn't believe what had just happened. As the bartender helped her up, she cursed Devon out, calling him every name in the book. Devon just shook his head with disgust and walked off. When he heard Tader shout that she was gonna tell Spen he tried to kiss *her*, he stopped dead in his tracks.

"Yeah, that's right, ma'fucka!" Tader shouted, pointing her index finger in his direction. "You better believe that my girl's gon' take my word over yours! I've known her since elementary school, nigga! You better keep your mouth shut or your ass is out!"

Tader's words played in Devon's head over and over. He knew to take his word over her best friends since elementary school was not going to happen. Till this day, he kept his mouth closed about the incident, not wanting Spen to blame him for what happen. But the more Tader pulled off her sneaky stunts, the more Devon wanted to reveal the truth. Fuck it. He had to take a chance and hope that she realized the kind of person that Tader was.

"Spen," he muttered, rising up from the couch. "Before that bitch gets here, I need to tell you something."

Tader left the Waffle House feeling guilty as ever. She had just tied the knot to have Terrell killed and now she was on the way to comfort the person in which she betrayed the most in the past. A part of her felt relieved because Spen still hadn't mentioned the incident with Crispy yet. She hoped that it never came up. All she had left was Spen so if she lost her, she didn't know what she was gonna do. As she got into the driver's seat of her Chrysler, she buckled her seat belt and turned on the radio. Mariah Carey played through the speakers. Tader adjusted her rearview mirror before pulling out of the parking lot. Before she headed over to Spen's place, she wanted to stop by her house and grab a few things. There was no way that she was staying at her place with everything that had went down. She knew by now that the police had run the prints for the gun that Terrell was shot with and she was scared to death of being arrested for the charge. She didn't know where she was gonna go, but she would get the hell out of Dayton the first opportunity she got. After she got a few items from her house, her next objective was her money. She just spent the last six grand she had on a hitman, so now she needed to find another way to stack some chips and fast. If she wanted to leave Dayton, she couldn't do it with an empty wallet. She had to come up with something and it had to be fast. Her mind wondered off to the men she messed around with. There had to be a few of them left that she was still on good terms with. If she had to spread her legs a few more times to get some extra bread, then so be it. As she pulled into the driveway of her home, she began to reminisce on all the good times she had. She hated that she had to leave. She felt like she was leaving so much behind. She took a deep breath and reached for her door handle when all of a sudden, the doors locked. Tader was startled for a moment. *What the fuck?* She asked herself. She hit the unlock button on her keys but the doors immediately locked back up. Tader grabbed the door handle and started jerking it. She didn't understand what the fuck was going on.

After jerking on the door for some time, she finally let it go and tried to hit the unlock button again. Like the first time, the doors just locked back up. Tader started getting nervous. She took a deep breath and tried to relax. The car was quiet besides her heavy breathing. Out of nowhere, a frightful laugh emerged from the backseat of the car. Tader's heart dropped. To say she was terrified would be an understatement. Before she could make another move, she felt a tight grasp wrap around the nape of her neck.

"Guess who?" A voice whispered in her ear.

Tader was shaking uncontrollably. "Da....Da....David," she replied, stuttering through her words.

"Wrong answer, bitch!" The voice replied.

Tader tried to calm herself. She knew that if she panicked, she was ass out. After counting down from five in her head, she tried to snatch away from the grasp but soon felt her muscles being cramped together as an electrical force shot through her body, leaving her unconscious.

After hours of waiting for Tader to arrive, Devon grew impatient. He couldn't sit any longer. He was ready to break loose. He slipped his jacket on and looked at Spen who sat on the loveseat still enraged. He didn't know if it was the picture that had her more upset or the fact that he finally told her the truth about he and Tader's situation. "I gotta make a run," he told her.

Without looking up Spen asked, "What kind of run?"

Devon grabbed his keys from off of the coffee table. "I need to stop by the office and go over a few things. Afterwards I might go have a drink."

"So you're just gonna leave me here by myself?"

Devon asked, "Do you wanna come?"

Spen let out a heavy sigh. "Whatever, Devon. Just go ahead and get drunk and leave me here to deal with Tader by myself."

"I asked you did you wanna come," Devon argued.

"No, I don't wanna come!" Spen snapped. "Just go, okay.

Go get drunk and party all night for all I fucking care."

Devon shook his head. "Look, I'll be back in a few, a'ight." With that said, he was out the door. He understood that Spen was upset, but he was upset his damn self. Fuck going past the office; he was headed straight to the liquor store. Devon needed a drink. He was frustrated, irritated and exhausted all at the same time. It seemed as if nothing could go right for him. Every time he went right, everything else went left. He was sick of it. Trying to be Mr. Perfect just wasn't working for him. *Nobody's perfect, D*, he told himself. *So you gotta stop trying to be that person and just be yourself.* Devon wished that his older brother Delvyn was still around so that he could confide in him. Delvyn always gave Devon the best advice. Unfortunately for Devon, Delvyn left for the Army years ago and barley made contact. Devon always knew that he could talk to his parents, but nobody would listen to him like Delvyn would. That's why most of the time, he always kept quiet. When he pulled up to the liquor store, he went inside thinking he was only getting one bottle but instead he came out with four bottles of Gin. He really planned on getting fucked up. He wanted to drink all of his problems away. He debated on if he wanted to go back to the condo and get drunk or head to another spot. He knew Spen would have a fit if she saw him walk in with four bottles of liquor, so he decided to head elsewhere. As he pulled up to a stop light, he felt like his mind was playing tricks on him. He could've sworn he heard her calling his name. That nagging, squeaky, high pitched voice continued to call his name.

Devon turned to his right and there she was. The nightmare from hell had found him again. He rolled down his window, his blood boiling on the inside. "Aye, bitch!" He hollered. "Where the fuck did that picture come from?"

A wide grin spread across Crispy's face. "Did you break

up with her?"

"Answer my fuckin' question!" Devon yelled, with veins popping out of his neck and forehead. His brown skin complexion started turning red and his body felt like it was on fire.

"Bye, Devon," Crispy replied, stepping on her gas. She smiled knowing that he would follow her until he got his answer.

Just as she predicted, Devon sped up only putting enough gas on the pedal so that he and Crispy were even. "Answer me, damnit! Where the fuck did you take that picture?!"

"Spencer came to me and said she was looking for a good time. She's gorgeous, Devon. How could I turn her down?"

"You're fuckin' lying!" Devon argued. "You lying ass bitch!"

"I have no reason to lie," Crispy responded. "I'm on my way to get Ceddy, then we're headed back to Cali. Will you guys miss me?"

Devon let out a laugh that only the devil could repeat. He was starting to look crazy. "Miss you? Bitch, I won't give a fuck if you just crashed and died! You fucked up my life and then you try to bring my girl into this shit? Fuck you, Crispy!"

"You know what?" Crispy said, taking her eyes off of the road to look at Devon, "I hate you! You continue to blame me for your fucked up life but you've brought this shit upon yourself! You used me and all I did was get revenge on your ass. But even through all that, I still care about you! Ugh!" She screamed, pounding her fist against the steering wheel. "You're such a bastard, Devon! You don't deserve..."

"Whoa!! Crispy, watch the fucking ro....road!" By the time Devon could get his warning out, Crispy had rammed her Benz into a city bus. Devon slammed down on his breaks and hopped out of his truck. He rushed over to Crispy's car and saw her bloody head slammed against her shattered wind shield. "Fuck!!" He shouted. "Somebody call a fuckin' ambulance! Call a got-damned ambulance!!" He tried opening her smashed in car door, but it was no use. The wreck was too serious for him to open the door alone. "This shit is my fault," he said, pacing the street with his hands on his head. "I fucking told the bitch that I didn't care if she crashed and died! This shit is all my fault!!"

20

"What? Oh my goodness...Okay, I'm on my way!" Spen hung up the phone and ran upstairs to slip into some sweats and a T-shirt. She had just hung up the phone with Chatt and was disturbed to hear that she was in the hospital for rape and a broken jaw. Fuck Tader! She was gonna have to wait. Spen wasn't about to sit around waiting for her any longer especially when her little sister needed her by her side. After slipping into her netted slippers, Spen headed to the hospital. She wanted to call Devon to tell him where she would be just in case he came back, but then again, she had an attitude with him. She was pissed that he waited over two years to confess the truth about he and Tader's situation. It made her feel as if he was being sneaky about the whole thing.

Spen walked inside the hospital and headed straight for the elevators. She got off on the second floor and scanned the doors for Chatt's room number. When she found room 216, she rushed inside. She could've cried seeing her little sister look so horrible. She approached her bedside and ran her hand softly over Chatt's jaw. Only a man with a powerful hand could've done such a thing.

"Thank you for coming," Chatt said in a low tone.

"Girl, quit it," Spen replied. "I'm mad you didn't call me out here a long time ago! You know I would've flew out here."

Chatt sighed. "Sorry. I just needed some time to think about everything that's happened to me."

"Is it Dre?" Spen questioned, taking a seat on the edge of Chatt's bed. "I knew that ma'fucka was no good! Chatt, why did you try to hide it from me?"

"I didn't want you to worry about me."

"Damnit, Chasity! You know you can tell me anything regardless to if I'm gonna worry." Spen got quiet noticing the tears that started streaming down Chatt's face. "What is it, girl?"

Chatt took a deep breath. "Spen, there's something you need to know."

Spen wiped her face for her. "Girl, I gotta fill you in on a shit load too. I'm think I'm pregnant, Chatt."

Chatt tried to muster a smile. "Really? Oh my God, how?"

Spen laughed. "Devon didn't pull out the last time we had sex. It shocked the hell out of me girl, but I was so happy. But now, I just don't know."

Chatt tried to sit up. "What's going on with you guys?"

"I don't think we're gonna make it," Spen admitted. "I love him Chatt, I really do but, something's not there anymore."

"Don't give up on him, Spen. Devon's a great guy. He's loves you to death, girl. He wouldn't be human if he didn't

Triple Crown Publications *presents* . . . DAMAGE

make mistakes."

"I think he might have slept with Tader."

Chatt looked shocked.

Spen continued. "He told me she tried to kiss him two years back but he denied her and that's why they've been feuding all this time. But why would he wait so long to tell me?"

"Because that bitch Tader would've lied her way through it and made you believe her. I'm not saying I was there and saw what happen, but I know Tader and she ain't no damn saint."

Spen laid back and folded her hands over her chest. "You know, I think she might of set me up. Her and that bitch Crispy did something to me and I'm gon' get to the bottom of it. Wait till you see this shit, Chasity."

Chatt shook her head knowing that Tader and Crispy were a deadly combination. "I don't even wanna know. I got too much to worry about."

Spen noticed that Chatt had started crying again. "What's wrong, Chatt? Talk to me, girl."

"My mom is dead."

Spen covered her mouth. That had to be the last thing she expected to hear come from Chatt's mouth. She rose up and wrapped her in her arms. "I'm sorry, Chatt. I'm so sorry, girl."

Chatt cried into her shoulder. "Spen, I might be joining her soon."

"No, no, no," Spen replied sharply. "I don't wanna hear you talk like that, Chasity. Do you hear me? None of that talk, okay?"

Chatt pulled away from her. "Spen, I have...I have HIV."

Spen's heart dropped. She couldn't believe what she was hearing. She didn't want to hear it, nor did she wanna believe it. "Chasity, stop okay? You're making yourself

Triple Crown Publications presents . . . **DAMAGE**

miserable."

"The headaches, the fevers, the stomach aches. My doctor confirmed it. I'm dying, Spen."

By now Spen was crying just as hard as Chatt was, if not harder. "You are not fucking, dying! Do you hear me? You're not fucking dying, Chasity!"

"I can't run from this," Chatt cried. "It's already caught me."

"Just pray with me, okay? Pray with me, Chatt."

Chatt looked Spen in the eyes and told her, "A prayer can't save me this time."

Tader's head nodded off to the side as she tried to fight her battle with sleep. She was so tired, but she refused to drift off again. She was too nervous. She didn't know where she was or who had captured her. Her body ached horribly. Tader was so frustrated. She tried to jerk her hands away from the chair that she was duck taped to, but it was no use. Her hands and feet were taped tightly to the chair she was in and without any help, there was no getting out. Her eyes were also duck taped, preventing her from seeing anything. She released a frustrating scream. *What the fuck was going on?* The sound of a door opening got her full attention. She stopped trying to jerk away from the chair and tried to sit calmly. She heard a small set of footsteps approaching her. Goosebumps immediately appeared on her skin. The footsteps stopped right in front of her and Tader grew even more nervous.

All of a sudden, that frightful laugh she heard when she was captured in her car echoed throughout the room. This time, Tader was able to tell that the laugh came from a female. *But who?* Tader didn't fuck with any females besides Spen and Chatt, so whoever this chick was would surprise the hell out of her. The laughed stopped and Tader could smell the scent of a cigarette being smoked. Now she was really lost. She couldn't recall anybody whom she hung around who lit up cancers sticks. *Who the fuck is this crazy bitch?* Tader swallowed another gulp of saliva down her dry throat and started rocking back and forth in her chair. She wanted some got damn attention and this unknown female was gonna give it to her. She opened her dry mouth and was about to speak when her chest tightened, causing her to cough momentarily. She got herself together and tried again. "Who are you? What the fuck do you want from me?"

Tader could hear a smile in the females voice as she replied, "I'm you're worst nightmare, bitch. You fucked with the wrong kid."

Tader recognized the voice, but couldn't place a face behind it. "Who are you and what the fuck are you talking about?"

That horrifying laugh escaped her lips again. "You don't know me too well, but you know me well enough. I told my son I didn't trust you."

Tader grimaced. Her mind had to be playing tricks on her. She knew damn well this couldn't be the person she thought it was. "Who's your son?"

"You know who my damn son is!" The women snapped. "Fucking with your scandalous ass is the reason he's dead!"

Oh my God! Tader thought. "Please, I'm not the person who shot him!"

"Don't give me that bullshit," Momma Lee barked back. "You set my son up to be killed and you even brought me into the picture. I may be old, but I'm one wise ass woman. You're gonna pay for your sin's Ta'Ronna." She continued with that frightful laughter.

"I swear I didn't set him up," Tader cried. "It was all a

misunderstanding. You don't get it!"

Momma Lee bent down so she was face to face with Tader. She blew the smoke from her cigarette in her face and smiled. "No, my darling, I'm afraid you're the one who doesn't get it." She grabbed Tader's cheeks and sunk her long, sharp nails in as deep as they would go. "I've already handled your partner." She snatched her nails from Tader's cheeks, grinning when she saw the scratch marks that she left on her pretty dark face.

Tader started sobbing. "I don't know what you're talking about!"

Momma Lee smiled as she removed her pocket knife. She yanked Tader's head back and began cutting the tape from her eyes. Once Tader's vision was finally clear, the first thing she saw was David laying on the floor drenched in blood and cigarette ashes. "Guess who's next?" Momma Lee asked.

Tader's eyes bucked as she screamed, "Aghhhhhhhhhh!!"

"That's right, Ta'Ronna. Let it out!"

Tader continued to scream to the top of her lungs as the tears poured out of her eyes. She started shaking and within seconds she was vomiting. Looking at David's dead body put her in shock.

"Now," Momma Lee began as she reached into her purse and pulled out loaded .45, "as I recall, my son was shot to death and then there was an anonymous call to the police." She pointed the gun at Tader's chest. "Then you tried to hire someone to finish him off just in case he pulled through!"

"I...I didn't...." Tader couldn't get her words together.

"Don't lie to me. I've been watching you very closely." She shook her head. "You're gonna feel what my son felt Ta'Ronna."

Boom! Boom! Boom!

Triple Crown Publications *presents . . .* **DAMAGE**

Before Tader knew it, her whole world went black. Momma Lee gargled up a mouth full of spit and emptied it on her. She then jotted up the stairs, exiting the abandon building. Once she was inside her van, she lit a fresh cigarette. *What goes around, comes around,* she thought to herself as she pulled off. Before she pulled onto the highway, she stopped at a payphone and dialed 911.

"911, what is your emergency?"

"Yes, I'm calling because I heard gunshots near Kipling, and Cornell. You guys should really check that out," she said calmly before slamming the phone down. She looked up at the sky before she got back in her van. *All for you Terrell.*

21

Amazing Grace, How Sweet, The Sound....
Spen looked around the small gathering wondering where Crispy's family was. The only faced she recongnized was Ceddy's. She heard Devon sigh and grabbed his hand as they listened to the choir sing. She knew he felt guilty about Crispy's death, even though she constantly reminded him that he shouldn't. In his mind, it was his fault. Right before the accident, he told Crispy that he didn't care if she just crashed and died. Just moments after the words left his mouth; Crispy's Benz collided with a city bus, sending her crashing towards the windshield of her car. She died at the scene leaving Devon with a heart full of guilt. "I never meant for this to happen," he whispered to Spen.

"Shh," she told him. "We'll talk later, okay?"

Devon just shook his head. He was ready for the funeral

to be over. So much was happening around him and he didn't know how much more he could take. Spen was all he had left. He gripped her hand tighter and held on to her until the services were over.

"Come on," she told him as the small crowd stood. Devon followed behind Spen as she headed towards the front. She looked back at him and nodded towards the closed casket. "Go ahead."

Taking a deep breath, Devon stepped forward and placed down a rose. He stared at the photo of her stationed right next to the casket. "I apologize for everything," he stated in a low tone. He stared at the photo for a moment longer before walking away. Just as he and Spen were about to exit, Ceddy approached them.

"Can I borrow your man for a minute?" He asked, looking at Spen.

Spen looked at Devon then back at Ceddy. "Sure."

The two men walked off into a quiet corner. Devon crossed his arms and leaned against the wall. "I'm sorry man."

"Hun, it's not your fault. Accidents happen."

Devon was silent.

"Devon, I just wanted you to know that Ms. Crispy really cared about you. I know she put you through a lot, but despite the bull, she really had feelings for you."

"I know," Devon replied facing the ground. "I know she did."

Ceddy placed his hand on Devon's shoulder. "Hun, one day the two of you will meet again, and it'll be nothing but laughter when you guys look back on your past."

Devon looked up. "Thanks man. You have a safe trip back to Cali, a'ight?"

"I will hun, thanks."

Devon nodded and walked outside where Spen was

Triple Crown Publications presents . . . **DAMAGE**

waiting for him. "You ready?" He asked her.

"Yeah," she answered. "I already started the truck." She walked up on him and kissed his cheek. "You want me to drive?"

"Nah, I got it."

Spen stared out the window as Devon cruised the highway. She wanted to talk to him but she figured she'd wait until they reached their destination. She knew he probably didn't wanna talk at the moment anyway. They ended up listening to the radio the whole ride. By the time they reached Columbus, Spen was halfway sleep. Devon tugged on her shoulder, letting her know they were at the hotel. He retrieved their bags from his trunk then they walked inside. "I'll go get the key," Spen said.

When they got to their room, Devon disappeared into the bathroom. Spen heard the shower turn on and knew he was about to try and wash away his thoughts. She really hoped the news she had would cheer him up. While he was in the shower, she ordered them some food. Devon took so long that the food ended up arriving before he came out. "Devon, are you okay in there?" Spen asked, standing by the door.

"Yeah, I'm good," he replied, opening the door.

"Okay. Come eat with me." The silence continued as they ate dinner and Spen couldn't take it anymore. "Baby, please cheer up. I don't like seeing you like this."

Devon threw his fork down and shook his head. "Spen, all I wanted to know is where the picture came from. I promise you I didn't mean for Crispy to lose her life like that."

"I know, Devon. It wasn't your fault, okay?"

"It was!" He yelled.

Spen grabbed his hand. "Devon, it was not your fault. You can't do that to yourself."

"It just seems like I keep fuckin' up with every move I make. I'm really wondering why God hasn't called me yet."

Spen sighed, trying to hold in the water threating to fall from her eyes. "Maybe because He wants you to be here for your family."

Devon stared at her confused. "What are you talking about?"

"Well," Spen said, wiping the tears that finally fell, "a couple of months ago we made love and I don't know if you did it by accident, but—"

"Spen, are you sure?" Devon asked, cutting her off.

"Was it an accident?" She questioned, ignoring his question.

Devon stood up and pulled Spen up with him. He wiped her face and kissed her. "Everything else might've been an accident, but you having my child could never be an accident."

Spen shook her head, trying to stop crying. "Devon, let's make this work, okay? We have to work, I need us to work."

"We're gonna work. I promise you that."

Chatt swallowed the last pill she was supposed to take for the night before screwing the cap back on the bottle. She placed it back inside the medicine cabinet next to the other pill bottles her doctor prescribed her with. Chatt hated having to take a million medications a day. Sometimes she often wondered what would happen if she didn't take the medicine anymore. *I wonder if I would die in my sleep,* she thought to herself as she closed the medicine cabinet. She couldn't see her reflection in the mirror caused by the fog from the steaming shower water she was running. Chatt stripped out of her clothes and stepped into the shower, letting the water wash away her temporary pain. She knew DreStar was the person whom she contracted HIV from. She closed her eyes as a memory of them taking a shower together at her old apartment flooded her mind. *That bastard,* she thought as she erased his face from her mind. She hated him. DreStar had scarred Chatt so much that she didn't think she would ever be able to heal from the things he put her through.

The worst being when he took her mother from her. Chatt knew deep down inside that she and her mother more than likely would have never had a normal mother daughter relationship, but that still didn't make the pain any less when she heard the gun shot that ended Shawan's life. She would never be able to shake the image of Shawan with half her head blown off laying at the end of Dre's stairs. She shook her head from side to side as the tears from her eyes blended with the shower water running down her face. DreStar did nothing but make it harder for Chatt to trust any man. She was trying her hardest not to let him interfere with her relationship with Kilo.

Chatt didn't understand why her life had to be so cold. Ever since she was little, nothing but hardships seem to come her way. Now that's she older, she feels as if nothing has changed. She still seems to hit a brick wall with every path that she decides to take. Meeting DreStar had to be the worst thing that could've ever happened to her. Ever since day one, he was doing nothing but using her. Chatt often asked herself how she could be so stupid and blind to the fact that DreStar had only seen dollar signs when he looked at her. But she knew a lot of her blindness came from the fact that her heart was lonely and vulnerable. DreStar did such an excellent job of pretending to be interested in her. Chatt felt that she had finally found someone who accepted her flaws and all, but in actuality he only accepted her into the money making world of prostitution. DreStar did nothing but ruin Chatt's life.

After she washed her body from head to toe, she got out the shower and wrapped herself in a towel. Spen and Devon were gonna be in Columbus for a week, so she had their condo to herself. As nervous as she was, she invited Kilo to come over for the night. She talked to him about an hour ago and he told her he would be over in a few. A half hour had passed and he still hadn't showed. *I wonder what's taking him so long,* Chatt thought. She decided to go downstairs and watch television until he arrived.

Just as she stepped into the hallway, she felt her heart sink in her stomach. Standing there with a smirk on his lips and the entire right side of his face covered in pink, DreStar had returned. Chatt felt like she was gonna urinate on herself. "How...how...how did you—"

Before she could finish her sentence, her face lit up from the sting of Dre's forceful slap. "I'm never gonna go away Chasity. You can't run from me!" He sent his hand across her face again, this time sending her flying towards the ground. He put his foot on her throat and pointed to his face. "You see what you did to me? Huh? Do you see this shit!?" Chatt was trying her hardest to move his foot from her neck. She couldn't breathe and she knew that was Dre's whole purpose. "Nah, bitch! I'm in charge now!" Dre hollered. He removed his foot from her throat and kicked her in the face, immediately splitting both her lips open.

"You better kill me!" Chatt spat, coughing and spitting up blood.

"Or what? You gonna come back and kill me?" Dre taunted. He laughed as he watched Chatt struggle to stand. He let her get all the way to her feet, before he went at her again. "Come on, Chasity. Try to kill me!" Chatt tried to swing but Dre grabbed her arm and swung her against the

Triple Crown Publications *presents* ... **DAMAGE**

wall. Standing over her he said, "I hope you told your friend bye. Tonight is last time you'll be seeing any fuckin' thing!" He bent down and wrapped his hand around her throat so tight that Chatt thought it would crack. "You see Chasity, I could just easily pull out my gun and blow your head off like I did your mother's, but that would be no fun. I want you see my face while you die!"

Chatt closed her eyes while Dre slowly took her life from her. She knew he wanted her to die looking into his eyes, but she wasn't gonna let that happen. She knew she couldn't fight against him and win, so instead she accepted her fate. *I'm coming to be with you Shawan...*

Boom!

Dre was in shock as he felt a bullet rip through his stomach. Releasing Chatt's throat, he immediately grabbed the wound. *Fuck!* he grunted, looking at the face that was about to end his life. Dre knew it was over when he felt the cold tip of the gun touch his forehead.

Boom! Was the sound of the shot that splattered Dre's brains all over the place. Kilo looked at Chatt and hoped he wasn't too late. "Wake up lil mama." Chatt didn't move. "Come on, Chatt. Please," he begged, slightly tapping her shoulder. He put his head down in defeat when he got no response. *I was too late!*

Triple Crown Publications *presents* . . . **DAMAGE**

Two Years Later...

Dear Spen,
 I hope you get this letter in time. Thank you so much for writing me. I really thought you forgot about me. First off, I just wanted to say congratulations. I really wish I could be at your wedding, but hey, not everything works out like I want it to. I also wanted to apologize to you for everything. I know I betrayed you when I accepted the money from Crispy to help her set you up. And I hope you can look past what happened between me and Devon at the bar. I was drunk Spen, I really wasn't trying to take your man. Being in a cage for a while can really make you think. I've had a lot of time to talk with God. I almost had my life taken away from me, and girl when I'm say I'm thankful, you just don't know how much! Terrell's mom really wanted me dead, but God pulled me through that one. And even

though I'm behind bars, I'm happy I'm still breathing. I don't plan on being in here forever though. I'm not the one who killed my babe and I'm sure that'll come to light. If I could turn back time, I would go back to when you, me, and Chatt were still in school. Those were the good days; less drama unlike now. But I can't turn back time, so all I can do is continue to move forward. I hope that when I get out of here, we can be friends again. Let's put our past behind us Spen, I don't wanna go back. You and Chatt are the only family I have. I hope both of you can forgive me. You should write me more often. I love you Spen; and tell Chatt I love her too.

Always Your Friend,
Tader

Spen smiled as she folded the letter back up. She was happy that Tader was finally getting in touch with God. She was shocked when she first heard the news that Tader had been convicted. She was charged with first degree murder and sentenced ten years to life, with a twenty thousand dollar fine. Although Tader had betrayed her in the past, Spen hoped she didn't spend the rest of her life in prison. She knew Tader didn't kill Terrell. She might've been a scandalous friend, but she wasn't a killer.

Knock...knock...knock!

"Who is it?" Spen asked.

"It's me," Chatt answered. "What's taking you so long?"

"I'll be right out." Spen looked in the mirror one last time. Her hair and makeup were perfect and she looked beautiful in her lavender wedding dress. She walked over to the window and pulled the curtain back just a tad. It warmed her heart to see Devon, the man she loved waiting at the alter for her. Sitting in the front row was Devon's parent's, his little sister Kimmy, and his nieces and nephew.

Alongside them sat Kilo and Chatt, and on top of Chatt's lap was Devon Jr. Spen fanned her face, knowing she was about to cry. For once, everything seemed right. She was marrying the man she loved, she had a handsome son, and her best friend was still alive, healthy and happy. *Finally, the damage is done,* she thought to herself as she prepared to walk down the aisle.